DUPLICATES

ANDREW
NEIDERMAN

BERKLEY BOOKS, NEW YORK

DUPLICATES

A Berkley Book / published by arrangement with
the author

PRINTING HISTORY
Berkley edition / October 1994

ISBN: 0-425-14395-3

BERKLEY®
Berkley Books are published by The Berkley Publishing Group,
200 Madison Avenue, New York, New York 10016.
BERKLEY and the "B" design
are trademarks belonging to the Berkley Publishing Corporation.

PRINTED IN THE UNITED STATES OF AMERICA

10 9 8 7 6 5 4 3 2 1

Masterworks of Suspense by
ANDREW NEIDERMAN

THE SOLOMON ORGANIZATION . . .
his startling novel of a secret society

"Neiderman has woven a taut tale of horror made more horrible by its very plausibility." —*Library Journal*

ANGEL OF MERCY . . .
his newest thriller from G. P. Putnam's Sons

A dedicated nurse tries to save lives . . . while her demented sister destroys them.

THE NEED . . .
his shocking, erotic masterpiece of vampiric passion

"Deeply involving horror . . . vivid . . . engrossing!"
—*West Coast Review of Books*

AFTER LIFE . . .
a terrifying tale of love, death, and resurrection

A blind woman receives an ominous warning: "When your husband dies, don't let them bring him back."

SISTER, SISTER . . .
Neiderman's gripping psychological study in fear

Nature created something unusual in a pair of Siamese twins. No one knew *how* unusual . . . until it was too late.

PLAYMATES . . .
the shattering story of a mother and daughter "adopted" by a demented backwoods family

"Scary from first to last page."
—Dean Koontz, *New York Times*
bestselling author of *Mr. Murder*

To Sandor, a kindred spirit

PROLOGUE

ED WALTERS PLUCKED HIS CAMEL'S HAIR SPORTS JACKET OFF the hanger in his closet and slipped into it quickly. He had the feeling he had been standing there staring at it for minutes. He knew his wife, Jean, was already downstairs waiting.

It didn't always take me this long to get myself ready to go out, he thought.

Or did it?

Funny how little things like that about himself seemed so vague lately. Yesterday, he had stopped at the Thrifty Department Store on Main Street Sandburg to buy himself some after-shave lotion, but when he arrived at the men's cologne section, he had stood dumbly before the displays, unable to recall which one he favored. Mindy Lowe, the salesgirl, noticed how he was staring with confusion and asked him if he needed any assistance.

"You're not going to believe this, Mindy," he said, "but for some reason, I can't remember which after-shave I like. Isn't that stupid?" he asked, following it with a rumble of a laugh that seemed imprisoned in a chest within his chest. She smiled. The pretty twenty-year-old redhead leaned into him, her full breasts against his arm. She sniffed his face and reached for Drakkar.

"I know the male scents by heart," she said coquettishly. He was aroused; his heart began to thump and a wave of pleasant warmth settled in the pocket between his thighs. He could barely utter his thank you. Mindy Lowe enjoyed

1

the effect she had on him; he saw that and for some reason, it angered him. He had instant visions of tying her down and tormenting her until she pleaded for mercy. But it wasn't like him to think such things, was it?

He mused about it. At least that memory was vivid.

"Ed!"

"Coming," he called back, jumping as if his wife of ten years had caught him in an adulterous episode. He hurried into the bathroom to take one more look at his hair and brushed back the sides quickly. But as he started to put down the brush, he was hypnotized by his own image and his hand froze in midair.

It was happening again; it was definitely happening again. Right before his eyes, his face began to metamorphose. From top to bottom, it literally went from the face of a thirty-five-year-old to the face of a sixty-year-old. First, his hair changed from light brown to coal ash gray; his forehead widened and the creases deepened; his nose became more bulbous and drooped emphatically; and his mouth lengthened, the lips fuller, softer. His sharply chiseled jaw turned into a smooth round line and the skin under his chin became loose.

Then, as quickly as the new image appeared, it dissolved, first leaving him staring in cold fear at the skull and drained eye sockets and then, finally, reforming his own face, the flesh returning, the cerulean eyes glittering. Nevertheless, a bead of sweat had broken out along the middle of his forehead: proof that he indeed had been frightened and shocked by his own image.

"Ed, for God sakes! Can't we ever get to a movie on time?" Jean screamed.

"Coming," he mumbled, still unable to turn from the mirror. *"I'm coming."*

"So is Christmas," she retorted.

He pulled himself away from the mirror and charged out of the bedroom like a killer fleeing the scene of a murder.

Jean, her hands on the narrow hips of her tight jeans, stood waiting impatiently at the bottom of the stairs. She had her straw blond hair brushed down to her shoulders and wore a dark blue ribbon through it. Her bangs were cut neatly above her light brown eyebrows. Her almond-shaped brown eyes burned sharply with irritation and she pulled in the right corner of her mouth with disgust. Barely five feet five and weighing just over one hundred pounds, his diminutive wife looked formidable somehow. It was as if he saw her as taller, heavier, harder.

Sometimes, when he looked at her clothing in the closet or saw her small shoes, he felt almost as if he had entered the wrong house. These were the clothes of a stranger. His wife was a bigger woman.

Weird . . . these thoughts were so weird.

"I was just brushing my hair," he explained.

"We're going to see a film, Ed," she said as he came down, "not be in it."

"Sorry."

She shook her head.

"The woman is supposed to be the one who takes forever to get dressed, who primps endlessly, not the man," she lectured.

He smiled.

"All right, all right. Let's not make a federal case out of it. Did you lock the back door?"

"About an hour ago," she replied and started for the front entrance, scooping her purse off the dark pine table in the entryway of their two-story Cape Cod–style home. Ed turned and looked back up the stairway. It was as if . . . as if he were waiting for himself, as if he expected to see another Ed Walters, the real Ed Walters, come out of the bedroom and start down the steps.

"Now what?" Jean called from the open doorway.

"Nothing. Just making sure," he replied.

"Making sure of what?" she asked as he caught up.

"That I didn't forget anything," he said, unable to hide his irritability this time.

"We're only going to the movies, Ed. You have your wallet?"

"Yes," he said, patting his inside jacket pocket.

"So?"

"So let's go," he said as if she were the one holding them back now. He suddenly felt as if they were this elderly couple, two cantankerous septuagenarians who spent most of their day snapping and biting at each other.

The late June evening was warm, in fact balmy for the upstate New York community. Living only two blocks away from the business district of their relatively small community, the Walters would walk to the movie theater. Twilight lingered, and although there were pockets of deep, blue-black darkness between the houses and under the sprawling maples and oak trees, their street was still well illuminated. The glimmering lights of stores and cars ahead of them created an ethereal, quiet world, that soft, precious and short time when day retreated and night began to crawl over the horizon, dragging a blanket of darkness behind it. Only the brighter stars were visible this early.

For Ed it reinforced this feeling that he was living in a dream, moving at half speed through a setting where the sounds were subdued, people sometimes faceless, sometimes distorted, the ground beneath him occasionally becoming liquid, gooey, spongelike, his legs trembling, his feet disappearing and then reappearing, his own flesh sliding off his bones, melting and being left behind in a stream of blood and hair, the veins actually visible in the globs.

It sickened him and made his stomach churn. He groaned, unable to keep the disgust subdued as well tonight.

"What's the matter?" Jean asked.

"Nothing," he said quickly.

"You're acting very strange tonight, Ed Philip Walters," she said shaking her head. There it was again. Whenever she pronounced his full name like that—this deep sense of foreboding, this emptiness. He had stopped walking.

"What are you doing?" she demanded.

"What? Nothing," he said, catching up.

"Did everything go all right at work today?" she asked suspiciously. "Come to think of it, you've been acting weird ever since you came home."

"Work?" He was an accountant, he reminded himself, an accountant. "Sure. Well," he added, now remembering things in rushes, "we've got to pick up the slack. Tom's passing left us with a gaping hole to fill."

"Imagine what it did to his wife and family," Jean said caustically. "Suicide." She shook her head. "And none of you noticed it coming?" she asked.

Ed shrugged. "The man was no barrel of laughs, but depressed enough to take his own life?"

"Not that you would have noticed anyway," Jean said. "You didn't even notice I am wearing a new sweater tonight."

"You know, I thought that looked new," he replied. He had noticed it, but then again, all her clothes looked new to him these days.

Jean just grunted.

"How horrible it must still be for Bernice," she said, shaking her head. "She told me she never even knew he had

a pistol. That's so strange. Don't you think?" she asked him
quickly.

He nodded without speaking. There was a very faint
buzzing beginning at the base of his brain, triggered by the
references to Tom Storm's suicide. Images of a pistol barrel
flashed. He saw the tip of it press firmly against Tom's
temple. The report was muffled, but his head exploded.
Somehow, he didn't believe a man's head would come
apart as easily as a cantaloupe. Tom looked up with such
surprise in his eyes, but it had to be done. Ed didn't know
all the details and reasons why, but there were things he
had to accept on faith . . . like believing rain came out of
clouds. One part of him was honored, proud to have been a
contributor to the solution, but another part of him, a deeper
part, was troubled and irritated. Instinctively, he knew it
was that part that was causing these damn headaches. He
had told Dr. Randolph, but she didn't seem to care. Her indifference made him think it wasn't significant.

They were nearly to the corner. The buzzing became
louder. Jean was talking, but he didn't hear a word, just the
background sound of her voice: a monotonous hum.

As soon as they turned onto Main Street, Ed had that familiar feeling he was entering a movie set.

The traffic moved at its usual lazy pace down Main
Street, past the courthouse, which was the only stone building in town, past the barbershop where Moe Wolfer and his
assistant, Arthur, trimmed hair and held discourses on poli-
tics and business, past George's Soda Fountain and Confec-
tionery Store, an authentic mom-and-pop establishment
where sodas were still made with syrup and seltzer, past the
small grocery, the two bar and grills, the three clothing
stores, the two drugstores, all in turn-of-the-century build-
ings with flat roofs and picture windows.

Sandburg was a clean, quiet village that resembled a

Norman Rockwell painting come to life. It looked frozen in time, untouched by fast-food establishments, self-service garages, video arcades, and movie rental outlets. The streets were clean and wide, the sidewalks nearly spotless. People walked casually, smiled at each other, waved and held friendly conversations. One could feel safe here. At least one should, Ed thought. Why didn't he?

The movie marquee blinked before them, but Ed was having trouble reading the words. Everything seemed to be going in and out of focus. The buzzing moved up from the base of his brain and formed a crown of stinging noise, closing completely around the top of his head. He felt as if his skull were being pried open and turned to look at himself in a store window.

His image was clear, but what was that line down his forehead? It grew thicker and thicker, taking on the color of dried blood. Finally, it began to open; his head was literally splitting apart. He slapped his hands over his ears and pressed hard to keep it from happening, but he couldn't stop it.

Vaguely, he heard Jean complaining beside him. What was he doing now? Why had he stopped? What was he looking at? What was wrong with her? Didn't she see what was happening to him? His head continued to come apart like an egg, splitting, but what was emerging was terrifying—it was another head, another face—the face he had seen in the mirror.

He spun around, searching for a way to stop it.

The man approaching them had a smile on his face. That was all Ed would remember. That was the sole justification for what he did. Maybe, maybe the man was laughing at his pain, he thought, but even that thought died quickly. The man nodded, muttered a greeting, and started by when Ed spun around.

He struck him behind his head with his closed fist and the man went down on his knees.

How do you like it? he screamed, but the scream was only in his mind. Jean's scream was different; everyone heard her scream.

She clawed him back as he began to kick at the fallen man. When he looked at her this time, he was positive he had no idea who she was. She was certainly not his wife.

He swung his arm and caught her in the mouth with the back of his hand. She seemed to fly up and back, falling into a parked car.

The buzzing became intolerable. He slammed his palms over his ears. His head was nearly split in two. How could he stop it? Finally, his scream broke through and he was being heard. But no one around him would dare come near him. He screamed again and again, crying out for someone to help, but they gaped in fear and astonishment instead. Then their faces began to melt, their eyeballs falling forward on their cheeks and dangling by threads of muscle. Their flesh dripped off and splattered on the sidewalk.

He spun himself around and around and around.

Finally, he dove face first into the plateglass window of Feinstein's T.V. Repair Shop where he had seen his head splitting.

The glass rained down around him, drops of ice, cutting into his flesh.

Good, he thought, his last thought before going unconscious. Good.

It's not my flesh anyway.

1

DR. RALPH STANLEY LEANED BACK AGAINST THE PLUSH REAR
seat of the gray stretch limousine and gazed dumbly out the
window as the vehicle rolled silently up Sixth Avenue toward Central Park. The deluxe automobile with its small
television set, stereo disc player and bar was practically
soundproof. All of the Manhattan street noises were muffled. On the sidewalks the tourists threaded through the
homeless as if they were truly invisible. Here and there a
bag lady pushing a grocery cart stuffed with her worldly
belongings blocked their paths and forced them to acknowledge her existence. Some reacted to her pleading and
bought their way to clear conscience by thrusting a dollar
or a handful of change into her sooty palm. For Stanley, all
of it—the excited theater patrons and visitors from other
countries, the beggars, the street walkers, the business people—all were now the cast of some panoramic dumb show.

But Ralph Stanley's mind was elsewhere anyway. His
thoughts traveled back as if the mind really were a tape
recorder one could merely rewind. Images of people being
wheeled in on gurneys flashed. Ambulance lights revolved
and blinked, as did police patrol cars. Harry Robinson, the
Sandburg chief of police, was at his side mumbling fearfully, but Ralph didn't hear him. He was concentrating too
intensely on the sight before him: Ed Walters's bloodied
face and skull, his eyes open but glazed over. Ed's visual
system had shut down, as had most of his body.

What was going on inside his head? Ralph Stanley won-

9

dered. Storms of thoughts? Lightning images? A torrent of words, names, places, none of which made clear sense? All the boundaries were broken inside his brain. Memories mixed and created unholy, illogical patterns. He was literally sizzling from within, a core of molten brain matter was preparing to blow the top of his head off and explode in a volcanic eruption of blood and neural matter.

Nancy Crowley and he had exchanged guilty glances. She had been at his side during most of it and the clandestine nature of what they were doing, as well as the social and political significance, had a strange effect on the two of them. It wasn't the first time a nurse and a doctor had formed an intimate relationship while working together, of course; but it was as if the two of them were coconspirators and needed to be reassured that they could trust each other as well. They became lovers, but lovers without great passion.

"We better get him up to the fourth floor stat, Nancy," he told her. She nodded and took control of Walters's gurney. As they rode in the elevator with Walters, she checked his pulse and blood pressure. Both were indicating potential stroke. The necessary medical protocol flipped through Ralph Stanley's mind, but he wondered, why bother? Why not let this . . . this what, man? . . . die?

This was his fault, too, wasn't it? He was a part of this team, wasn't he?

His fault, he thought again. Afterward, Nancy and he had agreed—it was time to get out. That was what he was here in New York to effect—a clean break, a true escape.

The limousine stopped for a light and Walter Fryman lit a cigarette. Ever since they had left the restaurant, the government man hadn't taken his eyes off Ralph Stanley. Ralph had felt his glare, but he had chosen to ignore it. He never had liked this man anyway. Right from the beginning, Ralph had felt repulsed by him, by his cold, calculating manner. Fryman was a man in his fifties, maybe even sixty years old, but he had a wildness in his eyes that reminded Ralph of younger, more restless and less disciplined men; certainly not someone with so much authority and power.

That was the word though, wasn't it? Power?

What was it Dr. Randolph, his mentor, had told him a number of times: "There are two main drives in higher living organisms—sex and power. Sometimes, the two are interchangeable," she added smiling wryly, if what she did with her lips and eyes could even be called a smile.

"What's the matter, Doctor? You haven't said a word since we left the restaurant," Fryman asked, pulling Ralph out of his reverie. He blew his smoke into the ceiling of the limousine and brought his cocktail to his lips, his eyes peering over the rim of the glass while he drank. As street lights penetrated the limousine and the glow washed over Fryman, Ralph Stanley caught the glint of amusement in the government man's dark eyes.

"I guess I had one too many Rob Roys," Ralph Stanley replied.

"Oh? Want to stop for something?"

"No, I can send down for some aspirin when I get to my hotel room," Ralph said. He was ever so anxious to get out of this limousine and away from Fryman, away from all of them.

"It's rather a nice spring evening here, isn't it?" Fryman said looking out the window. "A bit too warm, if anything," he added.

"I was never especially fond of New York," Ralph Stanley said. Fryman smirked.

"Country boy at heart, huh?"

"Yes, I suppose I am."

"You can take the boy out of the country, but you can't take the country out of the boy?"

"Something like that," Ralph replied dryly.

"We used to sing, 'You can take the girl out of the cunttry, but you can't take the cunt out of the girl,'" Fryman quipped. He laughed at his own joke, but Ralph simply stared blankly at the street.

How had he ever gotten involved with such people? he wondered. What wrong turns did he make? Thank God he was getting out and returning to UCLA Medical.

"We're almost at the hotel," Fryman said. "Last chance to change your mind," he sang.

Ralph Stanley turned to look at him.

"No, I don't think so. I'm . . . burned out on this. I wouldn't be of any good anymore," he said.

"A man as young as you are, burned out? What are you, all of forty?"

"It's not a matter of age; it's a matter of intensity. When you're at something so hard and so long, it wears on you in ways you don't expect," Ralph Stanley explained.

"Too bad. You were, in Doctor Congemi's words, 'of inestimable value,'" Fryman said, speaking with exaggerated nasality and lifting his head to mimic Dr. Congemi's arrogant tilt. "All you geniuses," Fryman muttered and shook his head disdainfully. He took another long sip of his cocktail and leaned forward until he looked on the edge of his seat. "I hated college, every minute of it," he added, his voice filled with aggression. "Right up to the moment of graduation."

Ralph Stanley thought the man might leap at him.

"Why did you stay then?" he asked.

"My father . . . my father would have hunted me down and shot me as quickly and as easily as he hunted deer and coons," Fryman replied, but he didn't seem resentful about that. "The old man was a rock in body and thought," he said with admiration in his voice. "He taught me well.

" 'Walter,' he said, 'remember this: what doesn't destroy you, makes you stronger.' Understand?" he asked.

"Yes," Ralph Stanley said. He understood that such a philosophy would make Fryman contemptuous of him, too. In the government man's eyes, he was weak. Well, if morality made him seem weak, then so be it.

"Well, well," Fryman said. "Looks like we're here."

The limousine pulled up before the doorman who hurried to open the door for them. Ralph Stanley started to get out, but Fryman leaned forward and put his large palm on Ralph's right knee firmly. Their eyes met and Ralph Stanley saw Fryman's psychotic coldness.

"I don't suppose I have to remind you about your oath of secrecy, do I?"

"No," Ralph said quickly.

"This project's too important for any monkeyshines," Fryman warned.

"What project?" Ralph said. Fryman smiled widely.

"You know, I liked you, Doctor Stanley. Of all of them, I liked you the most."

"Somehow, I'm not sure that's a compliment," Ralph said and pulled himself up and out of the limousine.

Fryman's smile wilted quickly.

"I'm not getting out," he snapped at the doorman.

"Very good, sir," the doorman replied and closed the limousine door. Fryman watched Dr. Stanley enter the hotel. Then he turned to the chauffeur.

"Drive," he commanded. The limousine started away. Slowly, Fryman leaned forward and lifted the telephone receiver. He sat back and punched out some numbers. The voice on the other end was merely a whisper.

"Yes?"

"Make the withdrawal just as we instructed," Fryman ordered. "Understand?"

"Understood," the voice replied.

Fryman returned the receiver to its cradle and finished his drink in a gulp. A jam-up at the next traffic light stopped the limousine's progress. Horns blared. Pedestrians seized the advantage and flooded by, their arms and hips grazing the sides and windows.

"Damn it! *Get me the fuck out of here!*" Fryman screamed, his face distorted in agony. He had a wild animal's antipathy toward anything in the slightest way confining. Once, when he was caught in a terrific traffic jam on the beltway around Washington, D.C., he got out of his vehicle and walked, leaving the car still running, panting like a dumb animal on the side of the highway. He never doubted he would chew off his leg to escape a trap, just like the beavers and raccoons his father used to hunt.

Frustration handcuffed him and he wouldn't be handcuffed, even figuratively.

THE man in the black-and-white pinstripe suit sat in the darkness, not a muscle moving. He had his hands on his lap, palms down. In his mind commands rolled by like news bulletins. The same words were repeated, the same instructions. It was as if his eyes were turned inward. He had a momentary vision of himself—a man with a rubber face, the mouth shifting and twisting, the nose dipping and then shortening, the eyes bone white.

Vaguely he heard the sound of voices in the hotel hallway. Guests were talking and laughing on their way to and from the bank of elevators at the end of the corridor. After the phone call, he had just relaxed in the same chair, waiting. The process that had been initiated in his brain ticked on like the clock on a time bomb. He could almost hear it inside himself.

When he recognized that footsteps in the hallway were coming in his direction and had stopped at the door, he rose quickly and moved with stealth to a dark corner of the hotel room, away from the door. The click of the key in the lock sounded like the hammer of a pistol being cocked. Then the door opened and a wave of light rushed in, washing away the darkness.

Ralph Stanley found the light switch and flipped it quickly. Then he closed the door and walked directly toward the telephone. He and Nancy had made up their minds the hour after he had pronounced Ed Walters dead; they were going to expose them. They were going to bring it to an end before it was completely successful and out of control.

He had just lifted the receiver to call Nancy to tell her the first stage of their plan had been completed, when he sensed someone was behind him. He turned and looked into the intruder's eyes. They seemed as bland as Ed Walters's eyes had been. For a moment he didn't recognize him. Then he realized it was Sam Heller, Sam Heller who was just over a year old. What the hell was Sam Heller doing in his hotel room in New York?

"Sam?" he began, but Heller caught him between the legs with his closed fist. The blow was so quick and so unexpected, Ralph Stanley hadn't even had a good instinctive reaction and his legs closed a split second after Heller's fist contacted his balls squarely on center. The rush of pain crumpled him as a girdle of agony quickly tightened around his waist. It blew the air from his lungs as well. Helpless, he put up little resistance as Heller, with an incredible burst of strength and speed, spun him around and seized him at the neck and buttocks, driving him forward toward the balcony.

Ralph tried to protest and stop his forward progress, but the patio doors were already slightly open, so that when his body hit them, they blew apart. The momentum increased. Heller rushed him forward toward the railing of the balcony. Ralph managed to get out a single scream and straighten up some as Heller lifted him and cast him over the railing with seeming ease.

Dr. Ralph Stanley experienced the shock of denial when he went over. He seemed to be flying for a moment, and then the lights below exploded in his eyes as he dropped twenty-three stories. Mercifully, he managed to pass out just before he hit the door of the parked taxicab.

Sam Heller didn't look down to see the results. He turned with an automated jerk and walked through the suite and out into the corridor. He walked slowly to his own hotel room just up to the right and casually took the key out of his sports jacket pocket. He opened the door and turned on the lights. Then he went to the bathroom and brushed his hair. Satisfied that he looked neat, he put out the lights and left the hotel room. He was hungry; he needed a little snack, he thought.

Standing before the elevator, he smiled at two women when the doors opened and they stepped out. Then he got in and punched L for lobby. He felt rather tired for some reason and decided that as soon as he had something to eat, he would retire to his room, relax, watch some television and then go to sleep. He had an early plane to catch.

After all, he was anxious to get home to his wife and children.

MARION Boxletter forced herself to smile as she reentered the cocktail lounge from the ladies' room. She really hadn't had to go to the bathroom. She just needed to be alone for a moment and splash some cold water on her face. The piano player looked up and smiled back at her. He appreciated pretty women and Marion was a very attractive thirty-two-year-old brunette. She was five feet ten with a sleek, model's figure: perky firm breasts, a waist so narrow her husband could put his hands around it, and long, shapely legs.

A little more than a year ago, if she and Bob were vacationing in New York City like this, she would have requested the piano player do their song, but ever since her and Bob's nine-year-old son, Joey, and her brother, Brian, disappeared on a camping trip, she had felt like a zombie. Even if something made her laugh or if something tasted good or felt good, she would hesitate to enjoy it because it made her feel guilty to do so. At Bob's insistence, she had finally begun seeing a therapist, but all that had done so far was made her more aware of how deeply her sorrow went.

"You're being unfair to Sherri," Bob had finally declared. "Why destroy both children?"

She knew he was sorry he had put it so harshly, but what he was saying wasn't far from the truth. Their six-year-old daughter was almost without a mother these days. Marion was often distracted and often lapsed into long mental depressions. She thought she had been bad when her father died a little over two years ago. He had been the last of their parents to go, but unlike her mother and Bob's parents, her father had been a vibrant, active man right up until the day he keeled over. And Joey loved him so, she thought.

Bob had taken up the slack as much and as well as he could, doing as much as possible with Sherri, but his work at the computer company had grown more complex this last year. Actually, she finally agreed to this vacation more because of her concern for him than for herself.

Despite his strength, Bob had aged this past year. He was still a firmly built, six-feet-one-inch man with broad shoulders. An athlete all his life, he maintained a muscular body with just the slightest evidence of a pouch developing lately. But there were dark shadows under his eyes more often and his light brown hair looked thinner. They were a handsome couple, Marion thought; it was just that these days, they moved like mourners under a perpetual dark cloud.

As she crossed the plush hotel lounge with its soft blood-red leather-cushioned booths and marble bar, she saw the way Bob's college buddy Tim Watson and his wife, Clarissa, were staring at her. Marion was positive they had been discussing her and her condition. She had tried not to be a burden, a killjoy, but there were things she just couldn't help.

How could she look at a family with the children holding onto their parents' hands and not think of her own tragedy? How could she stop the nightmares, those dreams about Joey freezing to death in the wild, screaming for her, begging her to save him and finally closing his eyes and fading away in the snow? Somewhere, miles and miles deep in the forests, her baby's bones lay exposed. Wild animals had feasted on his flesh. God, how these thoughts tore her apart. It was as if something were alive in her brain, gnawing away every night. Soon she would be without a mind, and truly become the zombie she imagined she appeared to be now. She had had to stop going to college part-time. It had been her intention to eventually complete her degree and get certified to teach in elementary school, but that ambition was practically dead and buried.

"You all right?" Bob asked as she approached the table. She nodded. His dark brown eyes were full of concern.

"We're thinking about calling it a night anyway," Clarissa said. "And you two have to catch an early flight back to Ohio."

Marion nodded. She could see how anxious Clarissa was to end this. It hadn't been fun for her, not the way it used to be before the tragedy. Then, the two of them were like high school girls whenever they all got together. They used to have such good times on their shopping sprees through Bloomingdale's and Saks and Bergdorf Goodman. This time, they hadn't gone anywhere together. Marion was actually terrified of leaving Bob's side.

"I'll see you at breakfast, won't I?" she asked, half expecting them to come up with an excuse why they couldn't make it. She wouldn't blame them.

"Oh sure," Tim said. "Eight-thirty, right here."

"Well, then . . ." Bob said, standing. Tim and Clarissa got up quickly. On cue, Marion thought. They're all pretending to be spontaneous when in truth they've planned and discussed every little action. Everyone feels he or she has to tiptoe around me these days, she thought sadly, for she knew it was true.

Clarissa and Bob hugged; then she turned to hug Marion.

"Have a good night's sleep," Clarissa said. Her embrace was quick, perfunctory, as if she feared embracing her too hard would cause her to shatter like thin crystal.

Do I really look that fragile? Marion wondered.

"See you in the A.M.," Tim said, hugging her quickly, too.

"Good night."

Bob put his arm around her waist and the two of them started out of the lounge.

Outside the hotel, ambulance and police sirens wailed,

but neither she nor Bob paid any attention to them. They were both lost in their thoughts.

"I'm sorry I was such a drag," Marion said as they approached the elevators.

"They understood," Bob replied.

"Everyone has to understand. Poor Marion." Her sad, tired eyes became bright with anger, but it was anger directed more at herself than at anyone else.

"Easy, baby." He tightened his grip on her waist. "Hold it together."

"I'm trying, Bob. I really am."

"I know."

She took his hand and they both stepped back as the elevator door opened and people began to emerge. Sam Heller was the last to step out. He turned quickly toward the dining room, but not quickly enough for Marion to miss him.

She gasped, her fingernails digging into Bob's palm so sharply he had to cry out.

"Hey!"

"Bob, look," she cried, stepping forward.

"Huh?"

"It's Brian. It's my brother!" she cried and charged after Sam Heller. "BRIAN!" she screamed, but Heller kept walking. "BRIAN!"

"Marion, wait . . ." Bob looked at the people who had stopped to listen. He smiled weakly and then ran after her. "Shit," he muttered. She was almost at the man.

He saw her reach out and seize his wrist.

"Oh, no."

But when the man turned, Bob stopped in his tracks. It was Brian; it was his brother-in-law.

Heller spun around and stared at the frantic woman who gazed at him with wild eyes, her hands at her bosom as her shoulders lifted and fell with her excited breathing.

"What is it?" he demanded. He saw Bob approach slowly to stand by her side, his eyes just as maddeningly wide.

"Brian. It's me . . . Marion. What are you doing here? Where's Joey?"

"Brian?" Bob asked incredulously.

Heller looked from Bob to Marion and shook his head.

"I'm afraid you've got the wrong person. Sorry," he said and started away. But Marion chased after him and grabbed his shoulder, spinning him around again. People passing stopped to watch. Heller was conscious of the fact that they were gathering an audience. They won't like this, he thought. They won't like me being noticed. The realization drove a shard of fear into his heart.

"What the hell is this, lady? I told you, you've got the wrong person," he snapped. He didn't want to be too emphatic with his protest. That would cause a bigger scene and he still had a chance to escape relatively unnoticed.

"Where's Joey?" Marion demanded, ignoring his protestation. "Where's my son?"

"Son? Hey, mister, is this your wife?" he asked Bob.

"Yes. I'm sorry," Bob said, coming up beside her and taking her arm, "but you have an amazing resemblance to my brother-in-law and . . ."

"Hey, I'm not your brother-in-law, okay? Now I'd like to go get something to eat."

"Where's Joey?" Marion cried, tears streaming down her cheeks.

"Marion." Bob embraced her and pulled her tightly to him to prevent her from doing anything else.

"Why won't he tell us where Joey is?" she cried through her tears.

Sam Heller shook his head and started away again, this time moving more quickly.

"Bob, don't let him go," Marion pleaded.

"Easy, honey. Easy."

"But . . ."

He put his finger on her lips.

"Shh, shh," he said. "Obviously, it wasn't Brian. It's just a coincidence. That's all. He's a man who looks like Brian, nothing more. Just a coincidence," he repeated.

Marion turned and saw the pockets of people gathered about watching and listening. She sucked in her breath and wiped the tears from her cheeks.

"Come on, honey, let's go up," Bob coaxed softly.

She hesitated. It was as if Joey's spirit were slipping through her fingers.

"Easy, easy," Bob chanted. She permitted him to turn her toward the elevator. As they started for an empty one, she looked back after Sam Heller. He was already gone, but in his wake, she felt the ominous shadows of something terrible, something that resembled her nightmares.

2

MARION COULDN'T FALL ASLEEP, EVEN AFTER TAKING TWO OF the sleeping pills. What surprised her was Bob tossing and turning. Usually, he was so much stronger, almost always able to contain his emotions. Finally, she heard him get up and saw him go to the window to look out at the New York skyline.

The only other time he had been this restless was shortly after Joey and Brian were reported missing. She had been hysterical most of the time, and for a good part of the time, under sedation. Bob had gone out with the search party and had discovered evidence of Brian's and Joey's camp.

"Their tracks just seem to disappear," he told her after he had returned. "It was as if the two of them stepped onto the air and walked away."

"Walked up to heaven, Bob?" she cried shrilly. "Walked up to heaven?"

"Easy, honey," he said trying to embrace her, but she wouldn't be embraced; she wouldn't be consoled. Consolation led to acceptance and she would never accept.

"NO!" She backed away from him. "My baby's not dead and gone. He's not!" she insisted.

"Marion . . ."

"NO, NO, NO." She was pounding herself so hard that welts began to develop on her thighs. He had to seize her wrists and restrain her until she crumbled into tears and finally took another pill.

Those early nights, just like tonight, she would waken

and see Bob standing by a window looking out as if he expected Brian and Joey to come walking up to the house. She had fantasized it often.

"Hi, Sis," Brian would say. "Boy did we have a time. I bet you guys were frantic."

"Mommy!" Joey would cry and come running into her arms. Sometimes the fantasy was so strong, she sctually felt his body and woke satisfied. It had all been a nightmare. Joey was home, asleep in his room, safe. They were still a whole family, intact, together, forever, she and Bob, Sherri and Joey.

"Bob?" she said, and he turned from the hotel room window.

"Sorry. I didn't want to wake you."

"I haven't fallen asleep yet," she said. He was silent a moment. Then, he stepped toward her.

"It's almost as if we're being tortured," Bob said.

"I know."

"To come upon a man who resembled your brother so closely . . . why? Is it just that we're looking for resemblances, for hope and so we find it?"

"No, Bob." She sat up.

"It's a nightmare; it's more than a nightmare; it's a lifetime of torment and why? Why us?"

"Bob." She held her arms out and he came to her. She embraced him and he pressed his cheek to hers.

"I'm sorry," he said. "I just feel very angry tonight and it's hard to sleep."

"It's okay, honey." For once, the roles had been reversed and she was comforting him. She enjoyed it; it helped her. "Let's just lie here together. If we fall asleep, we fall asleep."

"Right." Bob's body trembled with a sob. Then they were both as still as they could be.

"Remember when we fell asleep in each other's arms in the back of your car after the fraternity dance?" she said. If only we could fall back through time and start over, she thought, with just this one foreknowledge: not to let Joey go with Brian on that camping trip.

"Yeah," Bob said. "Everyone thought we had gone to a motel for sure. I would have, but in those days, who had the money to spend on motel rooms?"

"It was more romantic in the back of your car," she said. "Maybe not too comfortable, but romantic."

He laughed. Then they were both silent again, lost in their thoughts.

"What a remarkable likeness," Marion muttered under her breath.

Sometime just before morning, they did fall asleep. The wake-up call shocked them both. Bob fumbled for the phone and thanked the operator. Then, without speaking, the two of them prepared to go down to breakfast and check out. They emerged from the elevators and entered the dining room looking like somnambulists. It brought a smile to Tim Watson's face.

"Look, Clarissa, zombies."

"Sorry, guys," Bob said as they approached the table. "We just couldn't get it together quickly this morning."

"No need to apologize," Clarissa said charitably. "We should be the ones apologizing. Timmy couldn't wait so he ordered a Danish." She gave her husband a glance of chastisement. He shrugged and continued to chew.

"So, Bobby-boy, what happened to the early riser who used to drive me crazy about making morning classes in college?" Timmy joked.

"Disappeared along with the jump shot from the corner," Bob said. He pulled out a chair for Marion.

"Stop teasing him, Timmy," Clarissa said. She smiled at

Marion. "It's no wonder you two had a hard time getting up. You must have had quite a night."

Marion looked quickly at Bob, wondering how he could have told them. He shook his head.

"Quite a night?" he said.

"It's all over the news," Timmy said. Bob and Marion held their quizzical expressions. "Don't you guys know?"

"Know what?" Bob asked quickly.

"Someone took a dive out of his hotel window last night. On your floor, too. You really hadn't heard?"

"No," Bob said. "We . . . well, we got distracted and then turned in early. We didn't even watch television, so we didn't catch the late news. Who did what?"

"It was some doctor from California, a research scientist," Clarissa replied.

"Jumped or was pushed?" Marion asked.

"Right now, they think jumped. Something about a suicide note being found. I don't know . . . details are sketchy," Tim said. "This city is getting crazy. Something in the air here, I think. The murder rate is on the rise, suicides, rapes. A corpse has to take a number down at the morgue."

Marion shook her head, but as she did so, someone caught her eye. She looked past the two tables on her right and saw him again . . . the man from the elevator, the man who looked like Brian. He was sipping coffee and reading a newspaper.

"Everyone ready to order?" the waiter asked.

"Yes," Bob said. "Marion?"

"What?"

"Breakfast?"

"Just coffee, regular," she said quickly and turned back to stare.

"You've got to eat something, Marion," Bob said. "We won't eat again until . . ."

"All right, all right." She looked up at the waiter. "Toast. Whole wheat."

As the others ordered, she stared at the man again, watching his every move. He didn't sit like Brian used to sit; he had stiffer, firmer posture, and Brian wasn't one to read *The Wall Street Journal,* but the shape of his head, his ears . . . He drained his coffee cup and folded his paper. She saw him signal for the waiter.

"Are you anxious to get home?" Clarissa asked. She vaguely heard.

"Marion?" Bob said.

"What? Oh, yes and no," she replied quickly. She couldn't keep her eyes off the man.

"Yes and no?" Clarissa said. She looked at Bob.

"Marion, what are you . . ."

His gaze followed hers and he saw the man get up from the table. For a moment he couldn't speak either.

"He's left-handed," Marion said. "He signed his check with his left hand."

"Who's left-handed?" Timmy asked. He turned in his seat.

"Marion," Bob said softly. "A great many people are left-handed."

"That's interesting news," Timmy Wilson said, turning back to them. He gazed at Clarissa, but she just shrugged.

Marion watched the man leave and then, suddenly, she stood up.

"Marion?"

"Excuse me," she said and headed for the man's table.

"What's going on?" Clarissa asked.

"Bob?"

They all turned to watch as Marion crossed quickly to

the table. She paused when she got there and read the bill. He had signed it, Sam Heller, Room 1203. Ingesting the name, she started to put the bill down and turn to go back to her table, when her eyes fell on the nearly empty water glass.

It is Brian, she thought. It is.

Without hesitation, she wrapped a napkin around the glass and gently lifted it, emptied the remaining water, and started back to her table.

"What's she doing?" Tim asked as Marion returned. Bob shook his head.

"What are you doing with that glass, honey?" he asked.

"Fingerprints," she said.

Tim and Clarissa exchanged uneasy glances as Marion placed the glass gingerly into her purse.

"He signed his name Sam Heller," she muttered. "He's staying in this hotel."

"Why would you want someone's fingerprints, Marion?" Clarissa asked.

Instead of replying, Marion got up again.

"Honey?"

"I'll be right back," she said and started for the front desk.

"Hey, what the hell is going on here?" Timmy demanded. "Why would she want some guy's fingerprints?"

"She thinks he's her brother," Bob finally revealed.

"Her brother? You mean . . ."

"Oh no, poor thing," Clarissa said. "Has this been happening often, Bob?"

"No," he said. He turned back to them. "The thing is the guy does bear a strong resemblance. He even had me going for a moment last night," he said and he described the incident at the elevator.

"I suppose such things are quite understandable,"

Clarissa said. "There was that story in the paper last week. Remember, Timmy? The one about the mother whose child had been stolen while she was shopping."

"Oh, yeah," Timmy said, but it was obvious he didn't remember.

"What about her?" Bob asked.

"She sees her child everywhere now. She even tried to take another woman's baby and had to be forcibly restrained. I think they called it the self-denial syndrome or something. It's part of a refusal to believe your loved one is gone."

They looked toward the front as Marion turned away from the desk and started back.

"I'm so sorry, Bob," Clarissa said. "So sorry."

"He's from Sandburg, New York," Marion said, sitting down. Her face was flushed with excitement. "Do you know where that is, Timmy?"

He shook his head.

"Sandburg? Never heard of it. Must be some small, upstate town."

"His signature was so different," Marion said looking back toward the table and the bill.

"So put it to rest, honey," Bob coaxed. "Put it to rest."

The waiter brought their food.

"Oh, I only ordered toast," Marion realized. She looked up at the waiter. "I think I'll have some scrambled eggs," she said. It was as if she had just woken up and realized they were at breakfast. Everyone at the table had to laugh. It was a welcome moment of relief.

NANCY Crowley couldn't take her eyes off the telephone all morning. Ralph was supposed to have called her last night and confirmed everything. She had her bags packed and waiting, but the call never came and here it was late morning and still he hadn't called. She had barely gotten a few hours of sleep, afraid every time she closed her eyes that she wouldn't hear the phone ring. She practically had it under her head.

Now she tried to occupy herself, make herself some breakfast, read, watch some television, but her gaze kept falling on the phone in whatever room she was in, as if her merely glancing at it would cause it to ring. It did ring once, but it was only Sue Cohen over at the hospital confirming the week's schedule. She tried to sound nonchalant, almost indifferent to the days and hours, but she couldn't keep her voice from cracking a bit when Sue asked her what she was doing on her day off.

"Nothing much," she told her. "Catching up on some reading and doing some long-overdue household chores. You know how I hate to clean."

"The man you marry better be into sharing," Sue said. "Unless of course, you marry a doctor and you have an army of servants," she added. Everyone was buzzing about her and Ralph, Nancy thought. No matter how discreet she and Ralph were, their coworkers picked up the vibes, be it a look, a touch, or a soft word.

Ralph was a good man, she thought. Despite all this, he is a moral man, a brilliant man who has been betrayed, deceived, exploited. The angrier she got at people like Dr. Randolph and Dr. Congemi, the easier it was to accept Ralph's significant contributions to this horrendous project. His intentions were noble; theirs . . . greed and simple lust for power. That's the way she saw it now.

She had to confess it wasn't always the way she envisioned it. When she had first become part of the project, she was honored. She had been asked to work alongside some of the best minds in the field and they had recognized her abilities and experience. She never really cared for Dr.

Randolph, but she did admire her achievements, and she did like Dr. Congemi, at least in the beginning. He looked like someone's kind old grandfather and spoke softly, quietly, with that Santa Claus smile and twinkling blue eyes. Even when he said things that might unnerve someone, he did it calmly, making it seem like nothing, like nothing at all.

"We'll have to maintain a tight lid of security on all this, Nancy," he had first explained. "Not because we're doing anything illegal, but because we're doing things that the public might not understand at first. Confusion, misinformation could bring down one of the most significant scientific advances in the history of animal behavior."

Nancy winced at that. She never liked the way some scientists referred to mankind as just another species in the animal kingdom.

"So when you leave here at the end of the workday, you must put it all aside. If people want to know what sort of nursing you do, you tell them intensive care and leave it at that. Understand?"

She nodded. It didn't seem all that terrible to lie and keep tight-lipped then, and the pay was nearly three times what nurses normally received. Then she met Ralph and there were even greater dividends. In time they grew to trust and confide in each other, and finally, they admitted their mutual distaste for what they were ultimately doing. The straw that broke the camel's back, as they say, was definitely Ed Walters. When Ralph had discovered what Walters had been used for, he went wild. She would never forget the night he burst into her apartment and told her.

"I'm an accessory to murder," he cried to her. "That's what I am. And all in the name of science, a project to better mankind. I should have known."

She calmed him down and talked him into staying the

night. That was when they began to plan their retreat. At
first, that was all they were going to do—leave the project
and start somewhere new. Ralph would return to UCLA
and she would return to nursing at a city hospital. But when
Walters was brought in and Ralph realized what was happening, they decided they had to do more. They had to end
it.

"It's the only way I can live with what I have done already," Ralph told her. She didn't oppose it.

"I don't mind us blowing the whistle, Ralph; I'm just a
little frightened."

"I understand," he had told her. "I'll do it quickly, so
quickly they won't have a chance to stop us and after that,
they won't be able to harm us without drawing enormous
attention to themselves. I have a good friend who works for
the *New York Times*."

It seemed reasonable. Anyway, she had learned to depend and rely on his judgment a great deal. He was so
bright, the most intelligent and clear-thinking man she had
ever been involved with. For the first time, she felt she had
something substantial in a relationship.

But why hadn't he called? It wasn't like him to miss
doing something he had planned himself. He was too organized, too orderly and concise. A more meticulous person
she couldn't find. She used to laugh at that, especially when
she considered her own habits. Ralph would come into this
apartment, she thought, and start cleaning up. I'm not a
slob, but anyone would feel that way when Ralph took control. It was all right; they both laughed about it. At least he
had a sense of humor about himself. That was more than
she could say about Randolph and Congemi. Dr. Randolph
especially thought she walked on water.

Ring, damn it, she thought. She wanted to phone his
hotel, but he had specifically instructed her not to.

"I don't want them tying you to me on this," he had said. "Not yet. I'll call you. Don't worry. Just be ready to leave."

Of course, she made sure no one had an inkling that she was planning to leave. It was partly because they had both become somewhat paranoid, but just to make sure no one even suspected her leaving, she went to the supermarket yesterday after work and bought nearly two hundred dollars' worth of groceries. She made a big show of it, too.

The house was stocked; she was scheduled for work; she hadn't cancelled a thing—not the newspaper, not the cable service, nothing. She kept her packing down to a minimum, too. The moment after Ralph phoned, she would pick up her two bags and rush out to the car.

Why should anyone be watching anyway? she thought. Why should anyone suspect? Ralph wasn't telling them until he was in New York and by that time, it would be too late for them to stop him, stop us.

"Ring, damn it!" she cried. This was no good. She was no good at waiting. She had to phone the hotel; she just had to find out why he hadn't done what he was supposed to do. She went to the phone and lifted the receiver, but then she stopped. What if she were messing things up? What if there had been some minor complication and Ralph just had to hold off? He would expect her to be patient, and not deviate from the plan.

But a phone call, she mused. How much of a deviation is a phone call?

If your phone's tapped, if his calls are being monitored, it could be a major deviation, she concluded and put the receiver back. She retreated to the living room, sat down and stared at the television set. A commercial for pet food reminded her about Fluffy.

The cat, she thought. She would have to leave it. Where was that little princess anyway? It was a ball of white fur with two luminous kelly green eyes. She could use its warmth and comfort right now; she wanted to hold it and have it purring in her lap.

"Fluffy," she called and got up. She went to the kitchen and looked under the table and around the cupboard, but it wasn't there. She went to her bedroom and got down on her hands and knees to peer under her bed. Often, during warmer days, it would settle in there and sleep. But it wasn't there either.

She stood up and thought. As she did so, she looked at herself in the mirror above the dresser. I look a mess, she thought. I didn't even run a brush through my hair this morning. Not that she had much hair to brush. She always kept her light brown hair short, clipped mid-ear and trim in the back. Rarely did she wear any makeup. Her dark brown eyes looked bloodshot and her lids drooped from lack of sleep. She wasn't a vain woman, far from it, but she thought the wrinkles around her eyes were too deep for a woman in her late twenties.

Tension does it, she concluded. Nothing ages you like tension. She shook her head at herself and brushed down the front of her blouse where it had picked up some lint while she had looked under the bed. Then she went to the front door and looked out over the sidewalk and lawn of the townhouse complex. As always it was picture-perfect quiet: a little traffic moving lazily past the driveway, only an occasional pedestrian. Most everyone else who lived in the Laurel Garden Estates was at work. She knew some of her neighbors were transfixed on the "Phil Donahue Show" or "Geraldo." A dog barked somewhere in the distance and then, just as she was about to close the door, she heard the thin wail of a siren.

Ordinarily, she would have thought nothing of it, but the hospital's ambulances had a distinct siren—a pulsating, high-pitched sharp scream that sliced through anyone within range and caused drivers and pedestrians to hurry out of its path. It was literally painful to hear.

The siren grew louder as the ambulance continued in her direction. From the amplification of the sound, she knew it had turned off Main Street and toward Laurel Avenue. Curious, she remained in the doorway and sure enough, the ambulance appeared on her street and then turned sharply into the Laurel Garden Estates driveway. She stood there watching as it came to a halt right in front of her unit.

The doors were thrown open and the attendants, without looking her way, jumped out and hurried around to the rear of the ambulance. The rear doors were jerked open and the taller, stouter attendant reached in and pulled out the gurney on his own. She saw his neck muscles thicken as he held the stretcher between his large hands and lowered it softly to the ground. Then the two of them rolled it up the walk.

Something must have happened to Mrs. Steiner, Nancy thought. The elderly woman lived alone next door. Nancy knew she was well into her seventies, but until now, she assumed she was in remarkable health. She always appeared vibrant, energetic and quite independent.

The wheels of the gurney rattled down the walk. Nancy folded her arms under her bosom and waited until the attendants reached her. The taller one pushed while the shorter one followed along, carrying a doctor's bag. She didn't recognize either man and she thought she knew all the ambulance personnel.

"Is it Mrs. Steiner?" she asked.

Neither replied. The smaller man unstrapped the bed of the gurney. Then the two of them turned to her.

"I'm a nurse," she explained. "Maybe I can be of some help."

"Are you Nancy Crowley?" the taller attendant asked.

"Yes." She smiled. Someone in the emergency room must have remarked about the proximity of the address.

The taller attendant looked at his partner.

"Seriously hyperventilating," he said.

"Yes," his partner said, nodding.

"Poor color, too."

"Blood pressure dropping rapidly."

"Pardon?" Nancy said looking from one to the other.

Without warning, the taller man reached out and seized her upper arms, pinning them close to her body and back. The shorter man quickly opened the bag and stepped up as the larger attendant forced Nancy back into her apartment. Before she could scream, the shorter attendant clamped a chloroform-soaked rag over her mouth and nose. She tried to struggle, but the big man's grip was firm and tight. She felt his fingers pressing so hard into her arms that he reached bone.

Vaguely, just before going unconscious, she thought, I'm going to have some terrible black and blue marks there. I bruise so easily.

Then she went limp.

The shorter attendant put the cloth back into the bag and closed it quickly. He moved the gurney to the door and the two of them lifted the unconscious Nancy Crowley and dropped her on the stretcher. They strapped her in quickly and began to roll her away.

Mrs. Steiner opened her door and stepped out. She had been peering out of her front window.

"What happened?" she cried. "What's wrong with Nancy?"

"Possible heart attack," the taller attendant called back.

"Oh dear, no," Mrs. Steiner said, clutching her hands to the base of her throat. "Such a young woman."

After they had loaded the stretcher into the ambulance and started away, Mrs. Steiner shook her head again and started back into her townhouse when something made her stop and think.

"That's odd," she muttered. "They weren't giving her any oxygen."

She stood there for a moment longer until she spotted Fluffy, Nancy's cat, meandering its way back.

"Oh, you poor thing," Mrs. Steiner called. "Here Fluffy. I'll feed you," she said and the cat, as if it understood, stopped and then turned to continue in her direction.

3

THE FADED YELLOW TAXICAB, A RETREADED CITY TAXI WITH its lettering under a thin layer of fresh paint and still vaguely visible, turned down the corner of Highland Avenue. The normally peaceful residential street in Spring Glen, Ohio, with its sprawling maples and hickory trees was bustling with activity. The public school, only four blocks away, had let out a little over a half hour ago, and its emancipated young inmates were exploding with excitement and activity. A number of boys were guiding skateboards down the sidewalk, some of them looking quite proficient and gliding from side to side as gracefully as surfers. In the Morrisons' large front yard and long driveway, a small group of neighborhood children were playing stickball, and off to the left, on the Collinses' driveway, a half dozen girls were jumping rope with a clump of boys jeering and teasing around them.

Marion gazed sadly out the rear window of the cab. If Joey were here, he would be with his friends doing all the things a nine-year-old boy should be doing. The screams and cries of the children were like tiny knives poking into the surface of her heart. She winced and choked back tears. Bob knew what she was feeling. The moment they had stepped off the plane and he had realized what time of day it was and what they would find on their block, he anticipated her reaction. He put his hand on her shoulder.

She turned and smiled up at him.

"I'm all right," she said.

38

"Sure?"

"Yes. I won't let Sherri see me this way," she added, knowing that was his chief concern now. She wiped away a tear that had settled on the crown of her cheek.

Bob sighed deeply and looked ahead. Their gingerbread house came into view. It had a detached garage and a sidewalk that curved up from the driveway. Neatly pruned hedges bordered the walk.

"Sherri left her bike on the front walk again," Bob commented as the driver turned into their driveway. The moment the taxi came to a stop, the front door of the house opened and six-year-old Sherri Boxletter burst out over the porch and down the front steps. She was followed by fifty-eight-year-old Joan Waley, the Boxletters' baby-sitter. Mrs. Waley, a widow without children, was a godsend, as far as Marion was concerned. The gray-haired, soft-spoken, gentle woman was just like a grandmother to Sherri and highly reliable.

Sherri ran down the walk, stepping around her bike, and flew into Bob's opened arms.

"Hi, Pumpkin," he said, kissing her cheek.

"Why were you away so long?" she complained and pursed her lips.

"It wasn't *soooo* long," Bob said.

"Yes it was," Sherri insisted.

Bob shook his head and looked toward the approaching Mrs. Waley.

"Sounds to me like you got into a bit of trouble," he said. Sherri started to protest, but instead turned to Marion.

"MOMMY!" She reached out for her and Bob shifted her into Marion's waiting arms and kiss.

"Hi, Mrs. Waley," Bob said.

"Hello there. How was your trip?" She paused, her arms down, her hands clasped.

"Terrific," Bob said. "But there's no place like home."

"That's why I don't bother leaving it much," Mrs. Waley replied. "How are you, Marion?" she asked, smiling and shifting her eyes just a trifle to see Bob's expression. More often than not they were in some sort of conspiracy to handle Marion's sorrow.

"Fine, Mrs. Waley, but I guess I'm not cut out to be a city girl."

"Who is these days?" Mrs. Waley asked.

The driver brought their bags around and Bob paid him. Along with the suitcases was a large shopping bag. Sherri eyed it covetously.

"Did you bring me something, Mommy?" she asked, not taking her eyes off the bag.

"That depends," Bob said. "Did she behave, Mrs. Waley?"

Sherri shot a quick, worried look at Mrs. Waley, who held her smile.

"Yes," she said. "She was a good girl."

"Except she didn't put her bicycle away, I see," Bob said. He gave Sherri a look of reproach and her little mouth began to quiver. "Just forgot?"

She nodded.

"Well, we have to try to remember more," he said and then smiled. "We brought you something."

Sherri clapped her hands together.

"What is it? What?"

Marion lowered her to the walk and Bob picked up the bag.

"Now let me see," he teased. "I know we brought something."

"Bob, stop teasing her," Marion commanded.

"Oh, yes, here it is," he said dipping into the big bag and coming up with a large black-and-white panda. Sherri squealed with delight as Bob handed it down to her. When she hugged it to her small body, the panda looked almost as big as she was.

"How will you play with it, Sherri? It's so big," Mrs. Waley said.

"Oh, no. It's just right," Sherri insisted.

Everyone laughed and headed for the house. Bob carried their bags directly up to their bedroom and began stripping off his travel clothes. Marion went with Mrs. Waley and Sherri into the kitchen to talk and have some tea. As he changed his clothing, Bob gazed out the window that faced the rear of the house. The swing set he had bought for Joey was still there. Sherri, who often seemed spooked by any of her lost brother's possessions, showed little interest in using it. One of the swings moved to and fro in the breeze as if the ghost of his missing son were waiting to welcome him home. He shook off the image and hurried to complete changing. He wanted to call into his office and get whatever messages had come in while he had been away. There was nothing like throwing yourself back into work to stem the tide of melancholy and depression, he thought. Ever since Joey's and Brian's disappearance, it was his only salvation.

Marion looked up from the kitchen table when Bob appeared in the doorway. She saw he was wearing a light jacket and preparing to go out.

"Where are you going?"

"Just want to stop over at the office for a few minutes. They had a problem with that new software from Disco-Tech and it's thrown everyone into a frenzy. You should hear Ted Scholefield complaining."

"You're not the only computer technician they have, Bob," Marion said, but she understood. "What do you want to do about dinner?"

"Let's just order in Chinese," he suggested. "I feel like curling up in front of the television set and drowning in sitcoms tonight."

"All right. Mrs. Waley, do you want to join us for dinner?" Marion asked.

"Oh, no, I . . ."

"Sure you do, Mrs. Waley," Bob said. "I know you love that Mu Shu Gai Pan."

Mrs. Waley caught that look in his eyes. He hoped she would hang in a little longer.

"Well, if I don't have to eat with chopsticks," she said smiling.

"Great. See you guys in an hour or so," Bob said. He looked at Sherri who had her panda seated beside her and was pretending to feed it tea. "Was the panda hungry, Sherri?"

"What?" She considered. "Uh-huh."

"You have to get him panda food, you know," he said.

"Oh Bob, you'll drive her crazy," Marion said.

"What's panda food, Mommy?"

"The same food your father eats," she said. Bob laughed and hurried out.

A few moments after he closed the front door behind him, Marion got up.

"Actually, I'm glad you're staying for dinner, Mrs. Waley. I have a favor to ask."

"Certainly."

"I want to run out myself for a few minutes."

"No problem, dear. It's almost time for 'Geraldo' anyway," she said.

"Thank you."

"Where are you going, Mommy?" Sherri asked.

"Just to run an errand, honey. I'll be right back. Mind Mrs. Waley," Marion said. She went out to the entryway

where she had left her purse and jacket and then went into
the garage and got into her car. In moments she was on her
way to the Spring Glen police department.

The station was at the rear of the town hall. The only
other time Marion had been there was to pay a parking
ticket. Like most small town police departments, it was relatively quiet and had none of the battered and abused looks
urban police departments had. Anyone apprehended for a
serious crime was immediately brought to the county courthouse for booking and incarceration.

There were only two patrol cars in front and the windows
were so dark that Marion at first thought it might be closed.
When she entered, though, she found a young-looking patrolman seated behind the main desk reading a *Car and
Driver* magazine. He had his feet up on an opened drawer.
He had light, reddish-blond hair and a very fair complexion, which, she imagined, made him appear even younger
than he was. He was so engrossed in his magazine that he
didn't hear Marion enter.

She stood in the center of the lobby, gazing around at the
bulletin board with its routine announcements and wanted
posters. A miniature grandfather clock hanging on the wall
to her right ticked loudly. The room was lit by three pairs
of uncovered bulbs. To her left a teletype machine rattled
monotonously and then stopped. The patrolman, finally
sensing her presence, looked up. The moment he saw her,
he dropped his feet off the drawer and swung around in his
chair.

"Oh, I'm sorry. Didn't hear you enter. What can I do for
you, ma'am?"

Marion approached slowly, clutching her pocketbook
close to her body.

"I was hoping to find a certain policeman . . ."

"Who would that be, ma'am?"

"Phil Siegler," she said.

The young patrolman nodded.

"Phil Siegler retired about a year ago, ma'am. He lives in Lauderdale Lakes, Florida, now. I think," he said, rising and turning toward the file cabinets, "we have his address."

"No, no, that's all right," Marion said quickly. "Maybe you can help me."

"Oh?" He looked at her curiously. "Please, have a seat," he said indicating the chair beside the desk. Then he returned to his own seat. Marion hesitated and then sat.

"I have what might seem to be a strange request," she said, placing her pocketbook on the desk.

"We have at least a half dozen of those a day," the patrolman replied, smiling. "I'm Harold, Harold Michaels," he added, extending his hand. Marion shook it quickly.

"Marion Boxletter."

Although the policeman had a youthful and friendly glint in his eyes, she sensed a deep-seated maturity, too. His smile put her at ease and she relaxed and went forward.

"My brother was arrested here about fifteen years ago."

"Oh?"

"He was a student then and he and another boy pulled a prank. They took a classmate's car, but the boy's father didn't appreciate the joke and he pressed charges. I know my brother was fingerprinted. How do you call it, booked?"

"Yes," Michaels said, widening his smile.

"Nothing bad came of it. I mean he didn't go to jail or anything, but would you still have his fingerprints on record?"

"Absolutely," Michaels said. "It might have been a prank, but booking someone is serious business." He straightened up in his chair, taking a more military posture.

He could be all policeman when he had to, Marion decided, but she was glad of that.

She reached into her purse and produced the napkin-covered glass, placing it on the desk beside her pocketbook. She took away the napkin to reveal the glass.

"Could you check the fingerprints on this glass against the ones on record?"

"Ones?"

"My brother's."

"I suppose so, but why?"

Marion sat back and took a deep breath.

"About a year ago, my brother and my nine-year-old son went on a camping trip and disappeared."

"Disappeared?"

"Completely without a trace . . . nothing. My husband even went on the search parties and found where they had been camping, but other than that . . . no clues. It was as if the both of them had been plucked up by a giant hawk," she added, remembering the way Bob explained the woodsman guide's reaction.

Patrolman Michaels's youth seemed to drain out of his face and be replaced by an older, more thoughtful and concerned look. He nodded.

"I'm sorry, but . . ."

"What does it have to do with this glass and the fingerprints?"

Michaels nodded.

"I think I saw my brother in New York yesterday, only he refused to acknowledge me and admit who he was."

Michaels's mouth opened wider. Then a thought occurred.

"Maybe it was just someone who looked like your brother, Mrs. Boxletter."

"That's why I want you to check the prints," she said. "The man used this glass."

Michaels stared at her a moment and then nodded.

"I'm not crazy," she said. "And I'm not a hysterical mother. But I can't sleep wondering."

"I understand," Michaels said. "Let me have the information, your phone number and address, Mrs. Boxletter," he added. "I promise I'll take care of it for you."

He smiled again and that youthful and warm look returned. It filled her with hope and convinced her she had done the right thing.

"All of this is just a mother's instinct," she muttered to herself as she returned to the house. "Just a mother's instinct."

NANCY Crowley opened the door to CCU and walked quickly to the nurses' station. Lois Miller looked up from a chart as Nancy approached.

"You're ten minutes late," Lois snapped. Her black eyes blazed as the lines around her mouth tightened and created little white pockets in the corners. She wasn't a particularly big woman, but her authoritative demeanor, the way she hoisted her shoulders and scowled, intimidated people.

"Sorry. I got tied up with Mrs. Hoffman in the business office again. This is the third time they've screwed up my check."

"You should be doing that on your own time," Lois replied sternly. The head nurse was famous for her military manner. She never hesitated to let a lesser employee know he or she was an underling. There were even some doctors who were afraid of her and to whom she would speak in a condescending tone, but she was too good at what she did to be chastised. Doctors wanted her looking over their patients because they could be confident everything that should be done would be done and done correctly.

"I'm sorry, but . . ."

"Everyone is dependent upon everyone else reporting promptly," she lectured. "You wouldn't like it if the nurse replacing you were ten to fifteen minutes late, would you?"

"If she had a problem, I . . ."

"Mr. Hodes in bed three has been given his sedation. Keep a sharp eye on Mrs. Wellington's monitor. She's gone in and out of fibrillation twice during this shift. Doctor Cummings will be arriving shortly to give you new instructions. The rest is self-evident," she said.

Nancy nodded and looked down the aisle at Betty Peters who was checking an I.V. Lois Miller gathered up her things and headed out without a good-bye. It was as if a shaft of cold wind had been sucked away along with her. Nancy released a breath and shook her head.

Good riddance, she thought and watched her disappear out the door.

"Captain Queeg on your back again?" Betty asked as she returned.

"Ten minutes, ten minutes and she makes it sound like I'm a chronic goof-off," Nancy whined.

Betty shrugged.

"You elected to come back to CCU," she said. "Even though you knew she was captain of the ship." Betty paused and tilted her head. "Why did you come back? You were on special assignment upstairs, making more money . . ."

"I don't know now," Nancy replied quickly. "I needed a change," she added to satisfy her coworker's curiosity. The truth was she couldn't remember being away, but she didn't want to say that. They would all think she was crazy. How-

ever, she could see from Betty's expression that she had her
own theories.

"Are you all right? I mean, is everything okay these
days?" Betty asked guardedly.

"Sure. Why?"

"No reason." Betty hesitated and then came forward.
"Well, everyone knows about Ralph Stanley and we just
figured you wanted to transfer because of him."

"Ralph Stanley?"

"Doctor Stanley," Betty said. Nancy's blank expression
unnerved her. Was this some sort of mental block, a way to
avoid emotional trauma? "I just assumed . . . that is, everyone assumed you two were becoming an item."

"Me and Ralph Stanley?" Nancy started to laugh and
then shook her head. "You've got to be kidding."

"You weren't involved with him?" Betty asked incredulously.

"In work, yes, but if you mean romantically . . . pleeezzz.
The man was as cold as a corpse. I don't think he smiled
twice. I can't imagine going to bed with such a man."
Nancy leaned toward her. "He probably had an icicle for a
penis."

"Really? I mean, that's the way some of us saw him, but
the way you two were with each other sometimes, we just
thought . . ."

"Believe me, Betty, I don't wonder why such a man
committed suicide. He probably got so he couldn't stand
living with himself," Nancy said.

Betty nodded, but continued to stare at Nancy Crowley
as she moved away to observe the heart monitor attached to
Mrs. Wellington.

Betty didn't know Nancy all that well, but still she felt
there was something different about her, something . . . odd.

Was she telling the truth or was all this just the mind's way of protecting itself against a great traumatic impact?

Oh well, she thought, Nancy was a good nurse, and here, in CCU, that was really all that mattered.

MARION almost slowed down to a complete stop before turning into her driveway. It had been nearly two days since she had brought the glass to the police department. She never told Bob she had done so and he hadn't asked anything about it. Both of them seemed to have a tacit understanding it was better not to harp on what had occurred in New York. The more they did, the more burdensome would be the weight of their sorrow. Instead, they had both fallen into their normal schedules. Bob was already intensely involved in a new computer project at work. He tried to get her to reconsider and resume her college work, but she claimed she was too busy taking care of Sherri.

Marion knew she had become overprotective ever since Joey's and Brian's disappearance. Before that, she would have permitted Sherri to walk to school with the other children on the block. It seemed silly to them and to Sherri that Marion would drive her to and fro, but she was terrified of someone abducting her. That nightmare played repeatedly on the screen of her dreams. She had become paranoid; she knew it, but she couldn't help it. It was as if she had come to believe she and Bob were just not meant to have children. Some higher force, some evil power had made such a decision. The idea was quite unreasonable. It was easy to criticize the logic, but the emotional baggage was too heavy to throw off.

She turned into the driveway, bringing Sherri home from school, but kept her attention on the patrol car parked in front of her house. Officer Michaels was alone behind the steering wheel. He looked into his rearview mirror and saw her pull in. As she came to a stop, he got out of his car and approached.

"Why is a policeman here, Mommy?" Sherri asked fearfully.

Sherri recalled her brother Joey vividly. They had been very close and Joey had reached the point where he could be relied upon to look after Sherri. He was a mature, intelligent little boy. Bob used to call him "my little man."

After Joey's and Brian's disappearance, Sherri began to have her nightmares as well, and it was decided she would attend a few sessions with Marion's therapist. The talks appeared to help, but Sherri would often stop playing or wander into a room Marion was in and ask, "When's Joey coming home, Mommy? I want Joey."

It took all Marion's self-control to keep from bursting into tears, but she knew that would be devastating to Sherri. In as controlled a voice as she could manage, she repeated the story, but she always left the ending unresolved. In Sherri's mind dozens of rescuers were still out there searching. Marion knew this was what she was thinking about when she saw Officer Michaels approach the house.

"Hi," he said, smiling.

"Do you have results?" Marion asked quickly.

He nodded.

"Maybe we could go inside to talk a bit," he suggested.

"Oh, yes, yes. I'm sorry."

"And what's your name?" Officer Michaels asked Sherri.

"Sherri," she said shyly. She seized Marion's hand as they walked to the front door. Officer Michaels followed them in.

"We'll go into the living room," Marion said, indicating the door on the left. "Can I get you something to drink . . . juice, a soda?"

"Anything but diet soda," he replied, smiling.

"Be right back. Please, make yourself at home," she said.

He entered the living room. Sherri rushed up to her room to change out of her good school clothes quickly, while Marion went to get the drink. Marion's fingers fumbled with the can of Seven-Up. It took three tries to pull the tab. Her hand shook as she poured the soda into a glass.

He just wants to ease me into disappointment, she thought. There's no other reason why he would make a personal appearance and be so nonchalant. She had been hoping, praying that somehow this bizarre incident would lead to Joey's return, and now, it looked like all that hope was dashed. With an empty heart, she made her way back to the living room.

Officer Michaels was standing and holding Joey's picture.

"This is your missing son?" he asked.

"Yes." Her lips trembled.

"Nice-looking boy," Officer Michaels said, shaking his head. "Looks like a bright boy, too."

"He was . . . he is," she quickly corrected.

The policeman smiled again and put the picture down on the table.

"Oh, your drink."

"Thank you." He took it and sat down. "Well," he said, "I did some investigating. Your brother had a life insurance policy with you as the beneficiary."

"He wasn't married and both our parents are dead. We had only each other," Marion said, sitting across from him. Her legs had become wobbly.

Before the policeman could go on, Sherri appeared in the doorway, holding her panda.

"Wow, that's a big panda. What's his name?" Officer Michaels asked.

"Mr. Panda," Sherri said, her eyes wide.

"Of course. What else?" Officer Michaels said, turning back to Marion.

"Honey, Mommy has to talk now. Go play in your room," Marion said.

Reluctantly, Sherri retreated.

"Beautiful little girl."

"Thank you. You were saying . . ."

"Anyhow, it would make no sense for you to come to tell me he's still alive. I mean, if there was some sort of conspiracy to defraud."

"I don't understand," Marion said, leaning toward him. "What are you saying?"

"Those prints on the glass . . ."

"Yes?"

"Some of them match your brother's."

Marion sat back, the blood rushing into her face so quickly, she thought she would go into a faint. She fought back the loss of consciousness. Not now, she told herself, no weakness, no emotionalism now.

"Then that man has to have been Brian."

"It would seem so, Mrs. Boxletter. Seeing that this involves a missing person and a possible kidnapping, I have already notified the FBI. Someone from their office should be calling you soon. There isn't much more a small-town police department can do," he explained in an apologetic tone.

"Oh, I understand. Of course," she said. "You've been a great help already. I appreciate it."

"Do you have any idea why your brother would do such a thing?" he asked.

"No. He would never do such a thing. I've been thinking about it, of course, and I think he's suffering from some sort of amnesia. Something happened out there that caused it, I'm sure."

"But what about your son?"

"I don't know," she said, not able to stop the tears now. "But we'll find out, won't we?

"Won't we?" She demanded a response from the young policeman when he didn't speak quickly.

"Yes, you will," he said. "Now, you will."

4

THE MOMENT OFFICER MICHAELS WALKED OUT THE DOOR, Marion shot upstairs and began packing. She would take only enough for a few days, she thought. She scurried about the bedroom frantically, pulling open drawers, selecting garments, and then rushing in and out of the bathroom with toiletries. Sherri heard the commotion and came into the bedroom.

"What are you doing, Mommy?" she asked. She held the panda in her arms and for a moment, it looked as though the panda had come to life and was wondering the same thing.

"What?"

Marion looked around. What was she doing? She didn't even know where Sandburg, New York, was. They lived in Ohio. Bob was at work. But as if purposely to reinforce her determination, her eyes fell on a picture of Joey with her and Bob when Joey was only two.

"I'm going to go get your brother back," she replied with determination.

"Can I go, too? Please Mommy. Please . . ."

"You?" She thought for a moment. Of course, they would all have to go. They should all be there when she finally located Joey. It would be a great comfort to him to see his little sister as well as his parents, and the quicker they were all reunited, the better.

"Yes, honey. You can go."

"Yaay," Sherri cried. "And Mr. Panda?"

"And Mr. Panda," Marion said, smiling. "Go get your little suitcase out of your closet and put it on your bed. I'll be in your room in a minute to get your things together."

"I have to have a suitcase?"

"We're going far away, honey, and we'll be sleeping in a hotel."

Sherri nodded, wide-eyed, and then rushed back to her room.

But first things first, Marion thought and sat down on the bed by the phone. She was going to dial Bob's office to tell him the news and what they would now do, but it occurred to her that Brian might have given the hotel in New York a phony address. He had lied to them; he might be lying to everyone. They would go all the way to this place in upstate New York for nothing.

Come on, Marion Boxletter, she coaxed. How can you solve this problem? How can you be sure?

Information, she told herself quickly. See if someone named Sam Heller has a phone number in Sandburg, New York; then call it and listen to his voice. She dialed the long distance operator and asked her to help find the area code. Once she had it, she dialed long distance information and asked for Sam Heller's telephone number in Sandburg. The mechanical voice recited it. She wrote it down quickly and then punched it out. The phone rang and rang. Finally, an answering machine picked up. She listened keenly to the voice. It didn't sound like Brian's voice; it sounded too formal, almost as if it were Brian imitating someone. Was it Brian—had he assumed someone else's identity? The message said he could be reached at "the bank." When he asked the caller to leave a message at the buzz, she hung up quickly. Still undecided, she called and listened to the answering machine again, concentrating as hard as she could on the vowels, the intonations. There were differences, but there was a similarity in resonance, enough of a similarity to convince her it was indeed Brian. It was worth the gamble.

Her heart was pounding so hard, she thought she might go into a faint. She closed her eyes and willed herself to be strong and then she dialed Bob's office and he picked up the phone himself. Another omen. It was as if he had been waiting.

"Bob, the policeman just left," she said quickly, her voice so full of excitement the words threatened to bottle up in the base of her throat.

"Policeman? What policeman?"

She told him about bringing the glass to the police station to have the fingerprints checked. He had not asked her about it since their return from New York, and she knew he thought she had given up on the idea.

"You actually did that?"

"Yes, of course. I said I would."

"And?"

"They were his fingerprints. That man in New York was Brian."

For a long moment, Bob was silent. She knew the incongruous set of events was hard to fathom.

"I don't understand," he muttered. "If it was Brian, why did he deny knowing us?"

"I thought about that," she said. "He has amnesia. That must be it. Something traumatic occurred out there on the camping trip and it caused him to have amnesia. He doesn't know who he is; he thinks he's someone else."

"But why would he think he's someone else? That doesn't make sense, does it?"

"I don't know, Bob," she said impatiently. "Whatever the reason, it's Brian."

Bob said the unmentionable, the theory that lingered in

the back of her mind like a persistent fly buzzing under a window drape.

"Maybe something terrible happened to Joey and that caused Brian's memory loss," Bob said softly.

"There's no point to our guessing and guessing now, Bob," Marion insisted. Gone was the weak, limp rag of a woman, the bereaved and destroyed mother, the mental invalid who had to see a therapist twice a week, the woman who could burst into tears at any time, any place. She had no patience for that helpless, delicate self. If she were ever to get her son back, she would have to have strength and courage. She would have to be a woman of action, demanding, strong, firm in her convictions and purpose.

"Well, what can we do?"

"We can go find him, Bob. I've begun to pack our things. We'll take Sherri along, too."

"Go find him? Go where?"

"To Sandburg, of course."

"But how do we know that wasn't something he just wrote, part of his confusion?"

"I just called him there," she replied, proud of her ingenuity. They didn't have to depend on the police.

"You called him?"

"His answering machine came on. I didn't leave any message. I think it's best we just go there and confront him."

"Go to upstate New York?"

"Bob, we're talking about Joey, finding Joey," she said, a bit shocked and somewhat annoyed that she had to remind him.

"I know honey, but . . ."

"But what?"

"Shouldn't we just leave this up to the police?"

"We left it up to the police before and they discovered

nothing. An FBI man was supposed to call me and hasn't," she said, forgetting to add it had been less than an hour since Patrolman Michaels had left the house. "This won't be a priority to them. They're busy chasing the ten most wanted or some such thing. Anyway, fate, luck, maybe even God has given us an opportunity, Bob. What kind of parents would we be to pass it up? If you don't want to go, I'll go myself," she concluded quickly.

"I didn't say I didn't want to go, Marion."

"Good then. While I pack, you use those wonderful computer skills and devices to find out exactly where Sandburg, New York, is and get us an itinerary and transportation," she ordered. She felt more comfortable taking command. As long as they were moving, doing, taking action, she had no time to be weak.

"You want to leave today?" he asked, incredulity still in his voice.

"We'll be in front of your office in forty-five minutes," she declared firmly. "I've packed all your things."

"What am I going to tell Ted?" he muttered to himself. She heard it and it made her irate.

"Tell him you're going to bring home your son who has been missing for over a year!" she screamed into the phone. "And if that's not good enough for him, tell him to go straight to hell!"

"All right, all right, calm down. I'm just talking out loud. I'll take care of everything. You just calm down, Marion, before you get into an accident or something and make this situation even worse."

"Don't worry about me. Be ready," she warned and cradled the receiver quickly. Then she jumped up and finished packing her, Bob's and Sherri's things. In less than a half hour, she had shut up the house and brought the bags to the door. Sherri stood there, holding her panda, her eyes filled with both fear and bewilderment. She had never seen her mommy this excited before. Marion led her out of the house and to the garage. Sherri hopped into the rear seat quickly and sat Mr. Panda down beside her. She gazed out the window at her house as Marion backed down the driveway.

Somehow, maybe it was because of her mommy's frenzy or because of the uniqueness of being rushed out to go on a trip, Sherri had the strange feeling she would never see her house again, never ride her tricycle on this walk or play on the lawn. And as they hurried down Highland Avenue and away, she even felt she would never see this street or talk to her friends anymore. The feeling was so strong she just had to say it, just had to mutter it into the window.

"Good-bye," she said and fell back on the seat, her arm drawing Mr. Panda closer to her.

SAM Heller pushed the clicker on his sun visor and watched his garage door go up, turning on the light simultaneously. Philip had left his bike too far off the wall again. He would have to get out and move his fourteen-year-old son's twelve-speed before he could pull the vehicle in. He had complained before about this. With an uncharacteristic burst of anger, he slammed the base of his open right palm into the steering wheel so hard, it sent needles of pain down the inside of his wrist and into his forearm. He threw the transmission into park and thrust open his door, muttering one obscenity after another quite loudly. When he seized the bike, he tossed it roughly against the wall. The tires hit first and the bike bounded back defiantly.

Enraged, Sam carried the bike outside and flung it off to his left. It sailed over the small section of lawn and hit the tops of the hedges that bordered his property and Bob and

Irma Longo's. The bike fell over onto their property, but Sam didn't seem to notice or care.

"Serves him right," he said and returned to his car. He drove in, turned off the engine and got out again, carrying his briefcase. He hit the button to close the door and entered his house. The first room off the garage was his office, and as usual, the first thing he did was go to his desk to check the answering machine. Diedra and the children were out of the house so long during the day that there were always messages. Most of the time, they were for Diedra, but no one was permitted to touch his machine, or anything on his desk for that matter, so she and the children never looked. People who wanted to contact him simply called him at the bank. But occasionally, insurance agents, brokers, dentist and doctor receptionists called the house instead.

The first two messages were for Diedra as expected. He wrote down the names of the callers. The third beep produced no message, just a silence. He hated that—he hated when people called and didn't have the courtesy to at least leave a name and number. This excuse about not being able to speak to a machine was pure crap as far as he was concerned. What did these people think he was going to do: play their voices in public and embarrass them? Then there was a fourth beep and again, no message.

He was about to shut off the machine when something about this fourth call caught his attention. He dropped his briefcase and replayed it, listening keenly this time. Yes, there it was—the distinct sound of breathing. No, it was more than breathing; it was a kind of whimpering, a tiny, almost mouselike sound. A woman's voice, he decided. Who the hell . . . was this one of Kelly's girlfriends pulling a joke? His twelve-year-old daughter was specifically forbidden to use this telephone line and her friends were not to call her on it. He had given in and bought the kids their own line just so they wouldn't tie up his and Diedra's. Even five-year-old Peter was getting phone calls from his friends already.

Sam turned off the answering machine and headed farther into the house. Charged into it was more like it. He found Diedra in the kitchen putting the finishing touches on their dinner. From the aroma, he concluded they were having roast chicken. His stomach grumbled in anticipation. Diedra was a great cook. Every time he thought that, a line was triggered in his mind: "You won my stomach over first, then my heart." Echoes of laughter, but laughter that sounded strangely hollow and artificial, like a laugh track on a sitcom. And the line seemed so out of character for him. He wasn't much of a romantic, or was he? It vaguely troubled him that he was unsure about that. Shouldn't that be something a man definitely knew about himself?

"Hi, Sam," Diedra said, turning and smiling.

"You had two messages," he snapped and put the slip of note pad down on the counter. She looked at it.

"Oh, Millie finally decided to call about Saturday night, huh? Why it takes her and George three days to decide if they want to join us for dinner, I'll never know."

"The way George is, it probably takes her that long to get an appointment to discuss it," Sam quipped, but unusually bitterly, Diedra thought. She held her half smile.

"I thought you liked George," she said softly.

"I like him, but only in spurts. A steady diet of George Miller can give you the gout," he replied.

"What's wrong, Sam? Something bad happen at the bank?" she asked perceptively.

"No." He paused. "Yes," he said. "That asshole Federman wants me to take over the commercial loans until they find a replacement for Cutter."

"That's not fair; that's too much responsibility," Diedra said quickly.

"I can handle it," he snapped back. "It's not that it's too much responsibility."

She wilted.

"There's no additional compensation," Sam explained. "He just expects me to do it for the sake of the bank, as if the bank is a country or a church. It's just a bank, for Christ sakes."

Diedra simply stared. Sam's eyes were dark and his lips were pale. She couldn't remember seeing such wrath in him.

"Well, maybe you should discuss it with him more," she suggested as calmly and as softly as she could. It sent him into a rage.

"Discuss it! Discuss it! You don't discuss things with Federman. He doesn't listen to anyone but himself! The man's a . . . a . . ." It was as if the words had choked up in his throat. He seized his own Adam's apple and turned white.

"Sam!"

"I'm all right," he said, backing away. "I'll just go take a shower," he said. He started out, but his shouting had attracted the attention of his children and they all came running in from the den where they had been playing a Nintendo game. The moment Sam's eyes fell on Philip, his temper returned. The fourteen-year-old felt the waves of anger flowing in his direction and actually stepped back.

"You left that damn bike in my way again. Didn't I tell you to make sure it was out of the way?" Sam cried, waving his fist at him.

"Yes," the boy said meekly. "I thought I did."

"You didn't, damn it. Now you can go look for it," he added and marched out the door, parting his children and driving them away from him. He pounded his way up the stairs and slammed the door of his bedroom shut behind him. The rage didn't ease up. It carried him through the bedroom to the bathroom, where he began pulling his clothing off, his fingers groping impatiently so that he ripped a button off his shirt. Midway through stripping, he realized he was tearing at the garments. It was as if someone had dressed him in someone else's clothing, clothing he didn't like. It was too conservative, too blah for him.

Did he really like this tie? And these damn button-down collars—they were so confining. He tossed the garments away from him, not caring where they fell. He didn't feel any relief until he was totally naked.

What was this? Why was this happening? Why was it that he suddenly would look at himself in the mirror and not like what he saw? Every once in a while at the bank, he would pause at his own reflection in the glass or in something shiny and wonder why he styled and brushed his hair this way. Had someone talked him into it— Diedra, perhaps? He liked his hair longer, didn't he? Or did he?

What did he like? What colors did he favor? What were his favorite foods? He chose things almost automatically these days and afterward, he always had a moment of doubt, a questioning, wondering why he had done so. It was as if he were just discovering himself, every day learning something new.

He didn't even know why he was working in a bank. Every once in a while, he would gaze outside and want to go charging out just to be in the sunlight, to breathe the air, to feel free. He should be doing something with his hands—construction, farming, mechanic; anything but sitting behind a desk and pushing a pencil. These longings had become so intense, they were bizarre.

And then, there was that damn third eye. Even now, as he recalled it, he felt it coming again. He closed his eyes in hopes that would stop it, but when he opened them, it was there—right in the middle of his forehead, just like that mythological giant, Polyphemus the Cyclops. Only, this eye in his forehead grew larger and larger every time he saw it. Now, it was at least a third of the width of his forehead. He tried to turn away from the mirror, but he couldn't. It held him in a hypnotic grip. He had to stare and watch as the rim of the eye expanded like a cancer, first tearing down the flesh and then forming weblike threads to span the empty space inside of which he could see chalk-white bone. The flesh would literally crawl over the webs and connect with flesh on the other side, making the eye larger and larger. Soon, he would be all eye.

He started to scream. He seized his own head between his hands and with all his strength, started to turn his head away from the mirror. His neck muscles resisted, but he pressed and pressed until little by little, an inch at a time, he was able to turn himself far enough so that he couldn't see his reflection. Only then did he feel any relief and only then, when he looked back, was the eye gone. It was all the same tonight.

Exhausted from the struggle, he sat on the commode and held his head in his hands. His breathing slowed, but he felt the sweat that had broken out along his neck and shoulders. When he sat back, however, his heart began to beat hard and fast again. Something different was happening this time; something new. Terrified, he sat there hoping it would stop, but wave after wave of heat rushed over him.

The shower, he thought. Get in that shower quickly. It would stop it. He jumped up and opened the shower stall door. As quickly as he could, he turned on the shower. He wanted it to be hotter than usual today. It was as if he intended to scald himself, sterilize his skin. All of a sudden he was feeling dirty, but dirty from the inside out, and not this shower, not a bath, nothing could make him feel clean again.

The hot water created a heavy mist on the glass. It was really too hot, but he forced himself to step under the stream. He had to cry out, it burned so; but he wouldn't retreat and he wouldn't turn down the temperature of the water.

Suddenly, though, he found himself shrinking. The water was melting his body. In moments he was less than three feet tall and diminishing. Between his feet, the drain loomed threateningly. He started to get out of the shower, but found that his feet were glued to the tile. He extended his arm to turn off the water, but he couldn't reach the handle. He was getting smaller and smaller, less than two feet, less than a foot. The holes in the drain became huge pits. He slipped on the rim and fell forward, now less than an inch big. He held onto the drain as best he could, but his fingers gradually slid off the metal and he fell through.

He dropped through the darkness, screaming. The descent seemed endless. And then he saw another man falling alongside him. Slowly the man turned his face toward him. It was Dr. Stanley, Ralph Stanley, and he was trying to speak, but when he opened his mouth, the flesh of his lips went stringy and pulled his mouth closed. Then his eyes closed. Sam screamed again, louder and harder. He was following Ralph Stanley down, dropping almost as fast as he was.

"Sam! Sam!" Someone was calling him from above.

He was shaking; his body was shaking.

"SAM, SAM!"

He opened his eyes. Diedra was kneeling over him, shaking his shoulders. Behind her, he could see the children gathered in the bathroom doorway, their faces all worry and fear.

"What?"

"Sam, what's wrong with you? You were lying here on the shower floor screaming." Her face was full of fear and confusion.

"What?" he said again. He looked up. The shower was off. In fact, he had never turned it on. The stall was bone dry.

"What's wrong, Sam?"

"I . . . I must have fainted or something," he said.

"Oh, Sam, you should go right to the doctor. I'm going to call."

"No, no," he said. "I'm all right. It's nothing."

"Nothing? Sam, you were hysterical. I couldn't stop you for almost a minute. The kids are terrified."

"It's all right," he insisted. "Go ahead," he said, waving at the door. "I'll take a quick, cold shower and I'll be all right. Really."

"Sam, please."

"Just do it," he insisted.

Diedra stared at him a moment.

"It's all right," he repeated, more forcefully.

"All right, kids. Let's go downstairs. Daddy's fine." She looked back at him and shook her head. "You better go to the doctor, Sam," she said and left him.

He sat there for a few moments and then he pulled himself to his feet.

What the hell happened? What the hell did happen? He ran his hands over his body to be sure it was all still there and then he breathed with relief. A dream, he thought, it was all just a bad dream. He turned on the water and it never felt better. He let it hit his face and run down his cheeks and chin. Finally, refreshed, he stepped out, dried himself quickly, avoiding the mirror, and got dressed for dinner.

By the time he sat down at the table, he had forgotten all about it, but his children sat quietly around the table, all of them still terrified. He smiled, a bit confused. Why was everyone so glum?

"Someone get in trouble in school today?" he asked.

They all shook their heads no.

He looked at Diedra.

"They're still upset about before, honey," she said softly.

"Before?"

His children looked surprised.

"Oh," he said, finally recalling, something. "Well, I told you, Philip, keep that bike out of the way of the car. Okay?"

"Yes, Dad," Philip said obediently. "I'm sorry. I won't forget," he recited, shifting his eyes toward Diedra to see if he had delivered it as they had rehearsed. She nodded.

"Good. So, let's enjoy our dinner," Sam said. "I'm starving."

They watched him tear ravenously into a chicken leg. He realized all eyes were still intently on him.

"What's the matter?" he asked quickly. "Didn't you guys ever see a starving man before?" He winked at little Peter, who finally smiled. The pall lifted and his family began to enjoy their supper, the children rattling on as usual about school, about other kids, about television.

Only Diedra seemed a little restrained, but by dessert, she was her old self, too, smiling and talking about their friends, plans for the weekend, things she had to buy for the house. It was as if the Heller family had passed through the same nightmare and woken up.

The best thing to do was try to forget.

5

SHERRI HELD ON TIGHTLY TO BOB'S HAND WITH HER RIGHT hand and clutched Mr. Panda to her tightly as she and her parents marched behind the other disembarking airplane passengers at the Newark, New Jersey, airport. Normally, she would have held on to Marion's hand, but her mother was walking faster and harder than her father. In fact, Sherri and Bob practically had to run to keep up. Marion carried Sherri's little suitcase and Bob carried theirs in his other hand.

"Slow down," Bob pleaded. "We're going to have to stop somewhere tonight anyway, honey. I told you, it's nearly a four-hour ride from here and we still have to get the rental car. You know what that's like. And we'll have to eat on the road."

Marion heeded his plea and shortened her steps.

"You booked everything through your computer; it shouldn't take us long," she declared.

"Yeah, yeah, but eventually you deal with real people. Come on, relax a bit, otherwise you won't be worth a damn by the time we do get there, and we don't know what's awaiting us," Bob pointed out.

"I can't help it," she said after taking a deep breath. "I keep thinking we might be only hours away from Joey."

"If he's there. The only thing we might have established is that your brother is there," Bob said. He hated being the realist; it made him seem like the cruel one, the pessimist,

69

but it was better to anticipate possible disappointment and lessen the impact of a letdown, he reasoned.

"If my brother is there, we'll find Joey," she pledged. She nodded at her own thought. "We'll find him one way or another then."

"I still think we should call the police and at least let them know what we're doing."

"No," she said, stopping in the corridor. "They'll screw it up. They'll call ahead or something, and with our luck, Brian will be gone by the time we arrive."

"I hardly think . . ."

"What's the difference of a few more hours, Bob?" He hadn't seen her this insistent and determined since Joey's disappearance.

"Okay," he said, nodding. "We'll call after we get to Sandburg and see what's what."

"Good." She reached down to take Sherri's hand. "You go ahead and see about the rental car. I'll take Sherri to the restroom and meet you at the desk. It will save time," she said.

Bob smiled. She was like a tank, forging ahead. Pity anything or anyone who gets in her way, he thought. Less than an hour later, the three of them were in the rental car and driving down the New Jersey Turnpike, heading for upstate New York and, he hoped, the answers to the puzzle and the end of the mystery that had gripped their lives so firmly.

It was a longer ride than either of them had anticipated, and Bob suggested they stop for the night.

"We wouldn't be able to get to him this late at night anyway, Marion," Bob explained. "We might as well be fresh and appear in Sandburg in the morning."

Marion finally gave in, exhausted herself.

Sherri was already asleep in the back when they pulled into a motel. After checking in, Bob carried her to their room, and Marion undressed her and put her to bed. Sherri barely woke up to realize what was happening. She did manage to keep her panda close by as she fell asleep.

"Couldn't be a more adorable sight," Bob said, looking down at her in the other double bed. "Sherri and her Mr. Panda."

Marion smiled and then looked at Bob. They embraced. He felt her trembling.

"Are you cold, honey?"

"No. I'm just afraid, afraid we'll find out the worst and have to accept it," she confessed, reverting, if only for a few moments, to the vulnerable and fragile woman she had been.

"Whatever awaits us, we've got to be strong, strong for ourselves as well as for Sherri," he said. She nodded, tightening back to her resolve.

"I'll be all right," she said.

"Good." Bob kissed her on the forehead. "You want to take a shower? I feel grimy from the trip."

"No, you go ahead. I'll watch a little television."

She lay back on the pillows and turned on the set while he went into the bathroom. But her attention wandered immediately. She rose and went to the window to look out at the parking lot and the highway. Somewhere, a few more hours up the road, her son might be waiting. Why had this happened? What was going on with Brian?

Her brother was always a strong, independent fellow. He was only two years older than she was, but in her mind, he always seemed much older. His quiet thoughtfulness made him that way. Even as a little boy, Brian evinced independence. He could play by himself for hours, go off alone, travel alone, eat alone, never relying on the company of others. Sometimes, she would think he was more reliable than their parents. He had a wisdom and a stoicism that she came to admire, even if she didn't understand from what well he drew upon to be that way. She wasn't that way, and at times, she wondered if they weren't children of different parents.

Oh, they looked enough alike, but Brian had this manner about him that set him off from the rest of the family. He was bright in school, but far from an egghead. He eschewed team sports and went for the ones that relied more on the individual's stamina and ability, like wrestling, cross-country running, skiing. She couldn't recall a single instance when he got in trouble in school. He never missed homework, or behaved disrespectfully, and he had an outstanding attendance record. She would never forget the awards assembly when she was only in the eighth grade and he was in the tenth. He was called up to receive a citation for not missing a single day of school that year.

Her parents were proud of him, even though they didn't always understand him. They were especially surprised and upset when he went off one day and enlisted in the Navy to become a Seabee. He had done nothing to indicate such an interest. His parents just assumed he was going to go to college and study electrical engineering or some such thing. When he came out, he went directly into the Environmental Protection Agency's enforcement bureau. Bob used to kid him about being a glamorized boy scout, but Joey sure took to him and looked forward to his every visit and every opportunity he had to be with his uncle Brian. This last camping trip wasn't the first they had been on together. Who would have thought there was any danger in his going away with Brian?

"What happened to you out there, Brian? How could you do this, be this way?" she questioned. She turned from the window. Bob was still in the shower, the water running.

Her gaze fell on the phone. It was a little past eleven o'clock; he was surely home, she thought.

She went to her pocketbook and found the slip of paper with the phone number on it and while Bob was still in the bathroom, called Sam Heller. The phone rang twice and began to ring a third time when he lifted the receiver and in a groggy, slightly angry tone said hello.

She didn't speak. She analyzed his voice, a voice not on the machine now. She wanted to hear him again and feel confident. Years and years of hearing her brother's voice came to bear.

"Hello, damn it," he said.

"What is it, Sam?" she heard a voice beside him ask. Who was that?

"Some asshole," he replied and slammed the receiver down.

His anger seemed different, unnatural, but the first hello was more like the Brian she remembered. How could he not remember her? How could he have looked at her in the New York hotel and not known he was looking at his own sister? Was amnesia that powerful and overwhelming? Not even a note of recognition, a pause, some confusion . . . nothing.

Total strangers, she thought sadly, we're total strangers whose hearts pound the same blood around our bodies. Surely, the power of that blood will overcome anything.

As soon as she heard Bob fumble with the bathroom door handle, she cradled the receiver and fell back against the pillow again.

"You ought to take a nice hot shower," he suggested. "It will help you sleep."

"Yes, I think I will," she replied.

In the morning, after they had had breakfast and he had gotten into the car after paying their motel bill, he turned to her.

"Why did you call him last night?" he asked. "What did you say?"

She had forgotten that the charges would be on their motel bill.

"I . . . just wanted to hear his voice again," she confessed.

"Did you say anything?"

"No."

"You could have spooked him, you know," Bob chastised. "That was why you didn't want me to contact the police yet."

"I'm sorry," she said. "I couldn't help it."

He nodded.

"Let's just get there and get it over with," he declared and they shot off, out of the motel parking lot, and onward, north to Sandburg.

SAM Heller almost overslept. Diedra hesitated to go back upstairs to wake him. Usually, he was up before she and the children were, but this morning, when she awoke, she found him breathing deeply and regularly beside her, his eyes shut so tight it was as if he were trying to keep a nightmare from getting in or a good dream from getting out. She thought he would wake up when she got up and started to dress, but he didn't even turn over. She had to see about the children first. Peter always had to be dragged out of bed and hurried along. But when they came down to the kitchen and saw their father wasn't at the table reading *The Wall Street Journal* as usual, they were very surprised, too.

"I'd better go up to see if he's all right," Diedra muttered and did so. He hadn't budged an inch. Worried now, she woke him, but he was sleeping so soundly, she had to nudge him to do so.

"Huh?" he said, blinking his eyes. She pulled her hand back from his shoulder quickly.

"It's late, Sam," she said defensively. "I knew you would be angry at yourself for oversleeping."

He looked at her in the strangest way. It was as if he didn't know her, she thought, and he was trying to figure out who she was.

"Sam?"

Without replying, he turned and studied the room. Then he sat up, still not speaking, and stared at his open palms as if he were a fortune teller.

"Sam, are you feeling all right?"

She could almost see his memory focusing in on her when he looked up at her this time.

"Diedra," he said as if he were surprised to see her. It brought a smile to her face.

"Yes, Sam. Who were you expecting to wake you, Lena Olin?" She was a movie actress he admired.

Suddenly, as if his whole life had come rushing back over him, he spun around and looked at the clock.

"Damn. Why didn't you wake me earlier?"

"I just thought you would wake up yourself, Sam. You always do."

He threw off his blanket and hopped off the bed.

"I've got so much to do today at the bank. Forget about breakfast. I'll order out," he snapped and hurried into the bathroom.

Diedra didn't know whether to laugh or cry. He was acting so peculiar these days, she thought. If he didn't phone the doctor, she was going to. Didn't their doctor once ask her to call if she ever noticed anything peculiar about Sam or the children? That was after that bad flu epidemic, the one that played havoc with people's equilibrium. There wasn't anything wrong with Sam's equilibrium, and he would be angry she called, but even so, she should do it, she thought.

She made a mental note. Some time today, she would call Dr. Randolph at the clinic. She hurried back down to check on the children.

In the bathroom Sam had a vague negative reaction to the shower stall. Something unpleasant had recently occurred in there, he thought, but he couldn't remember what it was. Had he scalded himself? Slipped? What? Shaking off the bad feeling, he stepped in and showered as quickly as he could. The hot and then cold water had the desired effect. He felt his body wake up all over and his mind cleared. As he dried himself, he began to review the things he had to do right away at the bank.

Every time I go away, this happens, he thought. I get buried in catch-up paperwork. He paused, the towel in his hands, still naked, and stared at himself in the mirror as if he were looking through a window at another person. It was the strangest sensation. Then, as if the other person asked the question, he said, "I don't remember," aloud.

The question was, "Why did you go away?"

"I don't remember," he repeated.

"How could you not remember? How long were you away? Where did you go?"

He stood there stunned by his inability to recall. The heat rushed into his face and then traveled down his body until he felt he had stepped into a pool of fire. It was so frustrating, but more important, it was so frightening. Unable to stand it anymore, he hurried out of the bathroom and went to his closet. He found the pinstripe suit still in the clothing bag and frantically searched the pockets. In the inside pocket, he found the receipt for the hotel room.

"New York City," he muttered. "I was in New York

City." He breathed in some relief and started to relax when the next question shot through his mind.

"Why was I in New York City? Banking convention?"

He struggled harder to recall, but something was blocking the memory, something powerful and dark. He could almost see the thick, lead wall dropped between his question and the answer in his brain.

Should he ask Diedra? How could he do that without revealing his horrible lapse of memory? She would get hysterical and call Dr. Randolph immediately.

He didn't want that. No, God no. The doctor would have him come back to the clinic.

Like the perennial boogieman who haunted the minds of young children, the clinic loomed forbiddingly in his psyche. He saw it as it was, a modern structure with no windows. All the air within was specially filtered. It was especially frightening to him at night when there was a lot of moonlight. Then, the walls of the structure looked enflamed and in his way of thinking, everyone within was being consumed in a great fire.

The image of fire brought back a distant memory, so distant it came in smokelike waves, each wave bringing a slight addition of information. There was a small fire . . . a campfire. He was in the dark in the woods and there was someone else with him, but he couldn't see who it was. All he could do was look into the snapping flames of the fire. There were other voices coming from the shadows and suddenly someone was stamping out the fire. Try as hard as he would, that was all he could recall. Was it a memory or was it a dream? Maybe it was something from a movie he had seen.

The harder he tried to recall, the faster the image left him and along with its leaving came a ribbon of pain that extended from each of his temples and around his forehead. It felt like someone who had placed a sharp knife there was beginning to cut in. The pain became so intense, he had to bury his face in his hands and press the base of his palms against his cheeks and push and push until he drove the pain back inside.

Grateful it had stopped, he shoved the receipt back into the suit jacket pocket and plucked out a different suit to wear. Then he hurried about the room, gathering underwear, socks, putting on his clothing and tying his tie. Finally dressed in a way that brought safe and secure familiarity, he went downstairs quickly. The children had already left for school. Diedra was cleaning up the breakfast dishes. He stood in the kitchen doorway watching her until she felt his presence and turned around.

"Sam?"

He didn't reply. He was nearly in tears. He couldn't remember his wife's name, or the names of his children. Worse, he couldn't remember what he was supposed to do now that he was dressed.

"Are you all right, Sam?" she asked.

"I . . ."

"You didn't want any breakfast here, right? I didn't make anything for you. You said you would order in from the bank," she reminded him.

The bank. Yes, the bank. It started to come back, breaking through like blood pushing past a blockage in an artery. He was vice president of Sandburg National. It was on Main Street, Sandburg.

"Right," he said, "the bank."

She stepped up to him and kissed him on the cheek.

"Have a good day, honey," she said. "I'll try to stop by to see you later this afternoon when I pick up our clothes from the dry cleaners."

"Good," he said. He had to get to the car, but where . . .

"If you're looking for your briefcase, you left it in your office," Diedra said.

"My office? Oh, right. Okay. Good-bye," he said and went out the correct door into the office where he found the briefcase. His name embossed in gold was on it.

Sam Heller.

I'm Sam Heller, he thought and laughed. What a wonderful thing it was to suddenly remember who you were and what you did. It was like being reborn, dead and resurrected.

I'm alive, he thought happily. He swung his briefcase and went out to the garage.

I'm alive. This is my Mercedes; this is my house. I'm rather well off, he concluded and bristled with pride. He got behind the wheel of his luxurious sedan and commanded the garage door to open. He started the engine and backed out.

Then, as if something were pulling him along, he made all the right turns and ended up in the bank parking lot, parking in his own reserved space. Mr. Heller, it said. He pulled his shoulders back when he stepped out of his car, and sauntered to the front door of the bank. Employees scurried about within, some eyeing him fearfully. Everyone had to look busy and efficient when he arrived, he thought.

They'd better.

With a slight growl in his voice, he said good morning to those who dared say it to him. Then he went into his office and got behind his desk. It was then that he saw the faces of his children and remembered who each was.

This wasn't the first time these horrible lapses of memory had occurred, he thought. It was getting harder and harder to come back, he admitted.

But come back from where?

He had to go see Dr. Randolph, he concluded reluctantly.

And then for reasons he was just beginning to understand, he added, "God help me."

The phone rang and the day began, ending all this self-pity. We've all got roles to play and jobs to do, he thought. Let's get down to it.

"ARE you sure of the directions?" Marion asked. Bob stared ahead. When he didn't reply immediately, she knew he wasn't sure.

"This place isn't exactly a famous spot," he finally said in defense. "Truth is, it wasn't on some maps. Too small, I guess."

"A good place for someone to hide out," Marion muttered. "But why? Why?"

Bob didn't say anything. He reviewed the directions and his visualization of the road map and watched for the four corners that were supposed to be appearing any moment. Seconds later, he saw what looked like a deserted gas station and then the four corners.

"This is right," he said with relief. They slowed down as they passed the station. It looked bombed out—the windows gone, the door swung open, dead wires emerging from where the pumps had been. A broken sign dangled. It read SAM'S FILL UP. Bob turned left as directed and sped up.

Just over the hill ahead of them, the gray building began to appear as if it were rising out of the ground. It grew and grew against the horizon as they continued. Against the backdrop of fields and forests, the modern structure looked ominous and incongruous. The absence of windows made it even more eerie.

"What is that?" Marion muttered. Sherri leaned forward and gaped, clutching her panda more tightly. Bob shook his head until he spotted the sign.

"Sandburg Hospital and Research Center," he recited.

"What an ugly structure."

"Probably one of those ultramodern places with controlled environments I've been reading about," Bob said. "Surprised to see one way out here though."

They couldn't take their eyes off it as they rode by. Moments later, cozy, quaint little homes nestled against the base of the mountain appeared. Nothing could be more in contrast to the cold, gray medical building behind them. Many of the homes had picket fences. All had neat, well-manicured and trimmed lawns and hedges.

"So clean . . . neat," Marion muttered.

"I feel like I just passed through some time zone and reentered the Fifties."

The lazy flow of traffic reinforced that impression. Although the vehicles they saw were up-to-date, as Marion and Bob drew closer to the village, they noted the vintage structures, the mom-and-pop stores, the wide, clean streets and old-fashioned street lamps. The sidewalks were wide and the people who moved up and down them looked relaxed and content. Missing was the frenzied pace of a more modern town. Traffic crawled, people stopped to speak to each other, store owners waved and greeted passersby from their entrances. Some of the advertisements and slogans painted on windows were definitely from a time gone by, Bob thought.

"Look at that—ice cream sodas, twenty-five cents."

"Must be a come-on," Marion commented, but she shook her head with amusement at the storefronts with the big awnings and the cardboard posters depicting styles and taste from years past. Was it just campy? What else could it be? These people weren't cut off from civilization.

Bob slowed down as he reached the center of town. He spotted a policeman standing on the right, arms folded, talking casually with a short man in a business suit. He pulled alongside and the policeman looked up with interest.

"Excuse me, officer." The policeman stepped off the curb and approached the car.

"What can I do for you? Lost?"

"Almost anyone who comes here is," the gentleman behind him quipped. The policeman laughed.

"No sir. We've come to Sandburg to see an old friend. We know he works in a bank, but," Bob said smiling, "we've forgotten which one."

"There's only two," the policeman said dryly. "Sandburg National and First Union. Who's your friend?"

"Sam Heller."

"Sammy?" He widened his smile and relaxed, leaning against the car. "That's the Sandburg National. He's their vice president."

"That's it," Bob said quickly. "Sandburg National."

"Keep heading straight one block and make a right. She'll be on your left."

"Thank you."

"My pleasure," he said and started to step away. But Marion couldn't resist. She leaned over.

"Is Sam Heller a friend of yours, officer?"

"Well, we're closely acquainted," he said smiling. "As is most everyone in Sandburg, ma'am. Sam's been here only about a year, but just about everyone knows him and likes him. Tell him Lou gave you directions," he added and tipped his hat.

"Thanks again," Bob said.

"About a year, Bob. About a year," Marion muttered.

"Easy, baby. Easy. We've got to stay calm."

Forcing herself to be obedient, Marion sat back, biting down softly on her lower lip, but her heart began to pound in anticipation, pumping so hard she thought she might pass

Saint Rose of Lima Parish
Paso Robles, CA
est. 1922

90th Anniversary 2012

Rev. Leo J. Foin	1922
Rev. Leo J. Beacon	1930
Rev. Patrick Leddy	1939
Rt. Rev. Micheal Sullivan	1940
Rev. Timothy Cummins	1954
Rev. Patrick Flood	1956
Rev. Brendan McGuinness	1960
Rev. Msgr. James Marron	1969
Rev. Douglas Keating	1974
Rev. James Henry	1991
Rev. Derek Hughes	1997
Rev. Micheal Volk	2003
Rev. Wayne Dawson	2007
Rev. Roberto Vera	2010

Monica
Higuera
13 years

10th Anniversary
September 8, 2012

Perpetual Eucharistic Adoration
est. September 8, 2002
at Saint Joseph Chapel
in Saint Rose of Lima Parish
Paso Robles, CA

out before they got there. Bob made the turn and they saw
the renovated nineteenth-century stone building. A large
brass plaque over the front entrance read SANDBURG
NATIONAL, SINCE 1905.

Bob pulled into the parking lot and found a space
quickly. Then he shut off the engine and sat back.

"Well, we're here." He turned to Marion. Her lips trembled. "It's going to be all right, honey." He squeezed her
hand and they all got out. Bob took Sherri's hand in his.
Clinging to Mr. Panda, she walked between him and Marion. They paused at the front entrance.   ✦

The bank looked quiet. Only two customers waited at the
counter on the left. But on the right, a woman sat at a desk
and listened quietly as Sam Heller spoke to her.

"It's him," Marion muttered.

Bob opened the door and they entered. The woman at the
desk looked up and Heller turned to see who had come into
the bank. Marion stared at him, her heart fibrillating because he showed no signs of recognition, not the least. She
stepped toward him.

"Brian," she said. "Don't you recognize me?"

Heller looked down at the woman who shrugged.

"Brian?" His eyelids fluttered and then his face turned
serious. "Wait a minute . . . I've seen you before."

"Yes, oh dear God, yes," Marion exclaimed. She looked
back at Bob, but he didn't react positively. He saw something else in Sam Heller's face and it wasn't friendly.

"You're the people who practically attacked me in New
York," Heller accused. "What the hell is this?"

"We know who you are," Bob said, stepping forward.
"You can't continue this charade, Brian."

Heller just stared a moment, deciding whether to ask
them to leave or continue. Something told him not to make
a big scene. He relaxed, his shoulders slouching.

"Oh God," he said, "what is this? Who the hell do you think I am? I can't believe you people tracked me all the way from New York."

"Can we speak privately?" Bob asked.

Heller looked down at the woman.

"Should I call Chief Robinson?" she asked.

"No, it's all right," he said. "Okay, right this way," Heller said indicating his office. "If we're going to play this game of mistaken identity again, I suppose we should do it in my office."

They followed him in. Immediately after he closed the door, he was at them.

"What the hell do you people think you're doing?" he demanded.

"Don't swear, Uncle Brian," Sherri said timidly. He gazed down at her, but he didn't smile. "Well?"

"We can explain it all," Bob said calmly. He held onto Marion's hand firmly.

Reluctantly, Heller went behind his desk. Then he indicated the chairs.

"All right," he said, sitting down. "Let's hear it."

Bob and Marion sat, Marion not taking her eyes off Heller for a moment.

"About a year ago, my wife's brother disappeared with our son on a camping trip."

"So? I mean, I'm sorry," he said, nodding at Marion, "but what the hell does that have to do with me?"

"You showed up here about that time," Bob continued.

Heller shook his head and held up his hands.

"We think something happened to you that caused amnesia," Bob concluded.

"Amnesia?" The word triggered his recall of some of the morning's events. Forgetting things was becoming a problem. But what did it have to do with these people? "Let me get this straight—you think I'm her brother and I went on a camping trip and became an amnesiac?"

"Yes," Bob said. Marion's unrelenting gaze made Heller uncomfortable. He tried to avoid her eyes.

"Look, Mr. . . ."

"Boxletter."

"Boxletter. I'm not her brother."

"Is there a ten-year-old boy with you?" Bob demanded.

"Joey," Marion muttered.

Heller gazed at her again and then turned back to Bob.

"Absolutely not. I'm married with three children, a son fourteen, a girl twelve, and a boy five. Here's their picture," he said reaching across the desk to turn a portrait picture in its frame around.

Marion and Bob stared in disbelief. There was Heller, his wife and three children.

"That can't be your family," Marion cried. "You're . . . either confused or . . . lying."

"Lying?" Heller sat back as if slapped. "Now look here, ma'am . . ."

"I checked your fingerprints against my brother's," Marion exclaimed, "and they matched!"

"Fingerprints?" Heller's lips trembled. He looked from Bob to Marion and back to Bob. Neither softened their gaze or let their eyes sway. He sat back as if he wanted to get away from them.

"Yes, fingerprints from your water glass back at the hotel in New York. I took it to the police."

"Police?"

Heller's face seemed to be crumbling. His cheeks shook as if he had been given an electrical shock and his eyes widened. His complexion waxed pale and his lips turned blue. For a moment neither Bob nor Marion could speak.

"You went to the police?" he finally uttered.

"Yes. I don't know if you are suffering from amnesia or if you're faking it for some reason, Brian, but there's no way you could have a wife and three children. No way. Now you tell us what happened to Joey or we're going straight to the police."

Heller gathered himself quickly. His color returned and he pulled himself up in his chair.

"That's exactly what you should do," he said.

"You don't think we will," Bob warned.

"I hope you will," Heller said firmly. "I want this to end. You go out here and to the right three blocks."

He sat back smugly. Marion stared a moment and then rose slowly.

"You don't have amnesia, Brian, do you?" she declared, her eyes small. "What are you hiding? What have you done and how does it involve Joey?"

Heller turned away. Those eyes were like pools of fire burning through his skin. He couldn't stand the scrutiny. It was tearing him apart inside. His stomach churned and voices, voices from nightmares past screeched. He had to escape.

"I'm not going to waste any more time with this," he said, rising. "I happen to be a busy man. Take your non-sense elsewhere," he commanded.

Bob got up.

"Come on, Sherri," he said, reaching for her hand. She grabbed it quickly.

"We'll be back, Brian," Marion promised.

"I doubt it," Heller said calmly. His calmness made her tremble. She marched out of the office quickly, Bob and Sherri right behind. They walked through the bank and out the front entrance without speaking. On the steps, Marion wilted. She clutched her stomach firmly.

"I think I'm going to vomit," she cried.

"Easy, honey." Bob helped her down the steps and toward the car, Sherri trotting right behind.

"Is Mommy sick?" she asked fearfully.

"Just take some deep breaths," Bob advised. They stood by the car as she did so. The color returned to her face. She closed her eyes and then opened them and gazed at the bank.

"Mommy," Sherri said.

"I'm all right, honey." She stroked Sherri's hair quickly to reassure her. Then she turned to Bob. "Bob . . ."

"I don't know, Marion. He was so confident. Maybe there is some incredible mistake," Bob said.

She shook her head.

"I'm more positive than ever." She looked around, her gaze falling on the street that came out on Main Street. Traffic weaved lazily along.

"My son," she said. "My son is here."

6

SAM HELLER FELT GLUED TO HIS SEAT. THE SWEAT WAS trickling down the sides of his neck and under his shirt collar. It brought a thin, chilling electric slice down both sides of his spinal cord. His eyes were transfixed on the closed office door. The Boxletters had left, but something of them lingered behind. It wasn't shadows exactly, but it was like shadows. Actually, it was more like images lingering on the retina, he thought, like when light remains for a second after the switch has been thrown and darkness comes crashing down all around.

In the Boxletters' case, part of their images remained—their eyes, especially, and especially Marion's. Their voices still echoed. Here and there over the office, words reverberated—words that wouldn't die away: Brian, Joey, brother. Despite his overriding annoyance and anger, he couldn't help feeling sympathy for the woman, and that filled him with a painful confusion, painful because it gnawed away inside his head. When he closed his eyes, he could actually see teeth chomping, scraping down on the thin membranes.

Part of him wanted to reach out and pull this woman to him so he could embrace her, but part of him wanted to reach out and seize her at the neck and squeeze and squeeze, anything to stop her from screaming and crying. The contradictions tugged and ripped his insides. He felt his stomach do flip-flops. The pressure that began to build seemed to center itself around his heart and then constrict and tighten. It was getting rather difficult to breathe, he thought.

What frightened him was he had to remember to breathe. Suddenly inhaling and exhaling had ceased to be an involuntary action. If he didn't think about doing it, he didn't and his face burned and his eyes bulged.

What happens when I fall asleep? he thought. Panic intensified. The moment I do, I die. I'll suffocate myself as soon as my eyes close.

The ridiculousness of this idea finally struck him funny and he began to laugh. The laugh became a cough and the cough a wheezing that drove him to pull himself up from his seat and rush to the window. He threw it open and thrust his head out to suck in fresh air. Deep breaths restored some semblance of normalcy. His heartbeat slowed and the heat left his face. Relieved, he turned around, intending to go back to work.

But his office was gone!

In its place was a dark forest and there, right where his desk should be, was a small campfire. A little boy was roasting marshmallows on a stick. There was the sound of a transistor radio to the left. He stepped toward the boy and the boy turned slowly.

Only, it wasn't a boy's face; it was the man, the man of his nightmares. All the skin was stripped from his head, making veins and arteries, muscle and bone vividly visible. His face crumpled and reformed, each time becoming something more distorted, more hideous—eyes bursting, nostrils separating, mouth stretching and snapping like a rubber band, teeth decaying, tongue flailing about in blood like an injured water snake.

He covered his own face with his hands and cried out. He wasn't aware of how loud he was screaming until he heard Martha Applebaum's voice. He lowered his hands from his face and saw that the forest was gone, the fire was gone, the hideous face was gone. He was back in his office.

"Mr. Heller! Mr. Heller, are you all right? Mr. Heller?"

"What?"

"You were . . . shouting so loud, Mr. Heller."

He stared at her and looked past her at the customers and tellers who were gazing back at him in astonishment.

"Shouting? Oh. Yes, I'm fine. It was just . . ."

It was just what? He had no idea what to tell her.

"Would you like something to drink . . . coffee, soda?"

"No thank you, Martha."

"As long as you're all right, Mr. Heller," she said, mercifully ending the scene.

"Yes, I'm fine. Thank you."

She stared at him a moment and then left. Everyone went back to their work. Heller returned to his seat. After he sat down, he tried to recall what he was doing. Memories of the Boxletters returned. He had sent them to the police. Yes, to the police.

He had to go there, too, he thought. The thought came more as a command emanating from that dark shadow at the back of his mind. Report to Chief Robinson, he told himself in a voice that seemed artificial, mechanical, computerized. He rose with the stiffness of a robot and started out of his office, not gazing to the right or the left as he moved through the lobby, and thus not aware of how everyone else was looking at him.

"Mr. Heller?" Martha said as he went to the front door. "Are you going somewhere?" she asked, but he didn't hear her. He didn't hear anything but that mechanical voice chanting—"To Chief Robinson."

He didn't even remember walking up the street or entering the police station through the back entrance. Suddenly, there he was waiting in a room. And Chief Robinson, as if he had heard the same voice and knew Sam had arrived, poked his head through the open door and said, "Just stay in here, Sam. I'll be right with you."

He sat down and smiled.

So long ago in another time, in another place, he was a little boy again. He followed the line of his arm up to his hand and saw that it was joined with a larger hand, a feminine hand with soft fingers and painted fingernails. That hand was attached to a smooth arm and when he let his eyes climb over it, it took him to the shoulders and the bosom. Above the bosom like some flower dipping in the sunlight was the warm smile, the loving smile.

He knew who it was, but he couldn't find the word. He closed his eyes and squeezed and squeezed until he brought the word out of his brain like the last drop of juice out of an orange. It kissed his lips as softly as warm rain. He touched it with the tip of his tongue and then he cried out with joy.

"MOTHER!"

Then, as if he had said the most forbidden thing, a curtain of darkness dropped with the weight of iron, slicing through her arm as it fell.

He was left holding the detached hand and wrist. Blood rushed out and it folded like cellophane. In seconds it wasn't much thicker than wax paper.

After that the trembling began. Somewhere, deep in the well under his heart, the vibrations started. They gradually grew in intensity as they climbed toward his beating organ. This was going to be it; this was going to be something.

He waited, almost happy it had finally come to pass.

BOB and Marion were silent in their car as he pulled out of the bank parking lot and drove toward the Sandburg police station. Even little Sherri, normally loquacious, sensed the heaviness in the air and kept herself as still as a doll.

"It was Brian," Marion chanted. "It was." She did it now more to convince herself than to convince Bob. He shook his head.

"Maybe," he said. "But there was a moment in that office when his eyes were so cold, so calculating and vicious, I thought this can't be Brian, not in a million years. Didn't you see it? Feel it?" he pursued.

Marion tried not to agree, but her head nodded.

"Something's changed him, made him that way."

"But married, with children?"

"I don't know; I don't understand," she said and the tears that had built in her eyes began to trickle down her cheeks.

"We'll get to the bottom of it all now," Bob swore as they pulled into the police station parking lot. This time, when they all got out of the car, Bob, impatient with Sherri's slow pace, scooped her up and carried her and her panda to the front door. She didn't complain. The deep silence and tension around her parents made her hold her breath from time to time. She looked from her mother to her father quickly and then pressed her lips together, determined to behave.

They entered the station and gazed around. Although the building was old, the lobby of the station showed no signs of age or use. On the contrary, there was the feel and the smell of newness—new furniture, new wall paneling, new light fixtures. The duty officer behind the counter looked to be no more than a man in his mid-twenties. He had short-cropped, sweet potato–gold hair and a face full of freckles. Dressed in a sparkling blue uniform with a badge that seemed to catch all the light and glow, he looked more like a policeman preparing for a parade than a man at his daily routine. He looked up and smiled at the Boxletters.

"How can I help you?" he asked.

"We've got a problem," Bob said. "A serious problem."

"Well, things that look serious now often turn out to be far less severe later," he replied with a wisdom that went far beyond his appearance. "Did you want to see Chief Robinson?"

Bob looked at Marion and then replied.

"Yes, we need to see whoever is in charge."

"That's Chief Robinson," the young officer said. "Let me tell him you're here. Your name is?"

"Boxletter, Bob and Marion."

"And Sherri," Sherri said. The policeman smiled.

"And Sherri. One moment, please," he said and went to a door behind him. He knocked softly and then stuck his head in, mumbled something and returned.

"The chief will be glad to see you," he said opening the gate. "Right this way, folks. First time in Sandburg?" he asked Bob as they entered.

"Yes."

"Thought so. We know just about everyone who lives here, even the pets."

Bob nodded.

"Good. That's what we were hoping," he said. He looked intently at the young officer. As he turned away he thought, he looks young, but his eyes look old.

Chief Harry Robinson was standing behind his desk. He was a tall, stout man, easily six feet three or four and weighing two hundred twenty-five or thirty pounds. He had very light brown hair with a predominance of gray moving insidiously through it. His brown eyes were hard and cold, like glass eyes, Bob thought. There was a tiny, rather artificial smile around his lips, the quick perfunctory greeting of a bureaucrat.

"Hello," he said. He indicated the chairs and the small settee to the right. "Have a seat, please. My name's Harry Robinson."

"Bob and Marion Boxletter," Bob said. "This is Sherri," he added lowering her to the floor. "Go sit down, honey," he said nodding toward one of the chairs. Marion sat down beside her and rubbed her hands together nervously. Bob hesitated and then took a seat. Robinson remained standing.

"Close that door please, Tommy," he said. The Boxletters weren't aware that the policeman had remained in the doorway. He and Robinson exchanged an almost angry glance, Bob thought, and then the policeman backed out and closed the door. Robinson sat down.

"How can I help you?" he asked.

"Marion, why don't you start, honey," Bob said. She nodded, took a deep breath and began. She started with Brian and Joey's disappearance, ran through the weeks of horror while the searching continued and was finally ended, and then she skipped right to their New York trip, described Sam Heller and how she had stolen his fingerprints. She ended by describing their confrontation with him in the bank. From the way she related it, it was clear she believed her brother had suffered some traumatic shock and lost his memory.

Robinson listened without cracking a smile or making a comment. His large eyes grew smaller at times, and at times he nodded slightly, but he showed no emotion, no feeling about the story one way or another. He didn't even look sympathetic when Marion described how much of a nightmare it had been to have a child literally disappear off the face of the earth. When she was finished, he sat back, took a deep breath, shook his head and then smiled.

"Well. Looks like we've got one helluva confused situation here," he began.

"That's putting it mildly," Bob quipped. Robinson's controlled reaction and stoic face was beginning to annoy him. This man is too intent on being who he's supposed to be, he thought: the policeman who is always a policeman. Under neath it all, we're all men; we've all got to show some emotion, feel some compassion, he reasoned.

"Yes, well, the thing is, I've known Sam Heller for a year, and I can tell you he's an outstanding member of the community and a fine family man. Furthermore," Robinson said leaning on his desk and finally breaking into something of a warm smile, "I assure you, old Harvey Kornblau at the bank does about as good a check on his new employees as can be done, probably better than the FBI."

"But . . ." Marion began. Robinson held up his hand in stop-traffic fashion.

"Also, that involves a thorough check for criminal records . . . so if he had the fingerprints of a man who had been arrested and booked for auto theft . . ."

"I took them to our local police," Marion insisted. "They ran the check."

"Um . . ." Robinson sat back again.

"Fingerprints don't lie, do they?" Marion pursued.

"No, but sometimes experts make mistakes, especially with smudged prints off a glass."

"That man is my brother," Marion insisted. She fished a photograph from her pocketbook and got up to drop it on the desk in front of Robinson. He took it in his fingers and studied it a moment.

"Looks a helluva lot like Sam," he admitted.

"Too remarkable and close a resemblance to be any sort of coincidence," Bob added.

"Um . . ." Robinson said again. Then he handed the picture back to Marion. "Well, all I can tell you is my wife and I have baby-sat Sam's kids . . . and none of them is a ten-year-old boy. If Sam is your brother and he's had amnesia or something for a year, where do the wife and kids fit in? And if he's faking this role for some reason, to what end?

Also, Mrs. Boxletter, if that was the case, why would he be eager for you to come see the police?"

"We don't have the answers," Marion snapped back, a little harder than she had intended. "That's why we're here."

Robinson nodded.

"All right," he said. "I'll run a fingerprint check through the FBI myself and I'll call your police department and speak with them. In the meantime," he added, swinging his gaze up sharply at Marion, "I'd like you folks to stay away from Sam. Don't go near the bank or his home."

"What if he runs away now that we've come?"

Robinson started to laugh, but stopped when he saw Marion was dead serious.

"I doubt he'd do that, Mrs. Boxletter. But . . ." he said, raising that big palm again, "I'll keep an eye on him. Fair enough?"

Marion nodded.

"I assume you folks will stay in town until I can get a fix on this?"

"Yes," Bob said.

"You might try the Dew Drop Inn. It's just south of town. Clean and cheap and," he said, turning toward Sherri and smiling, "they have a little fun park for children. It's run by the Hamptons," he added turning back to Bob. "Real nice folks. They make guests feel like family."

"Thanks," Bob said, surprised at the extent of the chief's endorsement. "When should we call you?"

"Give me a call late in the afternoon tomorrow. Or, if you're in town, just stop by." Robinson stood up. "I'm sorry about all this," he added. "It can't be pleasant for any of you, even Heller."

"No," Marion said. "It's an endless nightmare."

Robinson nodded. He remained standing as they all got

up and walked out. The duty officer opened the gate for them, smiling. When Bob turned back after opening the front door for Marion and Sherri, he saw Robinson standing beside the duty officer. They were both looking at them intently, almost . . . angrily, Bob thought.

"I didn't like that man," Marion said when they reached the car. "He's too cold, too indifferent. I don't trust him and I don't think he's going to help us."

"We've got to give him a chance, honey. What else can we do?"

"Go to the FBI ourselves," she suggested.

"Maybe we will. Let's see what he comes up with tomorrow."

"The only thing he got excited about was this stupid motel," Marion said. Bob shrugged.

"Maybe the Hamptons are his in-laws."

Marion smiled for the first time since they had arrived. She got into the car and they drove out and turned back onto Main Street. Neither spoke as they headed south.

"Are we going to the hotel, Mommy?" Sherri asked.

"Yes, honey."

"The one with the fun park?"

"You heard that, did you? Yes, we are."

"Good. Mr. Panda wants to go to the fun park."

"I'll take him," Bob said. "You can stay with Mommy."

Sherri laughed.

Marion rested her forehead against the window and stared out at the village, the people, the clean streets and sidewalks, the quiet, almost dreamlike movement. No one seemed to look their way or pay any attention to them as they drove down the street, and if anyone did gaze out at them, he or she seemed to be looking right through them.

It was almost as if . . . they weren't really there.

*   *   *

CHIEF Robinson paused after he opened the door on Sam Heller. The man was sitting back in his chair, his head tilted so he looked up at the ceiling, his eyes as far back in his head as they could go. His lips were pulled back, revealing most of his teeth to the gums. Robinson was reminded of the face of an orangutan. He noticed that Heller had his hands clamped down on the arms of the chair, and he was squeezing so hard that the veins around his knuckles and wrist were lifted sharply against his skin. His feet were placed flat on the floor, and he sat so still, he looked petrified, frozen, every muscle, every tendon, every bone in his body locked.

The chief shook his head and closed the door softly behind him after he entered.

"Sam?" Heller didn't stir. The chief moved closer. "Sam," he said, louder, more firmly. Heller didn't move. Unnerved by the sight now, Chief Robinson automatically dropped his right hand over the handle of his pistol before drawing himself any closer. Then he reached out with his left hand and nudged Heller's right shoulder. The man's body felt like it had been carved out of stone. His entire torso moved with the nudge, but his head held its weird position and his eyes didn't move. Amazingly, he didn't even blink.

"What the hell . . ." Robinson scratched the right side of his head and considered Heller for a moment without speaking, without moving himself. He'd better call Dr. Randolph, he thought, and get an ambulance on the way. He decided to first nudge Heller one more time and reached forward, touching the man's right cheek this time.

The moment his fingers made contact with Heller's cold, leathery skin, the man wrenched his head forward and screamed. It was a piercing, shrill cry that tore into Robinson and made him shudder. With lightning speed, Heller followed the scream with a lunge, seizing Chief Robinson's extended fingers and shoving them hungrily into his mouth. Before the startled policeman had a chance to react, Heller crunched down with the full force of his teeth, tearing quickly through the skin and breaking the bones of the forefinger and middle finger. The pain was instantaneous and shot up Robinson's arm like a bullet, ricocheting off his shoulder bone.

Instinctively, he swung out with his free hand and caught Heller in the cheekbone, driving him off the chair. Incredibly, he held onto Robinson's fingers until he fell over. Robinson drew his bloodied hand up and howled himself at the sight of his mangled fingers.

Heller slapped his hands over his ears and got to his knees. The screaming and the noise drew patrolman Tommy Wilson to the door. When he looked in and saw the sight, however, he stood gaping in awe.

"Get me a towel," the chief ordered and grimaced with pain.

"What the hell happened?"

"A towel!" Robinson repeated.

Wilson rushed from the room. On the floor Heller had sat back on his haunches and was rocking back and forth, his hands still glued to his ears, his mouth open in an enormous, silent scream that made his eyes bulge and his nostrils widen.

"Sam!" the chief cried. "SAM!"

Slowly, Heller lowered his head until those wild eyes, orbs of fire and pain, were focused on the chief.

"What's wrong with you?" Robinson asked.

In response, Heller leapt at him with a remarkable, cat-like agility. Before the chief could react, Sam had his arms wrapped around Robinson's waist. Pulling the astounded policeman toward him, Heller snapped at his crotch, his teeth coming down so hard against each other, the click sounded like a hammer against nails. Heller caught some of Robinson's pants on his second bite and pulled and tugged like a mad dog.

Tommy Wilson stopped in the doorway, his eyes wide, watching the chief trying to extricate himself from the rabid man. Wilson reached for his pistol.

"No," the chief said. "Just help me get him off!" he commanded. Wilson rushed forward and threw a headlock around Heller's temples and forehead and then, with all his strength, pulled back while Robinson tried pushing Heller away with his good hand. It took both men all they had to get Heller off.

"Cuff him," the chief screamed.

It was easier said than done, for Heller's arms were nearly immovable. Wilson struggled, tugging and pulling, making progress in little increments. Robinson, in terrific pain from the damage to his fingers, helped as much as he could. Finally, Wilson was able to connect the cuffs.

The moment Heller's hands were neutralized, he threw his head back. They heard him choking and knew he was swallowing his own tongue.

"Get a spoon, quick," Robinson cried. Wilson let Heller fall over on the floor and rushed out. He returned with a spoon. While Wilson held Heller's head back, the chief worked the spoon in and freed Heller's tongue. Heller chomped down on the handle, locking his jaw. The muscles in his face strained and his eyes went back in his head again. After a moment, he went limp and his eyes slammed shut.

"What the hell happened to him, Chief?"

"I don't know." Robinson let out a breath and fell back

in the chair. The pain in his fingers intensified. He closed his eyes. "Call the hospital," he said. "Get an ambulance. Move it!" he screamed and Tommy Wilson jumped up and rushed out.

Chief Robinson stood up slowly, moaning. He looked down at Heller and then made his way back to his office.

"Ambulance is on the way, Chief," Wilson called.

"Good."

"Want any help with your hand?"

"No, it's all right. Go stay with Heller."

"Right."

The chief struggled to get the receiver of his phone and place it against his ear and shoulder. Then he punched out the numbers, rocking with pain in his seat as he did so. It rang and rang. Finally, Dr. Randolph picked up her phone. Her hello indicated her annoyance. She hated interruptions.

"What is it?" she demanded instead of saying hello.

"It's Heller," Robinson said. There was a long silence. "There were strangers here," he said. "A man, a woman and a little girl. The woman claimed he was her brother. They confronted Heller in the bank and then came here. I've sent them to the Dew Drop Inn to wait, but Heller came here. I've called for an ambulance," he concluded.

"What?" she asked.

"The same sort of thing as Ed Walters, one of those rabid-dog seizures. I've got a couple of broken fingers restraining him," he added, but there was little compassion or sympathy.

"Go to the emergency room," she said. "I'll look after Heller," she added and cradled the phone without a good-bye.

Robinson hung up and sat back. The towel was stained with his blood, but he kept his fingers tightly wrapped.

Pressure made them feel better. He could hear the ambulance siren in the distance.

Something's happening, he thought. It's all coming apart.

7

THE SHORT, ROUND-FACED ELDERLY LADY WITH THE GRANNY glasses leaned over and rested her heavy bosom on the top of the reception desk to smile down at Sherri.

"My granddaughter is not much older than you are, sweetheart," she said. Her cheeks seemed to bloom when she widened her smile and brightened her remarkably green eyes. Set in this venerable but not terribly aged face, those eyes look out of place, Bob thought. They're too youthful, too bright and alive, the eyes of a child. Those gleaming orbs radiated a vitality that made Bob think of actors and actresses in Geritol commercials. Time had definitely been kind to Mrs. Hampton. Her skin was still smooth and relatively wrinkle-free. She looked like she had all her own teeth, and except for a few age spots on her cheeks and forehead, and that blue-tinted gray hair, she didn't evince any other suggestions of old age. This was truly an active senior citizen. Bob imagined her easily in her seventies, but remarkably well preserved.

"Chief Robinson recommended we stop here," Bob told her. "Highly recommended," he added, smiling.

"Oh, he's such a dear, always looking out for Charley and me, not that we really want to be too busy mind you," she said and followed it with a short, thin laugh. If any woman could play Mrs. Santa Claus, this is she, Bob thought. She leaned over the counter toward Sherri again. "We're too old to worry about making money.

"But," she continued, smiling at Marion now, "I have the

nicest room for you. It looks out over Daniels's pond and
sometimes," she added, raising her thick, gray eyebrows a
notch, "you can see the ducks and geese. Your room is
number fourteen, on the first floor," she explained.

"Thank you," Marion said. Bob could see from the way
Mrs. Hampton was only glancing at Marion from time to
time that she sensed Marion was upset and very nervous.
Sensitive old woman, he thought.

"And Sherri can play in the fun park until it gets too
dark, if you like. I'd be glad to watch her," she added. The
very suggestion threw terror into Marion. She stiffened
quickly and put her arm around Sherri's little shoulder.

"Her father will take her or I will," Marion said firmly.

"Of course, dear. Now," she said turning to the wall of
keys, "fourteen . . . yes, here it is. Everything you need is in
there, but if you want more towels, just call us and I'll send
Charley over. He doesn't move as fast as he used to, so
give us a few minutes," she said.

"Thank you," Bob said, taking the key.

"Just go out this door and turn right."

"Maybe you can recommend a nice restaurant for us?"
Bob asked.

"Oh sure. Go to Ray's Diner. It's just a mile or so back
toward town and he has a special menu for children, too,"
she said, her eyes twinkling at Sherri.

"Sounds good. Thanks again," Bob said and they started
out. "Nice little old lady," he muttered. Marion said nothing. She was increasingly feeling that nothing was what it
seemed to be here. Everything she looked at, including the
people, had an ethereal, unreal appearance. She, Bob and
Sherri were moving through some sort of bizarre dream;
they had fallen down some mysterious tunnel and like
Alice in Wonderland, landed in a world created out of

someone's imagination. She trusted nothing, no one, not even her own senses.

"There's practically no one else here," she commented as they walked toward the rear of the two-story motel and saw how empty the parking lot was. The motel wasn't a very large or elaborate structure and was very unpretentious. Except for the small wooden sign at the entrance, there were no neon lights, nothing to advertise what it was. The driveway and parking lot were made of crushed stone and the structure itself was all wood with clapboard in need of fresh paint.

"Sandburg's not exactly a hot vacation spot," Bob replied.

Despite the age of the motel, their room was very quaint and very clean. Unlike standard motels, the furniture looked authentic nineteenth century with real hardwood beds and dressers. The windows had pretty, light blue curtains that were freshly washed and pressed and the hardwood floor with its large oval rug was clean and recently polished. The fixtures in the bathroom were old, but well maintained and also immaculate.

There was a black dial telephone on the night table between the two double beds and a small television set in a modest entertainment piece. Beside it was a light pine desk and chair and a blue porcelain table lamp.

"Very nice," Bob said when they had checked it all out. "Don't you think?"

"Yes."

"Especially for the price. This place . . . this whole town, it's like someplace that has just lagged behind or ignored progress. Can't say I don't like it, even though people here probably think the personal computer is a piece of science fiction," he added, smiling. He wanted to lighten the moment as best he could and get Marion to relax. But she was unwilling or unable.

"I hate it," she blurted.

"What?"

"Everything is just . . . too nice," she said. "It's not real. People don't live like this anymore."

"What? Sure they do, honey. It's not much different from Spring Glen, is it?"

"Of course it's different. Don't you feel it, see it?" she insisted.

"See what?"

"Something . . . eerie."

"Oh Marion. You're just letting our problem influence everything else."

"Our problem? Our problem!" She grimaced.

"All right, all right," he said, backing up. "Take it easy. I'm just as unnerved by all this as you are, but if we don't relax, we're not going to be any good to ourselves as well as to Joey when we do find him." He gazed at Sherri who sat on her bed, clinging to Mr. Panda. "As well as you know who," he added.

Marion swallowed back her tears.

"Why don't you take a shower, honey?" he suggested in a softer tone. "I'll take Sherri out to the fun park and then I'll shower and we'll go to dinner, okay?" He moved to her and put his arm around her, drawing her to him so he could kiss her forehead. She felt so cold, so clammy.

"All right," she finally said.

"Great. What do you say, Sherri? Want to go look at the fun park?"

"Yes, Daddy." She hopped off the bed.

"Don't leave her alone," Marion warned. "Even for a moment."

"Of course not," he assured her. He took Sherri's hand

and they left the room. Marion went to the window and watched them walk off. The ringing of the phone frightened her and she gasped and held her palm against her pounding heart while it rang a second time. She stared at it for a moment and then moved quickly, thinking it could be the police.

"Hello."

"Hello, dear," Mrs. Hampton said. "Is everything all right with your room?"

"Oh. Yes, thank you," she said, her voice dripping with disappointment. "It's fine."

"I'm glad. You've come a long way and I don't want you to be disappointed," she added. It was a nice thought, a kind thought, a considerate thought, but it sounded so ominous. "Don't be afraid to call if you need anything, any time, any time at all," Mrs. Hampton sang.

"Thank you," Marion said.

This is ridiculous, she told herself after she cradled the receiver and saw her hand shaking. I've got to get hold of myself.

She undressed quickly and went into the bathroom to shower. It was a small shower stall with a bathtub. The rear wall of the stall had a glazed, thick window that permitted only light to enter. One couldn't see out nor could anyone sec in, yet while Marion was scrubbing herself down, she had the strange sensation that someone was watching her. She turned on the window quickly and thought she saw a shadow move across the glass. She waited and watched, but the shadow didn't return. After that, she completed her shower and got out, drying herself as fast as she could. Then, with only the towel wrapped around herself, she went out to the room to look out the window again.

She leaned to the right to catch sight of Bob and Sherri. From this perspective, she could see the whole fun park—

the slide, the merry-go-round, the swings and monkey bars, as well as the big sandbox. But she didn't see them. If they weren't there and they weren't back in the room, where could they be?

Panicking, she went to the door and stepped out to look farther, but they were nowhere in sight.

"BOB!" she screamed. She couldn't help it; she didn't care how ridiculous she looked or sounded. "BOB!"

Suddenly, an elderly man, mostly bald with two gray puffs of hair looking glued onto the sides of his head, came around the corner of the building. He carried a shovel over his shoulder like a rifle and held a pail in his left hand. He was wearing coveralls and a flannel shirt. His physique was thin, practically gaunt, but he walked with a determination and strength that suggested a man at least half his age, if not younger.

Marion didn't go back inside, even though she was standing there with merely a towel wrapped around herself. The old man's face was mesmerizing. His cheeks were so sunken, his skin so wrinkled and dry, he appeared to be a man close to one hundred. She thought of mummified bodies, stuffed animals, corpses.

But his eyes—he gazed at her the way a man half his age might, with lust and pleasure. He even had a licentious smile. This finally made her self-conscious.

"I was just looking for my husband and daughter," she explained quickly, tightening the towel around her bulging bosom.

"Oh, they're over at the pond," he said, "lookin' at the ducks."

"Thank you." She stepped back inside quickly and closed the door. Then she went back to the window and watched him continue on, his pace a little faster. The red shale on the tip of his shovel looked like dry blood.

If that's Charley, she thought, he moves fast enough, too fast, and Mrs. Hampton surely knew it. It was just another thing to reinforce her feeling that they were in a very strange place, populated by people who were odd.

CHIEF Robinson, sitting on the passenger side of his vehicle, kept the towel snug around his crushed fingers and stared impatiently out the windshield as Tommy Wilson made the turn into the Sandburg Hospital driveway. The ambulance had already arrived and the attendants were unloading the stretcher on which the comatose Sam Heller lay.

"Pull right beside the ambulance," Robinson ordered gruffly. Wilson turned sharply. As soon as he brought the car to a stop, Robinson got out. Wilson started to emerge, too, but the chief leaned back and barked, "You just go back to the station, Tommy. I'll call you to come get me."

"Right," the patrolman said, retreating to his seat. He watched the chief hurry through the emergency doors and then he backed out and drove off.

Dr. Lila Randolph stood waiting just inside the emergency room door and escorted the gurney carrying Heller. Robinson knew that the short, thin woman with what he had come to think of as microscope eyes had seen him entering too, but had ignored him. She directed the attendants to push the gurney into the awaiting elevator. Chief Robinson watched them. Dr. Randolph turned and examined Heller for a moment. Then she straightened up and looked out at Chief Robinson as she inserted her security card in the slot on the elevator, which would permit it to go to the restricted fifth floor. Her face was bland, the pale, almost sickly white, pockmarked cheeks as rigid as the surface of a brass statue. She looked directly at the chief, but showed no signs of recognition and certainly not the least bit of interest in his wound. The doors closed and Robinson continued on to get his fingers treated.

Almost two hours later, with his fingers in casts and his hand bandaged, he looked up in the examination room and saw Dr. Nelson Congemi, Dr. Randolph's associate, standing there and smiling in at him. Dr. Congemi was a fifty-nine-year-old man with a pair of gentle blue eyes, a soft, almost feminine mouth and round jaw. He was at least fifteen to twenty pounds overweight for his five-foot, eleven-inch frame. He had smooth shoulders and arms, the muscle definition almost nonexistent, which only illustrated his distaste for any form of physical exercise or exertion. The consummate scientist, Dr. Congemi behaved as though the demands of his body, the need to feed it and clothe it, to empty it and keep it warm and dry, were an annoying burden. He often forgot to eat, and Chief Robinson even heard rumors that the man kept a urine bottle in his office so he wouldn't have to interrupt his thinking by going to the men's room.

Dr. Randolph suddenly appeared beside him and eyed the intern who had treated Chief Robinson.

"Are you finished here?" she demanded.

"Yes, Doctor."

"Thank you," she said as a way of dismissing him, and the young doctor moved quickly to leave them alone in the examination room. As soon as he left, Dr. Congemi walked farther in.

"So Harry, tell me what happened."

"As I told Doctor Randolph, these people came to my office," Robinson began and described the Boxletters and what they had done. "Afterward I went to Sam in the back room, but I found him in some sort of daze. When I approached him, he went into that violent fit, the rabid dog fit," he added. He had been the one to label Ed Walters's behavior and liked it so much, he applied it to Heller. He could see from the way Lila Randolph smirked that she didn't appreciate the label. Dr. Congemi didn't crack his smile, and his eyes revealed serious concern.

"Where are these people now?" Randolph asked.

"I sent them to the Dew Drop Inn. They're waiting overnight for me to check out the fingerprints. How's Heller?"

"This is Fryman's doing," Congemi said, ignoring the question and shaking his head. "We've got to tell him," he told Randolph. She didn't reply. She stood there, thinking.

"Why is this happening?" Chief Robinson asked. The fury in Dr. Randolph's eyes cowed him and seemed to intensify the pain in his fingers. "I mean . . . can it happen to any of the others?"

"That's not your concern," Randolph snapped. "Right now, you should be more concerned about this Boxletter family. Who knows they're here?"

"According to what they told me, they didn't tell the police, if that's what you mean. Apparently, they just upped and left their home."

"Good," she said.

"We've got to call Fryman," Dr. Congemi reiterated. Lila Randolph ignored him and kept her eyes on Chief Robinson.

"I assume you've made sure the Andersons are under control."

"Andersons?" He looked at Congemi, but found no sympathy. "Well, no, everything happened so fast, I . . ."

"We chose you, Harry, because you were supposed to be efficient under pressure," Dr. Randolph said. "Find them and isolate them before any more damage is done," she commanded and walked out before he could reply. He looked up at Congemi.

"It's not my fault these people showed up," Robinson moaned. He was the one who took the pain and the injury. Why was she so bitchy?

"Just plug up the holes quickly, Harry. I'll take care of Doctor Randolph."

"Yeah, well if you ask me, that's what she needs the most, Doctor Congemi, someone to take care of her. Probably doin' it with a test tube," he muttered. He looked up at Congemi who smiled. "Lubricated," Robinson added and Congemi's cheeks shook as he laughed silently.

"Call me when everything's secured," Congemi said and followed Dr. Randolph's exit.

Harry Robinson slipped off the table slowly. Even though it was only his hand that had been injured, his entire body ached in sympathy. This had looked like such a cushion, such an easy way to make great money, and after what he had been through in Vietnam, he decided he deserved easy pickin's. Now it was turning into a whole other thing. He recalled how paranoid he had become in 'Nam, how every Asian face became a threat and every shadow dangerous because he never knew what was what or who was who anymore.

Now, he would walk down Main Street Sandburg and wonder if the little old lady who had been in and out of the research center would come after him with a hatchet when he turned his back.

Great way to live, he thought as he walked out of the examination room and headed for the telephone to call Wilson. He stopped and looked at the elevator as if Dr. Congemi and Dr. Randolph were standing there watching him.

"Wonderful work," he muttered. "You people are really making a better world."

"Excuse me, Chief," the emergency room nurse who had been standing nearby said. He turned.

"Nothing," he said. "I'm just talking to myself."

Because of the expression on his face, she didn't know whether or not to laugh, and he didn't encourage it. He had practically lost the remnants of the sense of humor he had once had, and when you could no longer laugh, what's the point? he thought.

Bob, Marion and Sherri came out of their room and got into the car quickly. With the sun dropping behind the mountains behind them, the shadows around the motel had expanded and stretched rapidly, oozing over the parking lot. To Marion it seemed as if only the motel and its immediate surroundings were in the twilight. The sunlight still fell strongly in the distance. Darkness had singled them out. It gave her the chills and she shuddered at the car door and embraced herself.

"I'm starving," Bob said. "How about you, Sherri?"

"Me, too," she said. "And Mr. Panda wants a hamburger and french fries."

"I thought Mr. Panda was on a diet," Bob joked.

Marion looked at him, feeling both anger and envy. How could he remain so calm, so cool, even-tempered and strong in the face of this horrible nightmare, and yet, she wished she could be more like him, at least for Sherri's sake. She knew that was why Bob was putting it on and she understood, but to her, right now, she expected the whole world to be depressed. Maybe that was why she had this bad reaction to Sandburg and its inhabitants. It wasn't reasonable; it wasn't logical; it wasn't even fair, but she couldn't help it. The whole world should be sympathetic and no one should laugh or smile again until her son was returned. Everyone here looked too well adjusted, too content, too stress-free.

Where's the anxiety and the pain, the tension and the turmoil that characterized the rest of the world?

She had the same unreasonable reaction to the restaurant when they arrived. It was a place of smiles. The hostess, the waiters and waitresses, the customers, everyone was pleasant and congenial, no rushing about, no pressure, no impatience. Ray's Diner was just that, an old-fashioned diner with imitation red leather booths, a black-and-white checked tile floor, an old jukebox playing Oldies but Goodies, a long counter with matching red-cushioned stools and racks of homemade pies and cakes. The only compromise with the 1990s was the formal hostess who greeted them at the door and the sectioning off of the dining area to non-smoking and smoking. She was a pretty teenage girl with light brown hair and cerulean eyes. With her saddle shoes, her pleated skirt and light blue cotton sweater, she looked like an extra from *Peggy Sue Got Married*. Her name tag read Nancy Selzer.

"Smoking or non-smoking?" she asked as soon as they entered.

"Non," Bob said. He saw there was another couple waiting on the side. "How long?"

"No more than five minutes. I have two booths paying their checks right now," she said. "Name?"

"Boxletter," Bob said and smiled at Marion. The hostess was trying to be professional, but in a place this small, taking names seemed silly.

Bob and Marion stepped away from the doorway to permit two truck drivers who had eaten and paid their bill at the counter to leave. They both smiled at Sherri, who stood as close as possible to Marion and clung tightly to Mr. Panda.

"I've got to go to the bathroom, Mommy," Sherri said.

"I asked you back at the motel," Marion complained.

"Down there," Bob said nodding toward the rear of the diner where he saw the restroom sign.

"Come on," Marion said, seizing Sherri's hand. They walked down the aisle and started to turn into the small hallway that led to the restrooms when Sherri stopped abruptly to look at someone in a booth. Bob started to smile, but Marion turned abruptly to tug her.

"Sherri, you said you had to . . ."

"Look, Mommy," Sherri said.

Marion's eyes lifted slowly, her gaze climbing over the legs and knees of the man and woman, over their faces and across to the inside of the booth where her son sat gobbling french fries mindlessly, his right forefinger and thumb stained with ketchup. For a moment, Marion couldn't find her voice. All the blood in her body seemed to rush into her head. Her heart paused and then pounded vigorously against her chest.

And then she screamed, *"Joey!"* and lunged forward, literally reaching across the table, coming between the plate of food and the face of the blond-haired, tall man sitting at the end. Her abrupt action took the boy by surprise and he dropped his hamburger and pulled himself back against the wall and the window to avoid her hands. The dark-haired, comely woman across the table snapped back as well.

"Marion!" Bob cried and hurried down the aisle. "What are you . . ."

The blond man shoved Marion's hands and arms away and started to stand.

"What the hell . . ."

"It's Joey!" Marion screamed at Bob. He looked and saw his son.

"Joey."

"What the hell is this?" the man said, standing firmly now between the boy and the Boxletters. His wife remained shocked, her mouth open, her eyes wide, staring up at Marion.

"That's my son," Bob said. "Joey, Joey Boxletter."

"What the hell are you talking about?"

By now the rest of the diner had come to a standstill. The short-order cook stood staring behind the counter, the waiters and waitresses all froze in the aisles and the customers stopped eating.

Ray Stine, a muscular man in his mid-fifties, rushed around the counter.

"What's happening here, Kurt?" he asked.

"These crazy people are saying Adam is their son," he replied angrily. He was at least three inches taller than Bob and much broader. He had the forearms of a lumberjack and the neck muscles of a professional wrestler. Angry, his muscles tensed, his fists clenched, he looked formidable, but Bob didn't step back.

"That is our son," Bob insisted.

"Joey," Marion cried.

The boy remained terrified, his back smack against the wall.

"Don't you know us?" Marion asked.

"Look, mister," Ray said, "you'd better leave before there's real trouble here."

"No!" Marion cried.

"I'm not leaving without my son," Bob insisted.

Ray turned to Nancy Selzer who stood nearby.

"Call the police. Quick," he commanded. She ran to the front. "Now just you take it easy," Ray coached. "Leave these people be and when the police come, we'll settle it all. Go on," he added.

"Move on," Kurt Anderson said threateningly.

"Bob," Marion said, seeing the formidable foe.

"How did you get that boy?" Bob demanded.

"I've taken about as much as I will," Kurt said, glancing down at his wife. "You've upset my wife, too."

"I don't care," Bob said. "That boy . . ."

He never had a chance to finish the sentence. Kurt Anderson hit him sharply in the solar plexus, doubling him over. Marion screamed.

"Hold it, Kurt," Ray shouted. He turned Bob away and forced him down the aisle toward the restrooms where he sat Bob down in an empty booth. Marion picked up Sherri and followed, keeping her eyes on the Andersons. Kurt Anderson watched them go, his eyes blazing, and then he sat down.

"Please," Marion begged Ray Stine, "don't let them leave. That is my son; it is. We've come all the way from Ohio to find him."

"All right, miss. The police will be here any moment. Just stay put until they come. The Andersons won't leave," he promised. Marion nodded and then turned to Bob, who was beet red.

"That son of a bitch," he muttered. He wanted to go back.

"Just wait, Bob. The man's right. Wait for the police."

Moments later, the sound of the siren was heard and they soon saw the patrol car, its bubble light turning, zoom into the parking lot. Marion recognized Tommy Wilson when he got out and was happy. At least he'll know who we are, she thought.

Wilson stopped at the Andersons' table first and heard their story. Then he approached the Boxletters.

"What's going on here?" he asked.

"That's my son, Joey," Marion said. "You know why we went to see the chief today. Here," she added, fumbling through her pocketbook until she found Joey's picture. "Look." She thrust it at him.

Wilson looked down at the photograph and then turned and looked at the boy with the Andersons.

"They do look alike," he admitted.

"That's my son," Bob said. "I don't know how they did it, but somehow, they kidnapped him."

"Anderson?" Wilson shook his head. "He works for the town water agency and is the assistant fire department chief. Been here a little over a year."

"Which is how long our son's been missing," Bob said sharply.

"This is weird," Wilson said. "Tell you what we better do—we'd better all go down to the station and get things straightened out, okay? I'll ask the Andersons to go, but let's not have any more trouble, okay?"

"As long as they go to the station," Bob promised.

"Fine. Just sit here," he ordered and went back to the Anderson table. He spoke to Kurt for a few moments and then Kurt Anderson, his wife and the boy slid out of the booth. Anderson continued to glare back angrily. When Joey stopped to gaze at them too, Anderson muscled him around and pushed him ahead.

"Joey," Marion muttered.

"It's all right, honey," Bob said, embracing her. "It's all right. Finally it's all coming to an end."

8

BOB, MARION AND SHERRI WAITED IN A ROOM IN THE POLICE
station. The Andersons had arrived before them and been
taken to Chief Robinson's office. Patrolman Wilson asked
the Boxletters to be patient and then left. That, Bob noted,
had been more than a half hour ago, and whatever patience
they did have was worn thin. Marion, seated beside him on
the wooden bench, went from periodic sobbing to empty
staring. Sherri, tired, hungry, frightened, was curled up on
Marion's lap, her thumb in her mouth as if she had reverted
to infancy.

"I can't stand it anymore," Marion finally whimpered.
Bob stood up abruptly and seized the doorknob, but to his
surprise and shock, the door was locked.

"What the hell . . ."

"What is it?" Marion asked.

"The door . . ." He tugged and shook it on its hinges.

"We've been locked in?" Marion lifted Sherri gently off
her lap and stood up. "Bob?"

"Yeah, yeah," he said angrily. He pounded the door with
his fist and shouted, "HEY! HEY, UNLOCK THIS DOOR,
DAMN IT!"

"I wanna go home, Mommy," Sherri whined, rubbing
her eyes and sitting up.

"Just a moment, honey," Marion said. She brought her
finger to her lips to indicate Sherri should remain silent.
They all listened, but heard nothing, no footsteps, no one
coming to their assistance. Bob looked at her and Marion

felt a cold hand move up the inside of her stomach and wrap its icy fingers around her palpitating heart.

Bob pounded harder on the door. Then he waited again, all of them silent. He looked around the holding room. There were no windows and very little furniture—just a couple of chairs, the wooden bench and a small wooden table. Beside the bench was a metal railing on which to handcuff suspects. There was nothing on the walls and the floor was a dull, hard wood.

"Why would they lock us in?" Marion asked.

Bob pounded again, this time finishing with a kick at the base of the door. They waited; they listened, but still they heard nothing.

Marion sat down again.

"I don't believe this," Bob said. "We're being treated like prisoners, like maniacs."

"Mommy?" Sherri embraced Marion and pressed her face to her bosom. Marion held her tightly.

"It's all right, honey. It's all right."

"Someone's going to really pay for this," Bob promised. Frustrated, he turned from the door and shoved one of the chairs hard enough for it to fall over and slide a few feet.

"You almost broke the chair, Daddy," Sherri said.

"I wish I had," he fumed. He sat back on the table and folded his arms across his chest. "That door's really bolted shut," he told Marion. "It's been made extra heavy and extra secure. They keep people they arrest in here, for God sakes!"

"Bob, take it easy," Marion suggested softly.

"Take it easy? Take it easy?" He stood up and went to the side of the room and started to pound the wall, but these walls were so solid, there wasn't even a reverberation. "It's like wood over cement," he cried, his hands stinging from the impact. "Why are they doing this?" he asked.

"Maybe they think we're some sort of insane family or something," Marion said. "I'm beginning to think we are." She looked up at him, her eyes dark and sad, her face drawn with depression. "Why didn't Joey recognize me? How could he not know who I am?"

"They did something to him."

"And Brian?"

"I don't know. I don't know," he repeated and lunged like a madman at the door, this time hitting it with his shoulder. The abruptness of his movement and the intensity and abandon with which he threw his body against the wood startled both Marion and Sherri.

He backed away from the door and lowered his head.

"Bob, you're going to hurt yourself," Marion said softly. She was afraid to raise her voice, afraid of the rage in him, a rage she had never seen more violent.

Suddenly, there was the distinct sound of footsteps, many footsteps. Bob backed up a few feet. They heard the door locks being opened and finally, the door itself swung in. Three rather sizeable ambulance attendants entered, followed by Chief Robinson and Patrolman Wilson.

"What the hell's going on here?" Bob demanded, eyeing Chief Robinson's hand. "Why did you lock us in?"

Another ambulance attendant, one much shorter and smaller, came up behind the policemen. He was carrying a doctor's bag.

"These are the patients," Chief Robinson said.

"Patients!"

"Bob?" Marion said and started to stand.

Two of the attendants rushed at Bob before he could react and seized his arms. They drove him back to the table. Marion screamed and hugged Sherri to her as the third attendant stepped over and grabbed her right wrist.

"Easy," he said.

Bob struggled, kicked and turned. Patrolman Wilson moved forward to take hold of his swinging legs. The small attendant walked farther in and then casually, as if he did this sort of thing every day, opened the bag and took out a syringe. He placed the needle in a bottle and filled the syringe.

"Just show me some skin," he said to the attendant near him, who proceeded to roll the sleeve back on Bob's shirt. The small attendant moved expertly to stick Bob's arm. Bob's struggle intensified, but it was as if he had been shackled down. He squirmed and screamed.

Marion tried to stand, but the third attendant had an iron grip on her right arm and Sherri was crying and screaming against her, too. In moments, it seemed, Bob's resistance began to wane and soon it took only one attendant to hold him back on the table. Seconds later, all protest went out of his body and he went limp. Marion screamed louder.

"What have you done to my husband? What have you done?"

The small attendant turned to her and was provided a section of her arm to inoculate. He did so quickly.

"What are you doing to us?" Marion cried. "Please . . ." She looked at Chief Robinson who simply stood by, expressionless. She began to feel her head spin, and actually sensed her eyes going back in their sockets. She tried desperately to remain conscious and she was very much aware of Sherri slipping from her grip.

"My baby . . ." she muttered and then collapsed. The attendant holding her arm grabbed her before she fell to the floor.

Sherri howled as one of the other two attendants picked her up.

"Easy, kid," he said.

She was sobbing so hard, she had lost her breath. Her

face was crimson. When she looked back at her two unconscious parents, she felt more terror than she had ever imagined, even in her worst nightmares.

The small attendant turned to her, smiling. He had beady
eyes and silvery black hair, but his lips looked so red,
Sherri thought he wore lipstick.

"Don't be afraid," he said. "This won't hurt," he
promised. She watched in horror as he brought the tip of
the needle to her little arm.

"Mommy!" she screamed in a final outburst.

In moments, it was all over. The back door of the station
was opened. The ambulance had been brought as close as
possible. The stretchers were wheeled to the room and the
Boxletters were lifted onto them.

Chief Robinson walked out to the lobby of the station
where the Andersons sat waiting. He brushed the Anderson
boy's hair with his good hand and smiled at Kurt.

"What's happening, Harry? Did you speak to those people?"

"Yep."

"So?"

"It's a bizarre story, Kurt. These two people were being
treated at the hospital for shock. Seems they were in an automobile accident in which their son, a boy about Adam's
age, was killed. Neither parent could face up to it and
they've been hallucinating, imagining their boy was kidnapped."

"Oh my God," Toby Anderson said. "That poor woman."

"Yeah, it's very sad," Robinson said. "Anyway, I called
the hospital, spoke to their physician, Doctor Randolph. I
think you know her, right?"

"Oh yeah, sure," Kurt said. "She's been our doctor since
Adam had that bout with pneumonia."

"Right. Oh, she asked if you two would stop by some-

time during the next day or so. She wants to talk to you herself about all this."

"Sure."

"I feel so terrible for those people," Toby said, shaking
her head. Instinctively, she embraced her son.

"Yeah, well, they're in good hands now," Chief Robinson said. He nodded. "In good hands."

They all turned to look out the front as the ambulance
sounded its siren and tore up Main Street Sandburg toward
the hospital.

DIEDRA Heller had her face buried in her hands as she sat in
the hospital waiting room. She had phoned the children
twice since she had been summoned to the hospital, but she
had been unable to tell them much more than they had been
first told. Philip had assured her everything was all right at
home. He sounded so mature, so much the little man. Sam
would be very proud of him, she thought, very proud. That
realization brought her to fresh tears and she sobbed until
she felt an ache in her chest and back.

For a while, as she waited for Dr. Randolph, she recalled
more pleasant memories. Words triggered images suc-
cinctly, almost as if her whole life was neatly filed in alpha-
betical and chronological order. "Introductions" took her
back to her first meeting with Sam at that discotheque in
Denver. He was a business student then. Who introduced
them . . . Mitchell Poppel, her girlfriend Lois's fiancé.
Mitchell was also a business student, but he wanted to go to
Wall Street and become a broker some day. "Love" took
her to those simple dates: their walks through the park, the
rowboat, eating in the coffee shops and making love in
Sam's studio apartment.

Oh yes, that little apartment with the kitchen so narrow
only one of them could be in there at a time, and his roll-

out bed. That made her smile. Sometimes, it didn't roll out so well. But their lovemaking, that always went well.

"Marriage" brought her to Sam's proposal after he had graduated and gotten that first job at the First National. He wasn't going to make much money, but with her working . . .

"What I mean to say is, we can manage." That's how he proposed—designing their accounts receivable column.

"You're so romantic, Sam," she teased him. "But I agree, a merger is feasible."

Honeymoon in Carmel, California, the beautiful beach, the restaurants, Monterey, the aquarium . . . all the memories ticked by like a home movie.

The early years, the struggle, Sam's slow but sure ascent in the banking world and then the great opportunity here in Sandburg. It did seem like a marriage designed by an accountant, she thought, everything so . . . neat.

But why should that trouble her? she wondered. Don't most people want an orderly, sensible life in which they improve continually? When things go so well, we complain because there's not enough excitement; when things go badly, we complain because there's too much excitement. We're never satisfied.

"Don't think about being satisfied; think about what you have to do next to make things go well."

Who told her that? Why was the thought so impressive and so all-consuming? She tried to remember how or where she had heard it. It wasn't Sam's advice. It wasn't her parents speaking . . . Friends? No.

Diedra looked up sharply. Dr. Randolph and her assistant Dr. Congemi were approaching, both looking glum. She bit down on her lower lip, but she couldn't subdue a small cry. She was wringing her hands so hard now, the skin around her fingers began to burn.

"Diedra," Dr. Congemi said, sitting down beside her quickly and taking her left hand. "I'm afraid we have some bad news."

She looked up at Dr. Randolph. Her eyes were so cold, her face as stiff as a mask.

"Sam?"

"He's gone, Diedra."

"Oh no," she said, pulling her hand back and burying her face in her palms again.

"It was an aneurism in his head. It just burst and we had little chance to do anything."

"Oh God, oh God," she moaned and began rocking herself back and forth on the chair.

Dr. Congemi looked up at Dr. Randolph sharply. She stepped forward and put her hand on Diedra's shoulder.

"You've got to be strong for the children," Dr. Randolph advised, but firmly, not with sympathy or softness. It was more like a command. Diedra looked up at her and nodded.

"I know," she whispered. "I know. It's my fault," she said. "My fault."

"Your fault?" Dr. Congemi smiled. "Why do you say such a thing, Diedra?"

"Because he wasn't acting right for days and I put off calling you and didn't nag him enough to come to see you."

"What do you mean, he wasn't acting right?" Dr. Congemi asked.

"He had these strange bouts of memory loss," she said. "I'd find him standing around, trying to recall the simplest things. And he was more violent and angry than ever, losing his temper over the smallest things," she explained.

Dr. Congemi continuously eyed Dr. Randolph.

"You should have told us," Dr. Randolph said, her tone unforgiving. She looked at Congemi.

"Wasn't she supposed to inform us if anything was unusual?" she demanded.

Diedra looked up at her curiously through her tears.

"What do you mean, supposed to?" she asked.

"Doctor Randolph means that after Sam was sick with that bad flu a few months ago, either you or he was supposed to tell us if anything else occurred," he said quickly. "That strain of flu sometimes affects coordination."

"Oh."

Diedra started to sob again.

"I'm going to call someone to help you," Dr. Congemi said. "Don't you worry about anything here. We'll see to all the arrangements for you. Just go home to your children."

Diedra nodded.

"Stay here. A nurse will be in to see you in a moment," Congemi added and stood up. "We are both very sorry. Sam was quite a man."

"Thank you," Diedra murmured. She didn't look up as they left. She just rocked herself silently. Somewhere in her brain she imagined a new category being created for the file: Death . . .

Dr. Randolph and Dr. Congemi paused outside the lobby and looked back at her.

"I'd say we've been incredibly successful here," Dr. Randolph said, nodding.

"Huh? I'd like to hear your reasoning," Congemi replied.

"Look at how deeply she feels his death. The emotional ties are as strong as they would be had they really been in love and married all these years. Don't you think that's remarkable?"

"Oh, I see what you mean," he said, looking back. "Yes, you're right."

"You don't sound as excited as I would expect you to be, Nelson," she accused.

"Excited? No, I . . . frankly, I wasn't thinking along those lines, Lila."

"Well you should be," she chastised.

"Really?" he said dryly. "I was thinking more of how we have failed with Heller. There happens to be a comatose subject up on the fifth floor and a lot of good information gone to hell," he snapped back.

Lila Randolph saw a nurse approaching.

"This isn't the place to discuss this," she said, moving toward the elevator. Congemi followed behind. She inserted her security card and the doors closed. Immediately, Congemi was at her again.

"It was wrong to let Fryman use our people. I told you from the start it would come to no good," he complained.

"Really? What did you expect me to do? You know he could cut off our funding just like that." Lila Randolph snapped her fingers right in front of Nelson Congemi's eyes. "Compromises have to be made," she added. The elevator doors opened on the fifth floor.

Unlike the other floors in the hospital, this floor was deadly quiet. Most doors were shut and there was no one in the corridor. Even the lights were different, their glow more subdued. It made it seem as if nothing much was being done up here.

The two scientists started down to the right.

"We've got a serious problem here," Congemi began again. "Both of the subjects Fryman employed have gone bad. Apparently, we can't tailor people to do the things he wants them to do without laying the proper groundwork or utilizing their own seedy backgrounds. He's going to have to be told that we don't have a new secret weapon after all."

Lila Randolph stopped walking and turned on him sharply.

"Are you crazy? If we did that, he'd pull out on us instantly."

"Maybe that would be for the best," Congemi replied. Lila Randolph glared at him.

"You would do that, wouldn't you, Nelson? You would just throw everything we've discovered and done together out the window, and now, when we are so close."

"How close are we, Lila? And close to what? Something that will benefit mankind or something that will destroy it?"

"You don't know the answer to that?"

"Frankly, I'm beginning to have doubts," Congemi said. Lila Randolph couldn't keep the look of utter disgust off her face. "But," Congemi said, relenting, "I guess you're right. We've come so far, we can't stop now, especially after all we've done already."

"Exactly, Nelson, and it would be wise for you to keep that in mind," she said, an underlying tone of threat in her voice. She softened. "In the meantime, we'll observe Heller and see if there is anything we can do to reclaim the body."

"Reclaim? What did you have in mind?"

"Perhaps a restart," she said. "Now let's see about the Boxletters," she added quickly, before Congemi could object.

He followed her down the corridor until they reached a door labeled INFORMATION TRANFERENCE. Dr. Randolph inserted her card in the slot and the lock snapped open. She turned the handle and they entered what a layman might think was a control room in a television studio. Above what looked to be a table of editing machines was a row of monitors. Behind the monitors was a glass wall, and through it, on the other side in a large room that looked like a hospital ward were Bob, Marion and Sherri Boxletter, all dressed in hospital gowns and strapped in mechanical beds, each raised to a forty-five-degree incline.

Each of the Boxletters wore what looked like earphones connected to thick wires that ran up into the ceiling, only the earphones had been placed on their temples, the cups tight and flat against their skin. Their bodies were also attached to the usual heart and blood-pressure monitors. That information was drawn back into the control room and numbers and graphs were visible on the consoles lined up on the right. A nurse sat as still as a statue before them.

At the center of the panel sat a nearly orange-haired technician whose milky face was only a shade or two from classifying him as albino. He had gray eyes and diminutive facial features with lips almost as orange as his hair, the strands of which were twisted into harsh-looking, wiry curls. He was a small-framed man with stumpy fingers and bony wrists, jutting out from a white lab coat a good two sizes too small. He spun around on his chair and smiled at the two doctors, revealing yellow-stained teeth set in rather pale red gums. The name tag above his left breast read PYLE.

"All set?" Dr. Randolph asked.

"Just give me the countdown," Pyle replied.

Dr. Randolph looked at Dr. Congemi.

"Nelson?" He stared at the monitors. "I want us to be agreed on this," Lila Randolph added. After a moment he nodded.

"Okay, let's begin."

Pyle widened his smile and spun around in his chair. He hit three switches rapidly and three monitors lit up. A split second later, the graphic depiction of each of the Boxletters' brains outlined in white came on screen.

"Ready," Pyle announced.

"Start the process," Dr. Randolph commanded, her eyes on Dr. Congemi.

Pyle pushed three consecutive buttons on the control panel before him and a red shading began from the center of each brain on the monitor, expanding outward slowly. As it did so, the numbers under the monitor began to climb—5%, 10%, 20% . . .

Behind the two doctors, computers hummed.

"Receiving on target," Pyle declared. He turned and smiled as if to say, "So what's new about that?"

Dr. Congemi looked away. Sanford Pyle was Lila's acquisition, not his. He had trouble stomaching the man, who, it seemed to Congemi, made love to the machines. In terms of the project, Congemi had to admit Pyle was an asset. The man was religiously dedicated to his technology and apparently favored it over human contact. His vocabulary was restricted to megabytes, rams, discs, and the like. Yet, curiously enough, he didn't seem to understand or perhaps care about the purpose of his work. Perhaps that was the attribute that recommended him the most to Lila Randolph, Congemi thought.

The numbers climbed and the outlines of the cortexes became more and more red until each monitor, except the one attached to Bob, beeped to indicate 100%; his stopped at 98%. A small area of white remained in the visual depiction of his cortex.

"That's his computer expertise?" Dr. Randolph confirmed.

"Yep," Pyle said. "Glad you guys didn't waste it."

Pyle then hit three different switches and all the pictures turned white again.

"Ready for input," he declared.

"Proceed," Dr. Randolph ordered and Pyle went to a second row of switches.

Up on the screens, the cortexes were invaded with a dark blue shading and beneath the screens the numbers began to click off again . . . 5%, 10% . . .

"Very good," Dr. Randolph muttered. "Let's take a look at Heller," she suggested. Congemi nodded and they started out of the control room.

Pyle spun around to watch them go and then gazed at the nearly catatonic nurse, the product of a rather narrowly targeted mind-tailoring. Pyle rose from his stool and walked over to her. Her eyes never left the heart and blood-pressure monitors.

"Whenever they turn me loose on another subject, I get turned on," he confessed. "But three at once!" He sucked in some air through his dry lips.

The nurse barely blinked. Pyle gazed at the closed door and then at the monitors. Everything was going well. He could almost feel the movement through the wires. The pulsations gave him a very quick and very hard erection.

"Man," he said, closing his eyes; then he zipped down his pants so his bulging phallus could climb freely. Still, the nurse didn't shift her gaze. She had a purpose and that purpose was all-encompassing. It was the way she had been transferred. But—and the two doctors were unaware of this—Pyle had added something. Why couldn't he play around too?

"Jackie," he said, and touched her shoulder. She turned her head slightly and saw his excitement. "Hi." He smiled. "Little Billie's come out to play again," he said.

Without comment, she brought her lips to his erection and took it in smoothly, all the while keeping her eyes fixed on the heart and blood-pressure monitors.

"I'M not sure this idea about restarting Heller is a good idea," Nelson Congemi said as he and Lila Randolph rounded the corner at the end of the corridor. "It might just be that there is some moral fiber, some element we can't touch."

"Really, Nelson, that's not a very scientific statement from a renowned scientist. You're not getting religious on me all of a sudden, are you?" she teased.

"No, it's just that . . . he could go brain dead and . . ."

"What's the difference in Heller's case?" Lila Randolph said dryly. "It's a loss anyway. We might as well take advantage of what's available and see what we can rescue."

"I don't like it," Congemi repeated as they entered Heller's room. He lay unconscious, electrodes attached to his head. Congemi went to the EEG printout and watched as the styluses jerked out their imprint on the rolling paper. He ripped off a sheet and studied it.

"Look at this," he said. Dr. Randolph gazed at the paper.

"Major activity in the uncinate region."

"Psychomotor epilepsy," she said quickly.

"I don't like this, Lila. Not one bit. We'd better tell Fryman so he at least waits before taking another one of our subjects."

"We'll see," Lila Randolph said and went to Heller's bedside. She stared at him as she continued. "We've done more than two dozen transfers over two years and tailored eight of them. Nothing like this happened to the others."

"Only the ones who were made into assassins. Coincidence?"

"Maybe."

"Lila, he's perverting our work."

She spun on him.

"It's a small price to pay, Nelson." Her eyes narrowed. "We're on the verge of the Nobel Prize. You want to panic and give up?"

He stared. It was surely possible—the Nobel Prize.

"Well, as long as we get Fryman to hold off on using another until we can correct the problem . . ."

"I told you, let me handle Fryman. Did you see to the corpse for Heller's coffin?"

Congemi nodded.

"Good. Make sure it's a closed coffin. We'll have to decide what next to do with the woman and children."

"Just leave them be," Congemi suggested. "Move on."

"Maybe. In the meantime, I'd better be sure the Andersons don't recall the incident."

"We're manipulating them like puppets," Congemi remarked.

"We do what has to be done to make this all work," Lila Randolph replied and then looked at her watch. "The Boxletters should be completed." She looked up, that wry smile on her face. "Or should I say Charles Corbin and Elaine and Melissa Stratton."

"You're getting to feel a little bit like God, aren't you, Lila?"

"Let's just say I can appreciate the power. I often wonder," she added, looking back at Heller, "if God does."

"Just be careful we don't find out too late," Congemi warned.

It was the first time in a long time that something he said brought a real smile and substantial laughter to Lila Randolph's lips.

9

BOB ACTUALLY FELT HIS EYELIDS FLUTTERING. IT WAS AS IF two small butterflies had landed on his brow and each had its wings flapping against his closed eyes. The sounds around him were caught up in a funnel. Around and around they spun in their journey to reach the top. The bottom of the funnel from which they emanated was dark. Each sound, each voice, broke the black surface below and burst like a bubble. Then up it spun, up toward the cloudy light above. Gradually, with every flutter of his lids, the light came into focus. He was staring up at a ceiling fixture in the center of a bland, white ceiling.

Feelings returned. The sheet and the blanket beneath and around him felt stiff, heavily starched. His limbs throbbed with the ache that would come from his being asleep for years and years. He was Rip Van Winkle stirring back to life. As if to emphasize that point, his heart began to pound harder, louder, and a sudden rush of blood flooded his face, bringing with it a wave of warmth as if life itself were a pool into which he had been dipped.

"Mr. Corbin?"

He heard the voice, but for a moment he couldn't find the person talking. Then he moved his eyes to the left and saw Dr. Randolph standing beside Dr. Congemi. A puff of dull black hair with a number of strands stained gray fell over her dry forehead. She peered at him so intently, her eyes so small, he felt he was on a slide at the base of a gigantic microscope and she was looking down at him through the lens.

He shifted his gaze to Dr. Congemi, who was staring with a similar look, albeit not as intense. Neither doctor offered a smile. There was nothing warm in their faces, nothing that suggested sincere concern. All Bob saw was anticipation.

"Mr. Corbin, do you know where you are?" Dr. Randolph asked.

Bob turned to look around and saw the light, white cotton curtains on the hospital room window sway gently in the slight breeze coming through the opening. Aside from a single chair and a food tray on wheels, there was nothing else in the room. The small closet door was closed as was the door to the room itself. The walls were that aseptic white, not a stain, not a blemish on their powdery surfaces. The odor of rubbing alcohol caressed the inside of his nostrils. He turned back to the doctors and nodded.

"Where are you?"

"In the hospital," Bob said.

"Good," Dr. Randolph replied and nodded with satisfaction. "Very good."

"Why is knowing where I am such an accomplishment all of a sudden?" Bob inquired.

Both doctors finally smiled.

"Mr. Corbin, you fainted at your desk in the research center this morning," Dr. Randolph said.

"I did?"

"You had an attack of hypoglycemia, Charles. You gave us all quite a scare," Dr. Congemi said and shook his head sternly.

"Oh," Bob said. There was a fuzziness around all his thoughts.

"We had no idea when you started work at the research

center that you suffered from hypoglycemia," Dr. Randolph added, a definite tone of reprimand in her voice.

"I'm sorry, I . . . I haven't had an attack in five years, so I thought I was over it."

"Now, Charles, you of all people should know that you'll never be over it. You can only keep it under control by judiciously watching your diet," Dr. Congemi said. He wore the expression of a loving grandfather, reprimanding his naughty grandchild.

"I know. I'm sorry," Bob said and started to elbow himself into a sitting position. But the room spun on him. "Wow . . ."

"Easy, Charles. You have to come back slowly, carefully," Dr. Randolph said. "Don't try to do too much too quickly or you'll have a relapse."

"This was a bad bout," Bob realized and nodded with his eyes closed.

"Yes it was," Dr. Randolph said. "However, I doubt there has been any lasting harm. But, to be sure, let's test your memory, okay?"

"My memory?" Bob opened his eyes. "I don't think it has ever affected my memory."

Dr. Randolph smirked at Dr. Congemi. He shrugged.

"You can't think of every little thing, Lila," he said. "Especially when you're doing something rather quickly."

Dr. Randolph showed no signs of placation. She was a perfectionist who hated to see a staple out of place.

"It can and it does, Charles," Dr. Randolph said, turning her attention back to Bob. "You're just not aware of it."

"Oh."

"Anyway, let's see if anything's happened now. Where do you live?"

"Live? Currently, I'm at the Dew Drop Inn until I find a permanent place."

"Where were you working before you came to us, Charles?" she followed quickly.

"In San Jose, California, at Digisoftware."

"Good. Now, what about your family, Charles?"

"Family?"

Bob felt his lips begin to tremble and his eyes water as the images rushed down upon him. Everyone was singing Christmas songs. He had his eyes off the road for only a few seconds, but when he turned back, there was that red pickup truck, the driver's head back as he tipped a bottle to guzzle some whiskey.

Bob slammed his eyes shut to drive out the memory, but it wouldn't go. It was stuck on the insides of his eyelids— the shattering of windshields, the scream of metal, the collapse of dashboard and ceiling, a shard of broken glass streaking through Clara's face, tearing out her cheeks, the blood gushing, and then Brenda's little body, floating like a rag doll over the seat and landing limp and broken between him and Clara. How had he survived?

"Charles?"

He swallowed and, with his eyes still closed, replied.

"My wife and daughter were killed in an automobile accident three years ago. Drunk driver. Oh God," he muttered, bringing his hand to his face. "It's still as if it happened yesterday."

"Easy, Charles, easy," Dr. Randolph said, taking his hand from his face. The contact caused him to open his eyes. He saw the way she looked at Dr. Congemi, an expression of arrogance on her face. She turned back to him.

"You're doing very well, Charles. You're getting your life back together. We're all very pleased with your work at the hospital and very concerned that you return to your duties as soon as you are able. You're going to like it here in Sandburg, like it very much. You'll find how everyone

cares about everyone else. It's a real, new start," she con
cluded.

"Yes," Bob said. "I'm grateful."

Dr. Congemi stepped closer and smiled warmly.

"Charles, believe me, you're going to feel like someone
who died and was resurrected," he promised and patted him
on the hand.

"Thank you, Doctor."

"Rest up, my boy. We've got lots for you to do," he assured him. "Work," he added, his face serious, "work is the
only way to overcome great tragedy and sadness."

"Let's not tire him out on our first visit," Dr. Randolph
said sharply. Congemi gazed at her and nodded.

"Get a little more rest, Charles," Dr. Congemi said. "In
the morning we'll get you on your feet."

"Thank you. Oh," Bob said as they turned toward the
door. "It's coming back to me."

"What is?" Dr. Randolph asked quickly, her face concerned.

"I was right in the middle of a computer printout when I
got dizzy."

"It's all right," Dr. Congemi said laughing. "Jeff Liv
ingston took care of all that."

"Great. Thank him for me if you see him," Bob said.

"Will do. Rest easy," Dr. Congemi said and he and Dr.
Randolph left.

Bob lay back. He was feeling stronger and more awake
every moment. He usually rebounded quickly from a
seizure anyway, he thought. It was nice to be in the hands
of people who were obviously taking a personal interest,
too. Lucky he answered the ad for this job and made the effort to take the interview. They were sufficiently impressed
with his background and experience and hired him on the
spot. What he liked about these people was they didn't treat

you as just another employee. The moment he was hired, they got on the horn to help arrange a place for him to stay, important and necessary people for him to meet; in short, they did everything possible to make his transfer and relocation as smooth and as painless as possible. They even found him a personal banker, got all his finances in order, introduced him to a dentist, found him an accountant, familiarized him with the community. Hell, in no time at all he began to feel he belonged. It was almost as if he had been here all his life.

It was wrong not to tell them about his hypoglycemia, stupid, in fact. How did he expect to hide such things from doctors, for Christ sakes? He just didn't want to do anything to ruin his chances for the job, but he almost lost it because of his subterfuge. Of course, he thought, smiling, he could always claim he just forgot. It was part of his illness—look at what Dr. Randolph just told him—memory loss was a possible side effect.

Actually, he wasn't feeling all that sharp about his past. Sure, some memories were vivid, too vivid, but others . . . seemed so vague—his parents, his early childhood, even his education was hazy.

And he had the funniest reaction every time Dr. Randolph called him by his name.

"I'm Charles Corbin," he told himself. "Charles Foster Corbin," he recited as if it were a line in a play to be memorized.

Maybe, he told himself, it isn't a bad idea to lie back here and quietly review my life. Make it like a game— think of a fact, a place, a date and see if I can recall exactly why I should know it.

Let's see, he began, St. Mary's hospital, Brooklyn . . . that's where I was born. He laughed.

Dr. Congemi was right: this was going to resemble a resurrection.

"THAT hesitation over his family made me nervous," Dr. Congemi said as he and Lila Randolph headed down the corridor toward his office. "And then, when his lips began to tremble and he turned white . . ."

"I thought that was all rather touching," Dr. Randolph said, a smug smile around her thin, pale lips. "Such vivid memories, such trauma."

"Lila, smugness is unbecoming to a person and dangerous to a scientist," Congemi said. Lila Randolph laughed.

"Come, come, Nelson. There's nothing to say we can't enjoy and be proud of our accomplishments here, especially when they go so well."

"I'm not saying no . . . in fact," Congemi said, pausing, "I'm always a little amazed to see it myself, to see how utterly metamorphosed they are."

"It is exciting, isn't it, Nelson?" Dr. Randolph said, her eyes filled with as much passion and exhilaration as possible for the usually emotionless scientist.

"Yes," Congemi confessed. "I suppose that's primarily why we do it."

"Really?" Lila Randolph stepped back. "And here I thought all this time that your primary motivation was to better mankind," she said, her sarcasm dripping.

Congemi smirked and they continued on. As soon as they opened the door to his office, Charlotte Schwartz, his secretary, stood up, her eyes wide. She nodded at the closed door of his inner office.

"What?"

"Mr. Fryman is here with someone. He's very agitated," she added.

"I keep forgetting," Dr. Randolph said dryly, "that Chief Robinson is his man, not ours."

"Thank you, Charlotte. Why don't you take your lunch hour now," he added. "I won't need you until two-thirty."

"Okay, Doctor," she said, surprised at her good fortune: an extra hour for lunch. She gathered up her purse, shut down her word processor, and left.

"Here we go," Congemi said and opened the door to his inner office.

Walter Fryman was standing by the window impatiently, his hands behind his back. One of his associates sat in Dr. Congemi's chair, behind his desk, cleaning his fingernails with a switch blade. The moment he heard them enter, Fryman spun around.

"Walter . . ." Dr. Congemi began.

"What the fuck is going on?" Fryman demanded. He stepped forward, his hands on his hips.

Dr. Randolph closed the door softly behind them. Nelson Congemi didn't respond quickly. He simply stared at the infuriated government man. Fryman had always terrified Congemi somewhat. He was uncomfortable in his presence and forever suffered pangs of conscience dealing with the man. He didn't have Lila Randolph's ability to rationalize away the blatant truth: Fryman was nothing more than a legalized gangster, a psychotic with a license to act out. That was the way Congemi saw him and his view of the man was not something he could hide easily.

"Please, let's hold our voices down," Lila Randolph said coolly.

Just as Nelson Congemi had difficulty dealing with and talking to Walter Fryman, Fryman had difficulty with Lila Randolph. The stoic, cold scientist confused him. He hated her, but at the same time recognized that she had twice his intellect. He didn't see her as a woman, either, which added to his confusion. To him she was some sort of laboratory creature, a product of the very world of science in which she dwelt. That made her unknown and unknowns frightened him.

"I wanna know what the story is here," he said more calmly. "How come neither of you called me to tell me three people arrived looking for a subject, huh? How come?"

"It all just happened," Dr. Congemi said. "Very quickly."

"Telephones work pretty fucking fast," Fryman said. "I thought you scientists were smart." His associate smiled.

"Do you mind?" Congemi said, coming around his desk. His chair, his drawers, his papers were as personal to him as was his underwear. He couldn't remember the man's name. All of Fryman's so-called associates had the same gruesome look, which blurred their names, names that were similar as far as Congemi was concerned.

Fryman looked at his associate.

"Bruno," he said and jerked his head to the left. The man smiled, got up reluctantly, but stepped aside just enough for Congemi to pass. Congemi took his seat quickly, finding some security behind his desk.

"Well?" Fryman said, looking at Congemi. He was more comfortable facing him; he recognized Congemi's fear of him.

"Apparently, the man you people picked up on the camping grounds last year was recognized in New York when you sent him there to neutralize Doctor Stanley. As you will recall," he added, glancing at Lila Randolph too, "I was not in favor of using the man and the boy. Sticking with no-name derelicts has had its advantages and . . ."

"Sam Heller was perfectly isolated here until you asked us to tailor him, Mr. Fryman," Dr. Randolph added quickly, more to justify her own decision than anything else. But

Congemi saw it as an opportunity to voice a chronic complaint.

"That's right. What puzzles me is why, with your access to an army of professional killers," he said, eyeing Bruno, "you need to use our people."

"Your people!" Fryman looked from Randolph to Congemi, his face crimson. "Who the fuck do you think you people are . . . gods? You're no more than I am, fucking employees of the government, and as such, you happen to answer to me," he added, poking himself so hard Congemi flinched in sympathy.

A stillness rode the air for a moment. Fryman calmed, his body relaxing. Then he nodded and took a seat.

"All right," he said. "What happened to Heller?"

Congemi looked at Randolph. Fryman caught the glance.

"This thing is falling apart?"

"Oh no," Dr. Randolph said. "Quite the contrary. Matter of fact, we've been able to capitalize on these unfortunate circumstances."

"Is that right? I'm listening," Fryman said. He caught the way Congemi gazed uncomfortably at the man with the knife. "Bruno," he snapped, "will you put that fucking knife away and take a fucking seat."

The muscular six-feet-two-inch man snapped the blade closed obediently and sat down.

"Go on, Doctor," Fryman said.

"From what we've learned, it appears these people, the Boxletters, came rushing here after they suspected they had seen Mrs. Boxletter's brother."

"So?"

"Not having time to explain to anyone or tell anyone where they were going or what they were doing. The woman, ingeniously, stole Sam Heller's fingerprints in

New York and ran them through her local police department, but decided against seeking police assistance."

"Lucky for us," Congemi inserted. Fryman simply smirked.

"So how does this prove beneficial to the program?"

"Well, we have three new subjects, of course, but I . . . we have an opportunity now to test one virgin area."

"Virgin?"

"Untested," Dr. Randolph said quickly.

"Which is?"

Dr. Randolph smiled and leaned against Dr. Congemi's desk.

"Does the emotion of love depend on the existence of memory?"

"Huh? Spell it out, will you," he said irritably.

"In other words, if two people married and in love were metamorphosed and reintroduced, would they fall in love again or, even more intriguing, would they still be in love perhaps?"

"What's the big fucking difference?" Fryman asked, hands out.

"It's very important to our research to know whether emotions lie outside of sensory input," Congemi offered. "Memory is simply a sum total of that sensory input. Another way to put it is does the emotion of love, and perhaps therefore, the emotion of hate, lie somewhere outside the memory? Are people in a sense chemically attracted or repulsed by each other?"

"If there is some validity to that theory, no matter what you teach people you will not be able to stop them from hating," Dr. Randolph quickly added. "Arabs will always hate Jews, French will always hate Germans, blacks and whites will always hate each other, on and on. And the same would be true for love relationships, which might interest you more."

"What do you mean?"

"It may be impossible to get certain people to hate certain people," she replied dryly.

"I don't know," Fryman said. "I don't like using these people. We might just be better off getting rid of them."

"We'll be monitoring them better than any of the others. They literally won't be out of our sight or hearing. If a serious problem arises, we'll terminate the experiment."

Fryman thought for a moment. It was apparent to both doctors that what they were saying was sufficiently beyond him for him to offer much argument.

"What about Sam Heller?"

"We're trying to retrieve him, and see why he went bad on us," Dr. Randolph said. She gazed at Congemi quickly. She didn't want him to offer his theory of morality being too deep and causing problems.

"Two of the people I use go bad. I don't like it," Fryman said. "That's got to be fixed. Otherwise," he threatened, "some important people in high places might pull the financing out from under all this and get us to disband."

"We'll solve the problem," Lila promised quickly. She shot a forbidding glance at Congemi, who simply looked down.

"Um . . . all right, but the moment something unusual happens, you call me."

"You get your information pretty quickly, Mr. Fryman," Lila Randolph said pointedly. Congemi looked up sharply, amazed at his associate's courage.

Fryman stared a moment and then smiled.

"That's right, Doctor, so don't ever think of trying to hide something from me."

"Mr. Fryman," Lila Randolph said, "we're all in this together, partners, all wanting the same thing—to do some good for mankind and our country."

"You got it, Doc, only switch the order of priorities," Fryman said.

"Pardon?"

"To do some good for our country and then mankind," Fryman said. "Okay," he said to Bruno and the two of them stood up. "Someone comes looking for the Boxletters, they vanish. Understood?"

"Understood," Lila Randolph replied.

Fryman nodded, happy with himself and the way he asserted his authority over the scientists. He nodded and then walked out. Bruno smiled at Congemi and followed.

Neither of the two scientists spoke for a long moment. Then Lila Randolph turned to Nelson Congemi. He saw the fury and anger in her eyes.

"Perhaps one day we'll get the opportunity to metamorphose Mr. Fryman and tailor him to fit our needs and design," she said, obviously voicing a fantasy.

"You can't be serious," Congemi said, leaning forward.

"Why not? That's your biggest problem, Nelson. You limit your imagination. Nothing could be more detrimental to a research scientist," she added and left him.

Sadly, he realized she was right.

Two days later Bob Boxletter sat in real estate agent Dorothy Seymour's car, and let her drive him out to see a townhouse for lease-option. It was one of those bright, sunny days when a sea of blue sky fills the air with hope. He just knew he was going to find what he wanted today and really begin a wonderful new life, not that he could ever completely forget the sorrow and the tragedy behind him. As if it were all on some sort of periodic automated reminder, sort of like the automatic backup command on computers, the horrible memories would return, play themselves out vividly and then retreat to await their next scheduled appearance. It could happen when he slept or paused, or simply sat back to relax a moment.

"You're just going to love it here, Mr. Corbin," Dorothy Seymour assured him. "Everyone does."

"I love it already," he replied and she widened her smile. Unlike most real estate agents in his memory, she was soft-spoken and quite laid back. Not pushy, she evinced a strong sense of self-confidence. Obviously, she truly believed the properties and the area sold themselves. She was a guide rather than a saleswoman—no gimmicks, no carrot and stick, no transference, no devices, nothing but the product itself: Sandburg.

"How long have you lived here?" he asked.

"Oh, I'm a native, born and raised," she said, pulling to a stop. He looked up at the recently built townhouse, one of many set in the lap of the valley. On both sides of the development, the mountains loomed majestically. Behind the complex of homes were a half dozen acres of virgin forest, and all around them were smooth, rolling hills and fields. It was truly an idyllic setting.

"Breathtaking," Bob said and then a thought rushed over him as though he had unlocked it with some magic words: "My wife would have liked this."

"Oh, I'm sure." Dorothy patted his hand and got out of the car. He followed quickly and they walked up to the front of the available unit. "You're only a few miles from work and town," she said, opening the tall, light oak door.

He turned and nodded at the highway, which was practically devoid of meaningful traffic.

"After you," Dorothy said, stepping back. He entered.

"As you can see," she began, "all of the units are fully furnished and decorated. Of course, you can make any changes you wish afterward."

Bob gazed around. After the short, marble-floored entry-

way, there was a rather comfortable-looking living room
with a bay window that faced the long, flowing front lawns
and the mountain range to the east. It was freshly carpeted
in a plush beige nylon, all the colors in the sofa, chairs and
wall hangings coordinated. There was even a real wood-
burning travertine fireplace with a gas starter.

The unit had two bedrooms, one with a king-size bed and
one with a queen-size. They both came with matching
dressers and armoires. The main bedroom also had a small
secretarial desk and chair. The windows were draped in
bright curtains with patterns that matched the color
schemes in the carpets and bedding.

After he saw the fully equipped kitchen, which even had
a set of dishes and pots and pans, he shook his head in astonishment.

"All I need to move in is a toothbrush," he said.

Dorothy Seymour laughed. She was standing by the window in the kitchen, the one that looked out on the rear of
the development.

"That's exactly what Mrs. Stratton said."

"Mrs. Stratton?"

"Elaine Stratton, your neighbor." Dorothy nodded toward the view. Bob moved up to her and gazed out. Seated
in a lawn chair and dressed in a rather revealing two-piece
was a very attractive brunette. Even from this distance, he
could see she had diminutive facial features and a model's
figure—long legs, narrow waist, proportional, perky
breasts.

"She's a schoolteacher," Dorothy whispered, her lips
close enough to his ear for him to feel the puff of breath.
She was like the good, or for that matter, bad angel on
one's shoulder. "Divorced or widowed, I'm not sure," she
added.

"Oh?"

Suddenly Bob caught sight of a little girl stepping out from behind the corner of the patio. She carried a stuffed animal; it looked like a panda bear.

"She has a six-year-old daughter, adorable child. Well," Dorothy said, stepping back, "what do you think?"

"Pardon?"

"About the unit?"

"Oh," he said, smiling. "It's great. How soon can I move in?"

"Tonight, if you'd like," she said. "You'll find things are far simpler in Sandburg," she added. She produced the papers from her small leather case and Bob signed the lease. It was odd how he paused before bringing the pen to the line above tenant's signature. For a split second, he wanted to start his name with a B.

"Something wrong?" Dorothy asked.

"Oh, no, nothing," he said and scribbled *Charles Foster Corbin.*

"Foster. I like that. What a distinguished-sounding name," Dorothy said, holding up the document.

"My mother's maiden name," Bob replied. She smiled and they started out. Almost as soon as they appeared on the stoop, they heard Elaine Stratton calling.

"Mrs. Seymour."

Bob turned and watched her approach. She had a sleek figure, all right, he thought, with such a sexy way of tilting her head when she looked at him. Her brown eyes were so soft, he felt his heart stumble and then flutter. Was his face flushed or was that just the effect of the warm sunlight?

"Oh, I didn't mean to interrupt," Elaine said.

"That's all right," Bob replied quickly. She smiled, the brightness emanating from her eyes and rippling down her cheeks to settle comfortably around her sensuous lips. He was gawking like an infatuated schoolboy, but he couldn't help it. He didn't want to help it.

"Oh, Elaine," Dorothy said. "Let me introduce you to your new neighbor, Charles Corbin."

"Hello," she said, extending her long, graceful fingers. Bob took them eagerly into his own hand. How soft, he thought.

"Hi."

They stared at each other for a moment, and then Elaine flicked her eyes back to Dorothy Seymour.

"I just wanted to remind you about that dishwasher. I've called Mr. Borden twice this week."

"Oh yes. I'll see to it the moment I get back to my office."

"Trouble with your dishwasher?" Bob asked.

"It just hums."

"Drive belt must have slipped off," Bob diagnosed.

"You know about such things, Mr. Corbin? Mr. Corbin is a computer expert. He's just started working over at the hospital," Dorothy explained and followed it with a laugh. "Why shouldn't you know about it? I'm sure a dishwasher isn't half as complicated as a computer."

"You'd be surprised at some of the computerization that's going into the new kitchen appliances," he said and immediately regretted sounding too technical. He shot a quick look at Elaine, but she didn't seem put off.

"Maybe you can look at my dishwasher if it's not fixed by the time you move in," she suggested.

"Love to," he said.

"Well." Elaine looked at the smiling real estate agent and then back at Bob. "It was nice meeting you, Mr. . . . ."

"Corbin."

"I'm so terrible with names. I have to keep my seating chart in front of me for half the school year," she said.

"See you soon," Bob cried as she started back to her house.

"Well now," Mrs. Seymour said. "I think you made quite an impression."

Bob blushed.

"That's all right, Mr. Corbin. People have to meet each other somehow. Why not through a dishwasher?" she said and laughed.

Bob had to laugh, too.

He looked back and saw Elaine Stratton was seated in her lawn chair again; her little girl playing beside her. What an attractive woman, he thought. He couldn't help but wonder what had happened to her husband.

10

BOB STARED ABSENTLY AT THE COMPUTER MONITOR BEFORE him. The flicking light of the cursor had suddenly become mesmerizing. The pulsating electrical impulse had literally hypnotized him and he sat as still as a catatonic, only his eyelids occasionally blinking, his subdued, regular breathing lifting and dropping his chest slightly.

At first Jeff Livingston didn't notice. He had found the new man, who had been transferred from the research department upstairs, about as intense in his work as anyone he had come across when it came to computers, and like many of them, he found the same reticence when it came to conversation. Everything was an extraction, or reaction, as he liked to call it. Ask questions and you get direct, simple answers, nothing added, no embellishment. These programmers took on the characteristics of their computers: speak to them precisely or they won't respond, and they had an almost electrical ability to spot errors and point them out. At least he was still thinking of computers as tools and not icons. He imagined some of these people got on their hands and knees in the morning and said their prayers to a blinking monitor.

The truth was the fifty-four-year-old hospital bureaucrat longed for the simpler days. There was a time when this hospital was intimate and full of living people. Why, the business office had six employees then, now it had two; there used to be eight people rotating hours and days in admissions; and administration had no less than ten. When

153

they had an employees' gathering, they had a gathering. Now . . . now people were replaced by these damn computers.

He had been forced to learn about them to survive, but he wouldn't go beyond what was necessary and he avoided the in-service classes like the plague. He was confident that someday soon something would be added to the hospital's mainframe and he would find his pink slip waiting in his mailbox. It was inevitable, just like most of the changes ever since the research unit had arrived and taken over the fifth floor.

Why had they chosen Sandburg? He wished they hadn't, yet he couldn't argue with Moe down at the barbershop. Since the government had come to Sandburg with this project, whatever the hell it was, the town had benefited enormously economically. There were all those new housing developments, the influx of all sorts of professionals, money spent on municipal improvements, as well as improvements for the school. Sure, progress was profitable, Jeff thought, but there was a sacrifice. Something very subtle was happening to his little community. People were . . . changing, growing more urban in their thinking. Used to be a stranger was a stranger. It took time to accept him, and rightfully so. People had to earn trust.

But not these new people. Hell, they were accepted and incorporated into the village so fast, it made his head spin. Just the other day, his wife Patricia was saying she was going to try the new dentist. Imagine: a dentist arrives and sets himself up almost overnight and people who used old Doc Kaplan all their lives, people who swore by him, were thinking of giving the new man their business. They said it was time for "fresh blood." There was a term he despised.

"Blood don't get old," he told Patricia. "It gets richer like wine."

He glanced at the new man again and realized he hadn't stirred and wasn't flicking his fingers over the keyboard. He was told the man had a chronic ailment which, Dr. Congemi had explained, might affect his memory sometimes. It was why they felt they had to shift him from research to the hospital library. The work was too critical to risk errors. Like my work down here is not very important, Jeff mused. I'm the base of the totem pole, even below the bottom.

"If he's a bit confused from time to time, think nothing of it," the doctor told him. That was why he didn't question what Charles was talking about when he thanked him for completing some printout the other day. When Jeff mentioned it to Dr. Congemi, the doctor told him that Charles was referring to the day he had passed out on the job on the fifth floor.

"Charles?" he said, finally finding his stillness peculiar. "You all right?"

The man didn't stir.

"Charles?" He walked over to him and put his hand on Bob's shoulder. The contact had the effect of dropping a handful of ice cubes down Bob's neck. He shuddered and jumped.

"What? Wha . . ."

Jeff stepped back.

"Sorry, I thought you might not be feeling well. You were just sitting and staring for so long."

Bob gazed up at Jeff Livingston as if he had never seen the man before.

Christ, Livingston thought. What a nut case and they give him to me.

"Are you all right?" he asked. The way the man was focusing his eyes, Jeff got the impression he had been in a state of unconsciousness.

"Yeah," Bob finally replied. "I just got lost in a day-dream. It was the weirdest thing."

"What was?" Jeff asked, surprised the man was volunteering conversation.

Bob sat up and scrubbed his face with his dry palms.

"I was riding in a car with this woman and there was a child in the rear . . ."

"So?"

"It was the woman who lives next door to me, but we've just met for a few minutes. I hardly know her name."

"Is she attractive?"

"Very."

Jeff smirked and shrugged.

"Fantasy, that's all."

"Yeah," Bob said. "I suppose." He looked at the monitor. "I guess I'd better finish this up. It's almost time for lunch."

Livingston watched Bob work until he was satisfied he was all right. Then he went to his own terminal. He started to turn it on and stopped because he recalled a few weeks ago he had come upon that man in the corridor outside of the radiology suite just standing and staring ahead. It was odd because the man was standing in the middle of the corridor. He had almost walked by him, but when he smiled at the man, he saw that the man's eyes were like glass. So he paused and asked him if he were all right. When he didn't respond, he touched him and the man jumped just the way Charles had just jumped.

Another hypoglycemic? he wondered. He shrugged. This is a hospital, he reminded himself. Sick people come here.

He went back to work.

Bob rose from his chair at twelve o'clock sharp. Jeff Livingston shook his head.

"You're better than an alarm clock," he said.

"What's that? Oh. My stomach's the alarm clock. The rumbling's getting so loud I can't think."

"Hospital food. I don't know if your stomach's rumbling for it or anticipating it," Jeff joked, but Bob didn't laugh. He looked as if Jeff were presenting a serious biological question. Damn, these computer people are all alike, he thought again, no sense of humor.

"Maybe," Bob finally responded. He smiled, actually smiled. "I'll tell you when I return," he said and left.

Bob went down to the cafeteria, which was on the basement level of the hospital. It was a rather big cafeteria, recently expanded to handle additional personnel, as well as hospital visitors. The long neon lights and the wide, tall windows at the rear provided excellent illumination. The tile floors shone and the sparkling new, long, narrow tables looked immaculate. Bob moved to the line and began to choose his food. After he paid the cashier, he turned to find a seat and saw her.

She was at the last table on the right, her daughter beside her. Right now, she was leaning over speaking to the little girl softly. Probably trying to get her to eat her food, Bob thought and headed toward her, wondering what had brought her to the hospital. A nurse was sitting at the end of the table reading a magazine, but she didn't even glance up when he arrived.

"Hi," he said. Elaine Stratton looked up, obviously not recognizing him at first, he thought, because she blinked rapidly and held her half-smile frozen. "I'm Charles Corbin. Your next-door neighbor? We met the other day when Dorothy brought me to the unit." The way she was gazing at him, he began to wonder if it all hadn't been some sort of dream.

"Oh," she finally said. "Oh." Her smile widened. "I'm so

sorry. I was just a bit confused. You looked very familiar,
but for some reason, I thought we had met long ago, so I
wasn't trying to think of anything recent. That's right," she
added quickly, "Dorothy said you worked in the hospital."

Bob looked at the little girl who was staring up at him intently, her eyes blinking rapidly too.

"Hi," he said. "We never met."

"Oh. This is Melissa. Melissa say hello to Mr. . . ."

"Corbin."

"Corbin. Sorry, but I have this . . ."

"Problem with names. I know. You told me," he said,
smiling. "Mind if I sit down?"

"Oh, please, do."

He glanced at the nurse who was still concentrating on
her reading and then he pulled out a chair.

"So," he said, arranging the food on his tray, "what
brings you to the hospital? Visiting someone?"

"No, we had to have a follow-up exam, didn't we,
Melissa?"

"Uh huh," the little girl said, her eyes still fixed on Bob.
He smiled at her and then stared for a moment. There was
something about her eyes, the shape of her mouth. She reminded him so much of someone. But whom? Not his own
child. Brenda was dark-haired and dark-skinned and had a
much thinner face and was at least two years older.

"Both of you? What happened?" he asked.

"Something nearly very tragic. Carbon monoxide poisoning," Elaine said.

"Wow! How?"

"Leaky pipe in the motel we were staying in before we
got our unit. Lucky for us, the maid didn't pay attention to
the Do Not Disturb sign."

"That's kind of odd—carbon monoxide in a motel
room?"

"That was the diagnosis," Elaine said, shrugging. "It's an old place just outside of town, the Dew Drop Inn."

"Dew Drop Inn? I stayed there, too."

She smiled.

"Anyway, it left us groggy and all . . . even dopey," she added for Melissa's benefit and tickled her. "Right, Dopey?" The little girl giggled and then turned to Bob, her face serious again. "But fortunately, no lasting effects or side effects according to Doctor Randolph."

"Randolph? She's your physician?"

"Uh huh."

"She's mine, too. Not that I actually chose her," he suddenly realized.

"What do you mean?" Elaine asked.

"That's odd." He sat back. "I can't remember . . ." He sat forward to explain. "I'm hypoglycemic. I thought it had become less and less of a problem for me, but apparently, it hadn't and I had a seizure and went unconscious."

"Oh, how terrible!"

"On the job," Bob added. "When I came to, there was Doctor Randolph and Doctor Congemi, her associate."

"I see."

"I suppose I shouldn't be surprised I didn't remember much. It's one of the side effects," he said, shrugging. He started to eat.

"You lucked out getting Doctor Randolph. She's not going to win any personality contests, but she is a brilliant diagnostician."

"Yeah, I know. She and Congemi head up the research unit here."

"Are you a scientist involved with that?" Elaine asked quickly.

"Me? No. I'm just a plodder, but one who plods on computers. Right now, I'm assigned to the hospital library—

files, records, that sort of thing. I'm working on a program
to make them access faster."

"Sounds very complicated."

"It is," he said. "Actually," he said, leaning toward her,
"I'm brilliant and very talented." He gave her his most
charming smile. Her eyes warmed.

Melissa, feeling left out, lifted her stuffed animal so that
it was completely visible. Then she sat it on the table emphatically.

"Looks like a panda," Bob said, sitting back. "From
China."

"She won't go anyplace without it. It's like a security
blanket."

"Does it have a name?" he asked Melissa. "Wait, don't
tell me," he said, closing his eyes and pretending to think.
"His name is . . . Mr. Panda."

Melissa laughed, but Elaine's eyes widened.

"How did you know?"

"That's the name? Lucky guess, I guess," he said.
"No . . . ESP. For instance"—he gazed into her soft, brown
eyes—"I bet you're a chocoholic." He didn't know himself
why he said it, but it made her sit up.

"How did you know that?"

"Am I right?" he asked, surprised. She nodded.

"And how. I'm an addict. I've even got the stuff hidden
around the house."

"Funny, isn't it?" he said. "How sometimes, we just get
onto each other's wavelengths."

"Yes." She stared at him for a long moment. "Are you
settled in your apartment?"

"Almost. I just need some minor things . . . like food."

She laughed.

"A man alone," she said. "How about coming over for
some capellini with tomato and basil tonight?"

"Angel hair? I love it."

"Somehow, I knew," she said.

"This is kismet," Bob said, warming. She shrugged.

"Stranger things have happened and will happen."

"All right, I'll be there."

"Seven, okay?"

"Perfect. Don't make dessert. I'll take you to a diner that has the best double chocolate cake. It's called Better Than Sex."

"I hope not," Elaine said, her eyes teasing. Bob felt himself grow warm.

Coincidences, he thought to himself, aren't they just wonderful?

"THERE'S a glitch," Pyle said. Dr. Congemi and Dr. Randolph stared up at the monitor. Almost all of the cranial outline was in blue shading, but off to the right in the video graphic of Heller's cerebral cortex there was a red stain, barely visible.

"What's happening?" Congemi asked, squinting so hard the crow's feet completely crossed each of his temples.

Pyle swiveled around and peered up at him. The way the small-framed technician turned his shoulders and pursed his lips made him look more like a primped, middle-aged woman. Congemi swallowed his revulsion and waited for the response.

"Frankly, Doctor, I don't know," Pyle said. "This is the first time we've done someone over twice. I haven't done a thing different."

"Maybe that's our problem," Dr. Randolph said, nodding. "Let's clean him out and start again, only this time increase the speed."

"Sort of like a rush," Pyle said, liking the idea. To Congemi it seemed as if the milky-faced man experienced a vicarious metamorphosis himself every time he engineered one. He sounded jealous of the subjects.

"I don't know, Doctor," he added, changing to a more serious tone. "It's not like we're shaking something loose in there. What I'd like to do is isolate that memory pocket and try tailoring it."

"Only as a last resort," Dr. Randolph said.

"Could it be that some experiences are truly deeper than others?" Congemi wondered aloud. "That they go against our nature to such an extent they become indelibly printed?"

"That's utter nonsense," Lila Randolph said. "We've already established that memory is merely electrochemical. It's a tangible thing. Just as words can be erased on an audiotape or pictures on a videotape, memories can be erased from the brain."

"Except that one," Pyle said, nodding toward the monitor, his arms folded across his small, flat chest. His sharp elbow bones protruded emphatically and looked as if they would tear through his paper-thin skin.

"Precisely," Dr. Congemi said. He turned to Pyle. "Isolate it and tell us exactly what it is he refuses to forget."

"Oh, please, Nelson," Lila said. "Do you really think there's a conscious intransigence here?"

"Not conscious, no. But subconsciously . . ."

"You and your damn Freudian influences," Lila said, wagging her head disdainfully.

Pyle widened his smile. He loved to be present when the two scientists argued. Usually, Congemi retreated, but this time he seemed determined.

"I think it's important we know what it is this man can't forget." He turned to Lila Randolph. "It's almost as if something is haunting his conscience."

"Conscience is merely the sum total of learned repression. We're not born with it. We . . ."

"Don't give me a lesson in neo-naturalism, Lila. I'm not challenging any of that. All I am saying is this is a phenomenon we don't want to ignore." He turned back to the monitor and stared a moment. "It's like a scar."

"What do I do?" Pyle asked, smirking.

"Do what he asks," Lila Randolph said. "We have the time to waste I suppose."

"I don't like wasting my time," Pyle said with an unexpected defiance. Both scientists glared at him. "Just teasing," he said quickly. He began the process to draw out the newly added material and the blue shade started to retreat from the graphic. Beneath the monitor, the numbers ticked off in the negative: -5%, -7% . . .

"Someone's waiting for me in my office," Lila Randolph told Nelson Congemi. He nodded, but kept his eyes on the monitor. She smirked and left.

Dr. Randolph's office was on the opposite end of the corridor from Dr. Congemi's. It was of her own choosing. There were no other offices near hers. It was quite isolated. Most of her life, Lila Randolph had been a loner. She was an only child, and was quite precocious before school age. Her parents were medical doctors and her mother, because she didn't want the debilitation of a pregnancy, talked Lila's father into having his sperm and her egg joined in a laboratory and then implanted in a surrogate.

Even after Lila was born and brought home, Lila's mother eschewed the responsibilities of motherhood. A nurse was hired to take care of her during the first year, and after that a nanny was hired. Her parents made sure she was exposed to every modern learning tool, including computers, the result being she could read and write before she was four. They sent her to one accelerated school after another. She graduated high school at fourteen and entered Harvard under a special program.

Despite her ridicule of anything slightly romantic and her insistence that everything in the universe could be explained in scientific terms, she couldn't always repress her personal desires for some meaningful love relationship. Men had always been put off by her superior intelligence and analytical mind. Most were actually afraid of her. Her view of sex as something merely biological had turned her into a masturbator at an early age. If she was hungry, she would eat; if she felt sexual desire, she would satisfy it as best she could. She tried to fill her life with work and occupy her mind all her waking hours, but there were times when the fantasies invaded even her well-built fortifications. She hated that part of herself and was frustrated by her inability to eradicate it.

It was partly this personal interest in love relationships that caused her to seize the opportunity with the Boxletters. She wanted to disprove the existence of "love." People were drawn to each other for cultural, sociological, and practical reasons. Bells ringing, hearts fluttering, some magical, intangible quality of soul were all fiction. The Boxletters might go to bed with each other when they met as strangers now, but a revival of a deep affection would not occur. After she had played with them for a while, drawing them together again, she would insert a new love interest for each and prove that love, as the poets knew it, simply did not exist.

A part of her longed to prove this, and another part dreaded it, but she had denied that part of her any influence on her actions all her life. This was no time to surrender to weakness. Control love, control hate, and you effectively control the world, she thought, and despite what Nelson Congemi thought they and their work were all about, this was what they really were all about—power. All of the other benefits: a well-balanced, coordinated society, efficiency, control of disease, elimination of the criminal mind, etc., were simply side effects. But she would never tell him this; he was too weak to appreciate and understand. He was still living under the delusion he was a humanitarian. It nearly brought her to tears of laughter.

She opened the door to her office and stepped in quickly. Unlike Nelson, she did not employ a personal secretary. She didn't even want that much contact when she was working. She would dictate her notes and have them transcribed by computer. It was sufficient; she wrote no letters, carried on no correspondence, never ever received a personal phone call or made one.

Her office reflected her Spartan attitude. In it there was only her small desk and chair, one file cabinet, and one very uncomfortable-looking hard wood chair. There were heavy drapes over the two small windows, usually kept closed, and the office itself was lit with a single, large fixture at the center of the ceiling.

As soon as she closed the door behind her, the nurse sitting on the straight-back, hard chair stood up. She was a slim woman with small, dark eyes and a thin mouth. There was a fragility about her that was intensified by her obvious built-in fear of Lila Randolph.

"Well?" Lila asked quickly.

"They sat together and talked just as you expected."

"Good. And?"

"Here it is," the nurse said, fumbling with a small tape recorder in her hands. She held it out stiff-armed, as if she was afraid Lila would touch her. Lila plucked it from her fingers quickly.

"Go back to your regular duties," Lila commanded. The

willowy woman lowered her eyes and moved directly to the door. "And remember," Lila said, "tell no one anything."

"Yes, Doctor," the nurse replied obediently and quickly left.

Lila paused a moment and then sat down behind her desk. She unbuttoned the two top buttons of her blouse and sat back in her chair, staring at nothing for a moment. Her breathing quickened. Slowly, almost against her will, her right hand rose, glided softly over her small right breast and stopped when her fingers found her exposed skin. She let them linger there a moment; it had the effect of quickening her breathing. She closed her eyes and dropped her fingers to the top of her shallow cleavage. Her fingers moved in tiny increments under the loosely fitted bra until they touched her erect nipple. She moaned and squeezed her legs together. For a long moment she sat there enjoying the rush of warmth that mounted her thighs and spread like a sliver of silky glass to the clitoris of her vagina.

The realization of what she was doing and what was happening put her into a small panic. She sat back quickly, pulling her hand from herself, and bit down so hard on her lower lip she could taste blood. Finally feeling a semblance of self-control returning, she sat forward and fingered the small tape recorder. But her tactile sense surprised her. In her erotic imaginings, the tape recorder had suddenly become a penis. She squeezed her eyes shut, but that only intensified the image and the sensation. Reluctantly, she began to surrender again, only this time she brought the tape recorder to her lips and kissed the smooth edge softly.

Once again, the heat rose in her thighs. She moaned and let her legs fall away from each other. The exposure intensified the thrill and she brought her left hand to her pelvis, moving it in small circles faster and faster. Reaching a fevered pitch, she paused and pressed the play button on

the recorder. Bob Boxletter's voice was like the first thrust
of a man's penis into her. She couldn't help but welcome it.

"Hi. I'm Charles Corbin, your next-door neighbor. We
met the other day when Dorothy brought me to the unit."

Lila moaned louder. The seduction had begun. In the
subdued light of her office, she masturbated freely to the
rhythm of their words and reached her orgasm just as Bob
said, "It's called Better Than Sex," and Elaine replied in a
rather seductive voice, "I hope not."

11

BOB CHECKED HIMSELF IN THE MIRROR FOR THE FOURTH TIME. Every time he made a change in his clothing, switched from the dark blue shirt to the light green, or grazed his hair while doing something, he had to stop to be sure he looked all right. Everything looked coordinated, but did his hair look better swept a little more to the right in front or should he make the wave higher? Something else caught his eye; he leaned closer to the mirror. Damn, he missed a spot under his jaw when he shaved. He rushed back into the bathroom and cleaned the spot with a dry razor. After that, he stepped back for a final time and gave himself the once-over.

"I'm worse than a schoolboy on his first date," he told himself and laughed. Then he thought, this is a date, isn't it, and my first since . . . since the accident. I've got good reason to be nervous. It's been so long since I've been with a woman.

How long has it been? he wondered for a moment and then thought, that's odd: why should such a detail be gray? There was so much confusion lately, ever since his bout with hypoglycemia. He hoped he wouldn't suffer another seizure of that magnitude.

He started out of his bedroom and stopped. The photograph of Clara and Brenda loomed larger somehow. Of course, it's just my imagination, he thought, or my sense of guilt. He approached the picture in the gilded frame and took it into his hands for a moment. As he stared down at the pretty woman and child, he experienced a shotgun-like series of images: Clara laughing at something he had said, Brenda calling to him to help her with her homework, Clara and Brenda walking ahead of him in a shopping mall, all of them eating dinner at a restaurant, driving with Clara talking and Brenda jumping up and down on the rear seat . . . one image after another, flowing, streaming by like a trailer for a film.

Curiously, in all these images, he was mostly an observer—watching and hearing just as one sitting in a movie theater might be. Despite the vivid memory of the accident and the surge of horror and pain that followed, he found himself strangely aloof at this moment and drawn more to the promise in Elaine Stratton's eyes. It did fill him with guilt.

It's the burden that comes from living on, he thought. He returned the picture to the dresser. Clara would surely forgive me, wouldn't she? Why was it he couldn't be sure? He pressed his eyes closed hard as if that would help him remember. Tragedy leaves such gaping holes. He imagined his mind refused to recall certain things, blocked them out because they were too painful to remember.

But I've mourned; I've suffered. I must begin my resurrection or else jump into the grave beside Clara and Brenda, he concluded. That realization put new thrust in his steps and carried him quickly out of his apartment, across the grounds and to Elaine Stratton's front door. Melissa opened it.

"Hi, Pumpkin," he said. She giggled and ran back to the kitchen where Elaine stood sentry over boiling water.

"He called me Pumpkin, Mommy. He called me Pumpkin."

Elaine stepped out of the kitchen and smiled.

"Come on in, Charles."

"Brought some wine," he announced, holding up the bottle.

"Great."

Bob joined her in the kitchen.

"All these units are basically the same," he said, looking around. "Only yours has a more lived-in, homey touch. Are you a good cook?"

"You'll tell me. And be honest," she said, smiling. "The corkscrew's over by the bread box," she said, nodding. He was amused and warmed by how quickly she integrated him into the domestic activities. It was almost as if they had been together for ages. Melissa stood by watching him closely, fascinated with his every move.

"Wanna help?" She nodded enthusiastically. "All right. First, I'll get this into the cork," he said, doing so, "and I'll start the turn. Here, you give it a turn."

He squatted and looked closely into the little girl's face as she concentrated on her job. He felt this overwhelming urge to smother her in kisses and hold her close.

"Very good," he said and she looked up at Elaine proudly. "Do you do this often, Melissa?"

She giggled and seized the hem of Elaine's apron.

"It's been a while since she's had a man tease her like that," Elaine said.

"How long's a while?" Bob asked.

"Well over a year and a half," she replied. Their gazes locked for an instant, and in that moment, he felt her loneliness and hunger for love, a loneliness and hunger that easily matched his own.

"Everything's ready," Elaine said. "This is a perfectly timed dinner," she announced. "It must proceed on schedule."

"Aye, aye, Captain," Bob said, saluting.

"Please bring the wine into the dining room. Melissa, you go with Charles. I'll bring in the salad."

Without any shyness or hesitation, Melissa seized Bob's hand and led him out. He looked back and saw Elaine's smile.

"I love walnuts in my salad," Bob said after she brought it in and they had begun to eat.

"Funny," Elaine said. "I don't usually do that, but for some reason, as I was planning the meal tonight I reached for the walnuts."

"Glad you did."

After they spoke, they both paused and gazed into each other's eyes. They were both searching for something, some indication, some message. Bob found himself more and more intrigued by this attractive widow.

"So," Bob said, "what brought you to this idyllic little community?"

"After my husband died, I spent most of my time wallowing in self-pity. Finally, I got up one day and decided to finish my certification for teaching. Turned out I didn't need as much as I had feared and I got it after one semester and one summer session. Since we had no immediate family where we were, I decided to go for a completely new start. Answered an ad here, came for an interview and got hired. Next semester, I will be teaching fifth grade at Sandburg Elementary," she concluded proudly.

"How did your husband die?"

"Lung cancer. He was an addicted smoker. By the time he finally slowed down, it was too late." She looked down at her plate and then up quickly. "He went back to smoking after he was diagnosed. How's that for suicidal tendencies?"

Bob shook his head.

"We forget how fragile we really are." His eyes grew

small for a moment as his own family tragedy started to rise from the well of memory.

"I know your story," Elaine said quickly and then shrugged when he looked surprised. "I confess; I did some reconnaissance."

"Oh?"

"Talked to Dorothy Seymour. In Sandburg she's better than UPI."

Bob laughed.

Elaine got up and gathered the salad dishes.

"Want help?"

"No. Melissa will help me, won't you, Pumpkin?"

"You call her Pumpkin?" Bob said.

"Yes, I thought . . ." Elaine's smile softened into a look of wonder. "I just assumed when you did it, that you had heard me call her that."

"No, I . . . it just seemed right somehow."

Melissa took her dish carefully with both hands and marched out behind Elaine. Bob sat back and thought. Images, words, memories were getting so confused. It put him into a small panic for a moment. He felt himself warm, his face turn crimson. Was it the wine?

"Voila," Elaine declared, reentering with the bowl of capellini. Melissa followed carrying the serving fork and spoon. "May I have your plate, sir?"

"Thank you," he said. "And thank you, Pumpkin," he added, looking at the cherub.

He couldn't rave enough about the dinner. They sat and talked for almost an hour afterward, each one bringing up a memory, a reference that reminded the other of something similar. Although they didn't agree entirely on movies and music, they shared enough to make them more than compatible.

"Should I put up some coffee?" Elaine asked.

"Oh no. Remember, I promised to take you and Melissa for dessert. Better Than Sex," he added, smiling.

"This I got to see," Elaine said. "Give me a moment to straighten up. Melissa, go get your jacket, honey."

"Can I bring Mr. Panda?"

"Oh Melissa, do you have to bring him everywhere?"

"Sure she can. I know just what he would like for dessert, too," Bob said. Melissa beamed. Elaine sighed deeply and then smiled and relented. She could see that Charles Corbin was quickly taking on heroic stature in her daughter's eyes.

Bob drove them to Ray's Diner. It was very busy, every booth taken. Elaine wanted to give up the moment she saw the crowd.

"Let's see how long we have to wait," Bob said. He approached the hostess. When she looked up from her tablet, her eyes registered fear.

"Hi," Bob said, smiling with confusion at her reaction. "How long for a booth?"

For a moment she didn't answer; then she gazed down at her tablet and looked toward the end of the diner.

"Not more than five minutes."

"Great."

"Boxletter, right?" she said, bringing her pen to the tablet. She shook her head. She couldn't forget these people.

"Pardon?"

"Isn't your name Boxletter?"

"No. Corbin."

"Oh." She jotted it down nervously. "Five minutes," she repeated without looking at him. He reported to Elaine.

"Must be someone here who looks like me," he said and explained what had happened.

"They say we all have a twin somewhere. You don't have any brothers or sisters, do you, Charles?"

"I did. He was killed in Vietnam."

"Oh."

"Dorothy Seymour doesn't know everything," he said to quickly lift the cloud of despair. Elaine's smile returned. A few moments later, two groups left the diner and the hostess announced their booth was prepared.

"I'll order the Better Than Sex," Elaine said, "but I hope it's not true."

"What will you and Mr. Panda have, Melissa?" Bob asked.

"Can I have a piece of apple pie with ice cream on it?"

"Sure." He gave the order to the waitress. He and Elaine sat silently for a moment, gazing at each other, both oblivious to the noise and activity around them.

"It's a lot like coming back to life, isn't it?" she asked softly.

"Yes."

"Do you still miss your wife a great deal?"

"It's odd," he said, playing with the fork with his fingers. "I remember her vividly, of course. I can see her face before me, hear her voice, smell her perfume, the scent of her shampoo in her hair, and yet . . ."

"What?" Elaine leaned forward, her eyes intense.

Bob gazed at Melissa first. She was occupied with her panda and with looking at all the other people.

"I . . . don't feel any of it. Not the way I think I should," he said almost in a whisper. "It was a terrible thing that happened to us . . . horrible . . . I experience shock, but afterward, when I recall them, it's almost as if I'm thinking about someone else's wife and child.

"It's a terrible thing to admit now," he said, looking

down. He gazed up at her quickly. "I don't blame you for looking at me that way."

"I'm not condemning you, Charles. I couldn't."

"Why not?" he asked. "It's contemptible; it's . . ."

"I have the same thoughts about my husband," she confessed quickly.

"What?"

"Just what you said, exactly. When I go through the memories, I experience shock, pain; but when I recall him, it's like he was someone else's husband." She looked down and then up quickly. "I don't cry anymore."

Bob nodded.

"Maybe that's good. Maybe time and distance deaden our feelings so we can go on."

They stared at each other, neither completely convinced. The waitress interrupted them with the platter of Better Than Sex and Melissa's pie à la mode.

"More coffee?" she asked.

"Please," Bob said.

Elaine gazed down at the mound of chocolate cake. It was covered with a thick chocolate frosting, under which were three different layers of cake, each separated by a layer of chocolate mousse.

"You might be right," she said licentiously, "this might be better than sex."

Bob laughed and watched her dig in.

"Um . . ." she said, sitting back, her eyes closed. He laughed and absentmindedly took his fork and dug in.

"Thank God you're sharing some of this," she said. "Calories."

He laughed again, drank some coffee and ate a half dozen more forkfuls of cake while they talked. Suddenly, she put her fork down, her eyes wide in terror.

"What's wrong?" he asked.

"Charles, this cake. It's full of sugar."

"So?"

"You're hypoglycemic. You suffered a seizure recently," she reminded him.

"I forgot," he said.

"You just got out of the hospital and you forgot?" she asked, sitting back, a smile of incredulity on her face.

He stared at the cake and shook his head.

"How long a delay before your sugar level drops?"

"An hour maybe."

"Charles, you better get over to the emergency room and get checked out," she said.

"Right. I can't believe I was this stupid," he said, signaling for the waitress. "Sorry."

Elaine insisted on going with him to the hospital.

"It won't take that long," she said. "It's not late. Don't worry about us."

Melissa was sitting on her lap when he came out to the lobby after he had been examined.

"I'm all right," he said, shrugging. "My blood-sugar level is perfectly normal."

"Really? What did the doctor say?"

"I told him what had happened. He couldn't understand it. He called it a miracle and told me not to press for a second one."

"Charles, are you sure you're all right? Maybe you should call Doctor Randolph, too. An emergency room doctor is not the most . . ."

"Blood tests are simple enough. You don't need a specialist, Elaine. Besides, I feel fine."

He did look fine, she thought.

"How can you explain it?"

He shrugged. "I don't know. I guess I'm just . . . unpredictable," he said, smiling.

*   *   *

NELSON Congemi stopped in front of the unlabeled door and glanced behind him. This made him feel so surreptitious, so clandestine. So much of what they were doing was classified. The entire floor was restricted, but Lila Randolph had decided that this aspect of the new experiment was for his, Pyle's and her eyes only. The lower-level technicians had carried out their orders, ignorant of the purpose as usual. Only he and his associate knew that. Not even Pyle knew all of it, but it still made Congemi feel sneaky. Somehow, this was different.

He didn't voice his feelings; he knew how Lila would react and what she would call him. He wasn't sure himself about what it was that bothered him about it. Maybe, maybe it was prurient; maybe it was simply a sophisticated voyeurism. Maybe it was because he knew Pyle looked forward to it so much.

He inserted his card and the lock snapped open. Then he turned the door handle and entered the room. Lila and Pyle were seated at a console. Both turned, Pyle smiling, Lila smirking.

"You're late, Nelson," she accused.

"I don't like rushing dinner. Besides," he said, nodding toward the recorders, "it's all being taped."

"This is our first though," Lila said, not giving an inch. "You'd think you'd be as excited about it as I am. And as interested."

He blanched. Chastising him in front of Pyle infuriated him.

"Don't lose your perspective, Doctor Randolph," he retorted. "You'll make serious mistakes," he said, emphasizing *serious* and glaring down at her. His rage didn't faze her.

"Take a seat," she said. "It's already quite interesting and Pyle wants to explain the system."

"Did he tell you about the pocket of memory in Heller?" Congemi asked, looking at Pyle. Lila Randolph didn't turn around again. She waved him toward his chair and turned up the volume.

"We'll talk about it later, Nelson. Please," she said.

He sat down reluctantly.

"They've left her house, gone for dessert," Lila explained as if she were filling him in on some episode of a soap opera he had missed. "Go on, Pyle."

"Right." A fresh pink tint had formed around the edges of Pyle's eyelids. He spun completely around to face Dr. Congemi. To Congemi it looked like some form of irritation. Each of the red areas on Pyle's face was brighter, however. His orange lips looked positively luminous. It was the way his excitement reflected itself in his face.

"All of the bugs in their apartments are voice-activated. It's like the President's oval office," he added, his widening smile revealing more and more of his yellow teeth. "So every word they say, every sound they utter will be recorded here," he added, indicating the bank of recording devices.

"All of it," he continued, "is fed into the mainframe. If Doctor Randolph wants to, she can access a specific word and discover exactly how many times either of them used it. She can even analyze the syntactical arrangement of their sentences. One of my programs also considers intonation, stress, accent. Not only can we know what they say, but why they say it and how they feel about it," he added proudly.

Congemi nodded with reluctant approval.

"Sounds like you've covered it well, Pyle."

"Just doing what I'm paid to do, Doc, only doing it better than anyone else," he said. "Now Doctor Randolph knows how to operate all of this. Didn't take long to teach her, if you want a lesson . . ."

"No, that's fine. As long as one of us can do it," he said.

"Yes," Dr. Randolph said. "You can return to our other little problem now, Pyle."

"Aye, aye, sir," Pyle said, saluting facetiously. He got up and left.

Congemi looked down at the chair on which Pyle had been sitting as if he thought it had been contaminated.

"There's something quite revolting about that man," he muttered.

"No one's asking you to be in love with him, Nelson. He's good at what he does and he doesn't ask questions."

Congemi nodded and sat down.

"What are we going to do about this problem with Heller? It's just as I suspected—the assignment he committed for Fryman is as good as indelibly printed in his brain."

"Now Nelson, you know that can't be true. Pyle will soon discover how to erase it and that will be that."

"I don't know," Congemi said, shaking his head. "It's another reason why Fryman can't do what he wants with our subjects."

"If you tell him that, we're finished here," Lila Randolph said dryly.

The sound of laughter drew her attention back to the console.

"They've come back to her place," she whispered.

"Are you going to stay here and listen to this all night?"

"What am I going to do at home? Watch television?" she responded and in that response revealed the total absence of any life outside of her work. "Anyway," she said,

"it might turn out that these conversations are more enter-
taining."

Nelson Congemi nodded and stood up.

"I'm tired," he said.

"Go home, Nelson. I'll fill you in tomorrow," she said,
turning her back to him. She plugged in the set of earphones beside her, effectively channeling all the sound
there. Congemi looked at her for a moment and then left.

Lila Randolph sat back as soon as she knew she was
alone. She closed her eyes and immersed herself in the
scene.

"I should go home," she heard Bob say.

"You promised Melissa you'd kiss her good night after I
put her to bed," Elaine Stratton said.

"Right."

"Come on, honey."

Lila heard the distinct sounds of footsteps on the
stairs even though they were carpeted. She appreciated
the quality of their eavesdropping equipment. She
could hear Elaine washing Melissa's face, the splash of the
water in the sink, the sound of the little girl brushing her
teeth, the flush of a toilet. She thought she even heard the
snap of the blanket as it was drawn back to permit Melissa
to crawl in.

"We're ready, Charles," she heard Elaine call. His footsteps were distinctly heavier.

"I see Mr. Panda is tired too," Bob said. "Well then, have
a good night's sleep, Pumpkin."

She heard the kiss.

"You, too, Mr. Panda."

Melissa said good night and the two adults left the room.

"She's adorable, a little doll face," Bob said, going down
the stairs.

"Thank you."

"Does she miss her father a great deal?"

"Yes and no," Elaine said. Lila leaned forward in her seat as if she could look at them as well as hear them. "She asks questions about him from time to time, but I've never found her crying. Do you think that's strange?"

"I don't know."

The deep pause told Lila they were looking intently at each other.

"I'd better get home," Bob said in a much weaker voice.

"Don't," she heard Elaine say. The long pause was culminated with the distinct sound of a passionate kiss. Lila Randolph pursed her own lips and closed her eyes. In her imagination, made more vivid by the sounds she overheard, she saw Bob's hands moving over Elaine's shoulders, but it was like he was moving over her shoulders, too. She saw his lips travel down her cheeks to Elaine's neck, but she felt his lips on her. And then she felt the strength in his arms as he practically lifted the woman off her feet, drawing her closer to him.

There was a moan and then, "Oh Charles . . ."

Clothing rustled. Where were they? Lila scrambled to understand location and realized they were still in the hallway. What were they doing, lowering themselves to the floor of the hallway?

"Not here, Charles," Elaine finally said.

"I'm sorry . . ."

"No, don't go. I want you to . . . stay."

Lila heard their footsteps on the stairs again and watched the audio monitor trail them through the upstairs hallway to Elaine's bedroom. Once inside, their groping grew more frantic, their kisses longer, their moans deeper.

A moan escaped from Lila Randolph's own lips. They were on Elaine's bed now, and Pyle's super-sensitive microphones picked up the slapping of their stomachs, the grunts and moans, the ecstatic little cries and the distinct up and down movement on the bedsprings.

Lila's hands were all over her own body. Her pelvis gyrated as she pumped the air, almost in synchronization with the love scene on which she was eavesdropping. When Elaine cried out to express her orgasm, Lila was only moments behind her. She was so flushed and excited by the empathetic sex, she nearly missed the important dialogue.

"Oh God, that was wonderful, Bob," Elaine Stratton said.

"Bob?" There was a little laugh.

"Bob? I called you Bob?"

"I'm afraid so."

"But that wasn't my husband's name."

"Some old lover, perhaps?"

"No. Why would I call you . . . Bob? I feel so stupid. I'm sorry, Charles."

"It's all right. As long as you don't call me late for dinner," Bob said.

Lila Randolph was so excited by the combination of her vicarious sex and the turn of events, she thought her heart would pound an opening in her chest. Quickly, she scribbled down the tape numbers covering the moment.

Congemi might be right, she thought. Deep emotions might have a place so deep in the mind we are unable with our present technology to completely eradicate them. Perhaps we can't truly make good people do bad things or bad people only do the socially acceptable things after all.

She didn't like this tentative conclusion; it put a limit on her God powers just when she was beginning to enjoy them. For the time being, she would keep this to herself, she thought. It was too soon to make any conclusions anyway. Exhausted, she took off the earphones. She would listen again tomorrow. Now, she would go home and sleep.

It was practically the only reason she could think of to go home, but that didn't bother her. In fact, it didn't even occur to her.

12

To him it seemed as though he had truly been resurrected. Life had returned with all its force and power. Once again, he was looking forward to mornings. Sunlight cheered him; he had bounce in his steps. He cared about his appearance, his clothing, and most of all, his health. He had a reason to go on, to want to do well. Although his job wasn't as interesting as he wished, it still provided him an opportunity to excel and eventually get some sort of advancement. The most important thing was he had goals again; he had dreams.

Neither he nor Elaine had yet come out and said it specifically, yet he sensed they both were beginning to think in terms of a future together. He imagined her reticence sprang from the same fountain of fear as did his—commitments made one vulnerable to tragedy, unhappiness. Neither could stand to suffer a loss as great as the losses they had already suffered.

But life never had any guarantees, and everything that was truly worthwhile required risk. Since the dinner at her house, they had spent nearly every available hour together—going to the movies, shopping, going out to eat, and even going on a picnic.

Sandburg was such an easy, relaxing place in which to live. Absent was the tension and fast pace they saw everywhere else in America, in the world for that matter. People were friendly, content, and this atmosphere of serenity affected them and their relationship with each other. When-

ever people saw them out together, they smiled approv
ingly. It was as if everything and everyone around them
conspired to make their love and their lives together possible. No, he thought, more than possible, predestined. But
there were still obstacles, emotional hurdles to climb.

"I have to make a confession," he said to her one night.
They were sitting in her dining room having coffee. Putting
Melissa to bed together had become a shared daily ritual.
Afterward, they would either make love or sit and talk the
way they were doing now.

He looked down at his cup and turned it slowly in his
fingers. Elaine didn't speak; she waited with that gentle
smile on her face, her eyes searching hopefully.

"Since I met you," he continued, "I have thought less and
less about my . . . past." He looked up, his face a portrait of
inner turmoil. Her heart ached for him, for she knew exactly why he was suffering. "Every day, every moment
with you pushes my memories down deeper and deeper.
This morning, when I awoke, I lay there trying to remember my wife and . . . I couldn't. Every time I thought of her
face, I saw your face instead; every time I heard her voice, I
heard your voice. Even our lovemaking has intertwined
with the lovemaking I can recall between my wife and myself."

He looked down again.

"I don't mind it, but I feel . . ."

"Guilty?"

"Yes," he said, looking up quickly. He saw the expression in her eyes. "You too?"

"Exactly. But something even stranger happened to me
today. I looked at my husband's photograph, the one I have
in the glass frame on my dresser, and while I was gazing at
him your face imposed itself over his. It was
almost . . . frightening. I shook my head and looked again,

and still, you were there. Finally, you dissolved and he returned."

Bob simply stared.

"That happened to me two days ago," he finally said. "With the photograph of my wife and daughter. Instead, I saw you and Melissa."

The expressions of sympathy they both had for each other changed to looks of fear. Instinctively, Elaine extended her hand and he took it.

"Widows and widowers go through this, I'm sure," he consoled.

"It's never happened to me before. I had other problems; I went to a therapist, but . . ."

"Maybe neither of us had met anyone we cared about before," Bob offered. "It comes with the territory."

"What do we do?"

"Let it happen," he said. "That's what I wanted to confess—I don't care," he said firmly. "I want it to happen. I don't want to remember any other woman but you."

"Oh, Charles."

He got up and went to her. After he put his arm around her shoulder, she pressed her face against him and closed her eyes. He kissed her.

"Why should there be this . . . fear in us?" she wondered. "Why shouldn't we·simply love each other purely?"

"We're complicated; that's what makes us the higher creatures. We'll sort it out. I'm sure," he said.

But this conversation, these thoughts were not easy to shake loose. They returned continually, especially whenever he had a quiet moment at work. During his breaks, he would sit there and try to understand himself. The confusion was frightening and despite the pledges he had made to Elaine, he couldn't overcome the guilt he felt, especially when Melissa's face replaced his own daughter's.

One afternoon, Jeff Livingston interrupted his reverie with an uncharacteristic explosion of temper. Bob couldn't say he was crazy about the man, but they had gotten so they could work well together, and Jeff had indicated on a number of occasions that he was impressed with Bob's computer skills, even though Jeff didn't try to hide his revulsion for computers. He evinced a reluctant respect.

Bob and he rarely discussed their personal lives; everything said was usually centered around their work or the hospital, but Bob knew Jeff was married with three grown children, two living and working in Sandburg and one in the Air Force. Livingston knew about Bob's family tragedy and never asked questions.

"Damn, I don't understand this!" Jeff Livingston pounded the keyboard so hard, it jumped on the desk.

"What's wrong?"

"Every time I try to access this file, I get 'incorrect path or directory.' I'm not doing a damn thing different."

"Let me see," Bob said, rolling his chair over. He studied the monitor a moment and then began a string of commands that took him to the material via another directory. The information soon flowed smoothly again.

"Jesus, I never would have figured that out," Jeff said. He looked at Bob appreciatively.

"No problem. Who wants this information?"

"A technician named Pyle on the restricted floor. I don't know why hospital records concerning patients we had two years ago would be important to their research up there, but ours is not to question why."

Jeff accessed the printer and a printout began.

"Now I got my usual load to do," he said, patting a pile of documents. "But nobody thinks of that. Oh no. Just get it all done. That's all they know."

"I'm finished for now," Bob said. "Can I help?"

"If you don't mind taking a walk," Livingston said quickly.

"Sure. I can use the exercise."

"Take this crap upstairs for me, will you? I'm supposed to deliver this ASAP to this man Pyle on the fifth floor. When you get out of the elevator, turn right and go down two doors to one that's labeled LIBRARY. You'll find Pyle there or one of his assistants, I imagine."

"Right," Bob said, tearing off the sheets. He started out.

"Hold it. You need this to access the fifth floor." Jeff reached into his top desk drawer and came out with a slot card. "Shove it in the slot beneath the numbers first and then hit five."

"Gotcha."

"Thanks. I owe you one." Jeff would never say it, but he disliked most of the people who worked on the fifth floor, especially Pyle. Also, he had this suspicion that they were working on something potentially dangerous, something maybe contagious and he disliked exposing himself and felt very uneasy about it the two times he had gone up there. He couldn't care less what went on up there, and he resented having to put aside his regular duties to do something for them.

However, Bob didn't mind doing the errand. The way he was feeling, he would do everyone in this hospital a favor. A man in love is most generous, he thought and smiled. He moved spryly down the corridor to the elevator and inserted the card as he was directed to do. The doors closed and the elevator climbed to the fifth floor. When they opened, Bob was surprised at the poor illumination and the silence. The floor looked deserted; not a soul was in sight.

He shrugged and turned right, looking for the door marked LIBRARY and found it immediately. Two men, one in a lab coat and one in a suit and tie, were standing by a

line of long, narrow glass cabinets that ran nearly the length
of the room. In the back toward the right, he could see a
mainframe buzzing away. The man in the lab coat turned
and started toward him.

Why was this room called the library? Bob wondered.
He saw the name PYLE on the man's coat, above his breast
pocket.

"What are you doing here?" Pyle asked.

"I'm Charles Corbin. I work with Jeff Livingston."

"Where the hell's Livingston?" Pyle demanded.

"He's buried in work and asked me to bring this up,"
Bob said, looking past the pale-skinned man. The cabinet
appeared to be filled with computer discs.

"You tell Livingston that when he's asked to do something, he does it himself, especially if it involves this
floor," Pyle said. He looked at the printout and seemed satisfied.

"All right," he said, dismissing Bob with a gesture. "Just
go straight back to the elevator and down."

Bob saw the way the man in the suit glared at him. He
looked belligerent, on the verge of attacking him. Bob
turned and left, eager to get back to the elevator. But just
before he reached it, he heard someone talking. He paused
because there was something familiar about the voice. It
was someone he knew.

Who did he know working up here? he wondered and
crossed the corridor. A door ahead of him was slightly ajar.
He approached slowly, the conversation becoming easier to
hear. What he finally understood stopped him in his tracks
and brought heat so quickly into his face it was as if he had
been dropped in boiling water.

". . . But something even stranger happened to me today.
I looked at my husband's photograph, the one I have in the

glass frame on my dresser, and while I was gazing at him your face imposed itself over his . . ."

Bob stepped closer to the door. Was he hearing correctly?

"That happened to me two days ago . . ."

The sound of his own voice drove needles into his heart. He gasped and stepped back, his body beginning to tremble.

What was this? How could anyone . . . they were taped, he realized. Someone had taped his and Elaine's conversation. In her house!

He approached the door again, moving as quietly as he could, but maybe because he was trying so hard not to make a sound, his footsteps seemed to reverberate up and down the corridor. He saw a shadow moving toward the door from the inside and he stepped back into the well of another entryway. Whoever it was stood there a moment and then closed the door firmly. His and Elaine's voices could no longer be heard.

His heart pounding, he returned to the elevator and pressed the buttons quickly. The doors closed and he descended, his face, just hot with blood, now cold and pale.

"What's the matter with you?" Jeff Livingston asked as soon as Bob reentered their offices. "Everything go all right up there?"

"What? Oh. No. Pyle was angry you didn't deliver the papers yourself," Bob said. "Very angry, I'd say. I'm sure you'll hear about it." He handed the access card to Livingston.

"Jesus." Jeff shook his head and put the card back in the top drawer of his desk. "That ugly son of a bitch thinks he's a big deal around here just because he's got his own personally marked parking space. Forget about it. Fuck him. Don't let it bother you," Jeff said. He was about to turn back to his work, but Bob's appearance continued to interest him. "You feeling all right, Charles?"

"I don't know. I do feel a bit woozy."

"You've been watching what you eat?"

"What? Oh, yeah."

"Well, maybe you should go get checked out anyway. You look as white as Pyle and he's a sickly-looking bastard. Go on. I'll look after things here."

Bob stared at him a moment. Then nodded.

"Yeah, thanks," he said. "I will."

He left the office and hurried down the corridor, but instead of going to the emergency room he headed for the parking lot. In moments he was driving away, and not long after that he opened the door of his townhouse as quietly as he could and entered, moving on tiptoe through the corridor, eyeing every fixture suspiciously. His attention fell on the sprinkler system. He realized there were nozzles in every room in the house. He got a chair and stood on it to inspect the one in the corridor first. Sure enough, he discovered it wasn't a nozzle for a sprinkler; it was a tiny microphone. It was the same throughout the townhouse.

He left his house quietly and walked over to Elaine's. He rang the front doorbell, but after a while he realized she wasn't home. It was the middle of the afternoon. Unable to do anything else, he returned to his car and sat waiting. Nearly an hour later, she drove up. As soon as she stepped out of hers, groceries in hand, he shouted to her.

"Charles?" She smiled as he started toward her. "What are you doing here this time of day?"

"Don't go into your house," he said.

"What? Charles, what's wrong? I've got to go into the house," she said, smiling and thinking he was here to whisk her away on some romantic interlude. "I've got ice cream and milk and . . ."

He turned around and looked at his own unit.

"We can't go into mine either," he muttered.

"Charles?" She tilted her head. "What's wrong?"

"Quickly," he said, nodding toward her house, "put your groceries away and come right back out. Do it, Elaine. Quickly," he snapped. Her smile faded.

"Charles, you're scaring me."

"That's all right. I'm quite frightened myself, Elaine. Go on, put your groceries in the house and come right back out," he ordered more firmly. "We'll walk and talk."

"Walk and talk? Charles, what's going on?"

"Your house and mine . . ."

"Yes?"

"Are bugged."

"Bugged?" She started to smile again. "What do you mean, bugged?"

"Someone's taping everything we say and do."

SHE joined him on the front steps. He was pacing about, gazing at everything with a paranoid eye. Were there microphones in the hedges? On that pole? Buried in the lawn? Maybe those really weren't lawn sprinklers. He took her hand and led her away from the house and didn't speak until they were nearly to the gate of the development. Then he stopped and turned to her.

"All the nozzles for the sprinkler system are really tiny microphones," he began. "They're in every room in our homes and probably behind mirrors or in other fixtures."

"But why, Charles? Why would anyone be interested in what we say and do?"

"I don't know."

"How did you discover this?" she asked and he described what had happened on the fifth floor.

"You actually heard it?"

"Word for word, the conversation we had in your dining room."

"My God, I feel . . . so violated. All our moments together, our thoughts . . . our lovemaking," she said. He nodded. "We've got to go right to the police," she concluded.

"No, not yet," Bob said thoughtfully. "I was going to do that, but changed my mind."

"Why?"

"I can't prove I heard what I heard and the police might not be able to prove the institute and whoever is behind this placed those microphones in our homes anyway. Besides," he said, looking around, his face taking on that paranoid expression again, "maybe we can't trust them either."

"So what do we do? Nothing?"

"For the time being," he said, "we pretend we don't know those mikes exist, but I'm definitely going to do something."

"What?"

"I've got to find out what's going on, honey. That floor is restricted because the research is supposedly highly sensitive and valuable. Suddenly, I discover we're somehow part of that research. I want to know why."

"I'm shaking," Elaine said, embracing herself. "I can't help it."

He went to her and put his arm around her.

"Don't worry, no one's going to hurt us. I don't think that's their purpose or they would have done something to us already."

She stared at him.

"Charles, we really don't know all that terribly much about each other, so don't get offended by my question," she prefaced.

"I won't. You couldn't offend me if you tried," he said, smiling.

"Is there something in your past, something you did that would make you . . ."

"A target for a spy mission?" He laughed. "Hardly. I'm afraid I've led a rather commonplace existence until now. How about you?" he kidded. She shook her head, but continued to gaze intently at him. It made his heart beat faster. As innocent as he was, he could see that his denial wasn't convincing enough to settle her doubts and that disturbed him. His face reddened and a trembling began in his body as well. It made him shudder and sent a sharp pain through his head. He groaned and covered his eyes quickly.

"Charles?"

"I'm telling you the truth, Marion," he snapped with a belligerence that surprised even him.

"Marion?"

"What?"

"You just called me Marion," she said, a smile of confusion washing across her face.

"I did?" He thought a moment. Marion, Marion . . . "I must have gotten confused for a moment. I'm sorry, I just . . . this is all so unnerving."

"Charles, really. We should just go to the police," she insisted.

"No!" he said, pulling away from her. "Not yet. Just let me find out some more information. Then, we'll consider going to the police. All right? All right?" he repeated more firmly.

His wide eyes and stiff posture frightened her. She nodded.

"All right, Charles."

"Good," he said, looking around. "Good."

He walked her back to her unit.

"I feel like I can't even think private thoughts while I'm in there now," she said, looking at her door.

"I know." He smiled. "We'll have to check into a cheap motel in order to make love."

"It's not funny," she said, but she smiled anyway. "Where are you going now?"

"Back," he simply said. She seized his hand.

"Charles, be careful and the moment you find out anything . . ."

"I'll be back. Don't worry," he said and kissed her. She watched him get into his car and then, with reluctance and fear in her gait, she started to walk inside her house.

JEFF Livingston looked up with surprise when Bob returned.

"What happened?" he asked.

"I'm fine. It wasn't anything related to my condition."

"Good, but why didn't you just go home? It's practically the end of the day anyway."

"I wanted to finish what I started."

"They don't pay for overtime here unless they assign it to you," Jeff reminded him.

"It's all right. I'll have an easier day tomorrow."

"You're lucky," Jeff said, shaking his head. "You got all the time in the world. Me, I gotta go to the in-laws tonight for dinner and listen to my mother-in-law rant and rave about how my father-in-law gets under her feet since he's retired. Sounds exciting, doesn't it?"

"To tell you the truth," Bob said wistfully, "it does. I miss family, miss the get-togethers, the chatter. Not having commitments has its down side."

Livingston regretted stimulating Bob's tragic memories. He smiled, eager to joke his way out of it.

"Yeah, well, as I told my wife, if she let me out of this one, I don't think I'd make the same mistake," he said and began gathering his things together.

Bob sat at his terminal and began to work, pretending to ignore him.

"See you tomorrow," Livingston said and left.

Bob waited a good ten minutes and then got up and went to Livingston's desk. He was surprised to discover the drawers were locked. He searched the top of the desk, looked in the desk organizer and on the shelves nearby, but found no key. He thought for a moment and then opened his own side drawer and looked at the set of keys he had been given when he first began working. He had never seen a need to lock his desk. There were three keys on the ring, one obviously for the room itself. Hoping he was right, he tried one of the other two keys in Livingston's desk lock. It worked and he was able to get into the top drawer. He found the access card under some papers, scooped it up quickly, closed the drawer and left the office.

There was a shift change under way in the hospital. One set of nurses and aides was leaving as the other set arrived; consequently the elevators were busy. He stood by waiting, but he didn't take the first available elevator because he didn't want to go up to access the fifth floor in front of anyone. He wasn't sure who worked up there and who didn't and he was afraid that he might easily be recognized as an intruder at this hour of the day. Finally, he was alone when an elevator arrived. He took it quickly and inserted the card. The doors closed and he was on his way.

When they opened again, he stood there for a moment listening. Instinctively, he felt danger. He couldn't be discovered wandering around up here without permission. He poked his head out and checked the corridor. It looked as deserted and as poorly lighted as before. After another moment of hesitation, he stepped out and turned right. At the door marked LIBRARY, he paused and listened. He heard nothing, but he knew that didn't mean the room was unoccupied. These doors were exceedingly thick. He tried the knob and discovered it was unlocked. Searching his mind for excuses should he walk in on someone, he shrugged and decided, here goes nothing. He opened the door and entered.

There was no one in sight. Without any hesitation, he moved directly to the mainframe and studied it for a few moments, quickly gathering its capacities and some of its functions. But there were things about this unit that confused and puzzled him. He turned to the glass cabinets next and tried to open one of the doors, but it was locked. He brought his face to the glass and studied the labels on the discs within.

ANDERSON, KURT; ANDERSON, TOBY; ATWA-TER, WILLIAM . . .

People's names, he thought. Just hospital records? He moved down along the cabinet and read some more, stopping when he reached BOXLETTER, JOEY. The pain in his head returned, but with a vengeance this time, slicing across and down sharply, forcing him to groan and close his eyes. He waited. It subsided, but the intensity of the agony nearly had taken his breath away. It made his heart pound.

He returned his gaze to the discs and read on: BOXLET-TER, MARION; BOXLETTER, ROBERT; BOXLETTER, SHERRI . . .

Marion, he thought. Where had he just heard that name? Marion . . . Elaine. She said he called her Marion. But what would that have to do with anything?

He continued his movement down and stopped dead when he was in the middle of the Cs. There it was as clear as day—CORBIN, CHARLES. Was it simply his hospital records encased? And if so why was it kept up here on a re-

stricted floor where they were doing secret research? He
tried the cabinet door, but it was locked here too.

He gazed around the large room and hurried over to a
desk. Most of the drawers were empty, but the top drawer
was full of printouts. He perused one sheet quickly and determined it was some sort of program, and a very intricate
one at that. He put the papers back and felt along the inside
of the drawer until he reached a small plastic cup. When he
touched it, he heard the jingle of keys and pulled the cup
out. They looked like cabinet door keys.

He rushed back to the door of the cabinet that contained
CORBIN, CHARLES and tried each of the keys in the
lock. He was nearly at the end when one worked. He
opened the door and pulled out the file, surprised to discover that it contained at least a half dozen discs, each labeled in some code. He closed the cabinet and started out
when a new thought occurred.

He returned to the cabinets and tracked up the alphabet
until he reached the Ss. Sure enough, they were there:
STRATTON, ELAINE; STRATTON, MELISSA.

Once again, he tried all the keys until he found the right
one and opened the cabinet to take out Elaine's file. Then
he locked the cabinet, returned the cup of keys to the
drawer, and started out, pausing at the doorway to peer
down the corridor. All was still quiet.

He scampered out and hurried down the corridor, hanging close to the wall until he reached the elevator. This time
it seemed to take forever for one to arrive, and while he
waited, he heard voices at the other end. They grew louder.
Someone was approaching and at any moment would be
around that corner, he thought. Fortunately, the elevator arrived. He hurried in and hit the button. As the doors closed,
he heard the voices clearly. One of them was Dr. Randolph,
his doctor.

His heart was pounding so hard, he thought he might faint before he returned to his office and got to his computer terminal. When he did get there, his fingers were trembling so he almost couldn't insert the first disc. But he did and he fired up his monitor and heard the floppy disc mechanism grinding. In moments, the screen was filled with information, and what he saw held him in rapt attention so long, he never realized he was there for nearly four hours.

13

ELAINE WAS STARING AT THE TELEVISION SET, BUT SHE DIDN'T hear or see anything played over it. Her mind was elsewhere. The turmoil and the mystery had had the effect of stirring up memories, but in such a way as to confuse her. Suddenly, her past, something she could usually tap in a most organized and logical manner, became jumbled. Her own childhood became entangled in her recollections of Melissa's until she sat there wondering was that something that had happened to her or something that happened to Melissa?

The bewilderment eventually put her into a small panic. When she forced herself to concentrate, she found she had forgotten whether she had done something yesterday or last week; and then, when she thought about Charles, her confusion intensified further. When had they first met? How had they first met? She knew it couldn't have been that long ago, yet, just before, when she thought about a vacation she had taken years and years ago, she saw Charles in the images—Charles standing beside her, Charles sitting across from her in the romantic restaurant by the ocean, and Charles beside her in the bed in the hotel.

Why was all this happening? What did it mean? She covered her face with her hands and fought back tears.

"What's wrong, Mommy?" Melissa said. Elaine looked up quickly. Her daughter had come back downstairs and was standing in the living room doorway.

"Nothing's wrong," Elaine said, shooting a glance up at

the sprinkler head in the ceiling. "Why did you get out of bed, honey?"

"I had a bad dream," Melissa said and rushed to embrace her. Elaine stroked her hair as Melissa pressed her face into her lap.

"That's okay. Everyone has those occasionally. You want a glass of warm milk?"

Melissa lifted her head and nodded. Elaine kissed her and got up. Taking her hand, she led her into the kitchen. Melissa crawled onto a kitchen chair to sit and wait.

"Mr. Panda was crying," she said after Elaine had poured the milk into a saucepan.

"He was?"

"Uh huh."

"You mean in your dream?"

"Uh huh."

"Oh, I'm sorry. He's all right now though, right?" Elaine said, getting the mug out of the cabinet. Melissa shook her head.

"No, he's not. He thinks the bad men are going to get him," she said.

"Bad men? What bad men, honey?" Elaine asked. She smiled.

"The bad men in the dream, Mommy. They came and they poked us."

"Poked us?" Elaine drew closer. "You mean like this?" she said and gently shoved her right forefinger under Melissa's arm. She giggled. "It was only a dream, honey. Don't think about it anymore, okay?"

"I won't, but Mr. Panda will."

"Well, you'll just have to tell him to stop."

"He won't," Melissa insisted. Elaine stepped back and considered her a moment.

"Who were these men in your dream, honey?"

"One was a policeman," she said.

"A policeman? He poked you?"

"No. It was the other men, the ones in the white clothes."

"White clothes?" Elaine thought a moment. "You mean like doctors wear?"

"Uh huh," she said, nodding with excitement.

Elaine went back to her, this time squatting beside her and lowering her voice.

"What did they poke you with, Melissa? Just whisper in my ear."

Melissa did so and Elaine drew back as if she were able to see her daughter's nightmare played out on her face. For a long moment she didn't move. Then she bit down on her lower lip and stood up.

"It was just a dream, honey. You will soon forget it and feel better. And so will Mr. Panda," she added quickly. "It's nothing," she said, looking up at the sprinkler in the ceiling of the kitchen. "I'll give you your milk and then I'll go back up with you and read to you for a while, okay?"

"Uh huh."

Elaine turned back to the saucepan just in time. The milk had risen to the top and was about to spill over. She hurried to reduce the heat and pour the milk into the mug.

"I'll carry the milk for you, Melissa. It's got to cool a bit anyway. Come on, honey. Back to bed," she said and they walked out and up the stairs.

It took her nearly half an hour to get Melissa sleepy again. Finally, her daughter's eyelids closed and she drifted off. Elaine got up, put away the children's storybook, and started out of the bedroom. She knew it was only her imagination, but Melissa's Mr. Panda, set beside Melissa in the bed, seemed to be staring up at Elaine with worried eyes.

She had just settled back on the sofa and started to flick the remote channel selector to see if something on television would catch her interest and take her mind off her concerns when she heard a tapping on the window. She gasped, turned around and saw Charles looking in. Instantly, he brought his forefinger to his lips to indicate she should not reveal his presence. He beckoned for her to come out. She did so as quietly as possible. He was already down the walk and near the driveway. She hurried to him and they embraced.

"I was so worried about you," she said. "You've been gone so long."

He nodded and stared intently at her.

"We're definitely part of the research program," he said. Her heart began to pound.

"What do you mean, Charles? I never volunteered for anything."

"Neither did I, but we're part of it, along with fifty or so others who I'm sure don't know they're in it, either." Without saying another word, he led her to his car. She waited as he opened the door to reach in for something. He brought out a few computer discs.

"What is that?"

"You and me."

"You and me? I don't understand," she said, gazing at them in his hand.

"There are computer discs for Melissa, too. I've been viewing them on a monitor. That's where I've been so long. What these discs contain," he said slowly, "are our entire conscious memories, our life histories, much of it in our own words like stream of consciousness."

She took a step back as if the discs were spoiled with radiation.

"I don't understand. Why would anyone . . . what are they doing with it? How did they get it?"

"I don't know exactly, but I discovered something about our memories—they've been altered."

"Altered?"

"Tailored, changed in subtle and not-so-subtle ways. For example, I graduated college as a marine biology major, but I don't remember a damn thing about it and I'm a computer technician, yet I had no experience with computers in my recorded past. Recalling my recent hypoglycemic seizure and what didn't happen when I took you and Melissa for dessert and ate too much sugar, I went into the hospital records and discovered there was no such diagnosis. Lab results show a normal blood sugar. Hypoglycemia has been added to my memory, probably in order to explain my unconscious state."

"Maybe that was just a clerical error by someone in the hospital, Charles."

"I considered that. But there was something else in my past that's impossible to cover or mistakenly leave out."

"What?"

"My appendectomy." He unfastened his pants and zipped down his fly. Then he lowered his briefs. "You've seen me naked, but you can check for yourself—there's no scar. This body never had an appendectomy."

"This body? Charles, you're not making any sense."

"I am," he insisted, fastening his pants. "When you were fifteen, you had a bad bicycle accident, remember?"

"Yes. I hit a pothole and spilled. I was lucky because I hit my head, but there was no concussion. How do you know that? I never told you. Did Melissa tell you?"

"No. It's on the disc. As I said," he said, holding up the disc, "all your conscious memories."

She shook her head, the significance of what he was saying finally dawning on her.

"All my memories . . ."

"Yes. That bike accident . . . there was a lot of bleeding . . . scary bleeding. You were screaming because the blood ran down your cheeks."

"Yes," she said. "I hit a large pebble and it caused a severe head wound."

"Which scarred you, only your hair covers it well, so you were never self-conscious about it, right?"

"Yes," she said, looking down at the discs in his hand. "My God, Charles, my thoughts, even my feelings . . . I feel naked, worse than naked. My very soul feels exposed. I can't accept this; I can't."

He opened the car door and turned the vanity mirror on the passenger's visor so she could gaze into it.

"Find the scar," he challenged.

"What?"

"Find the scar. It shouldn't be hard to do. Scars are scars; they don't go away."

Slowly, she leaned in and pulled her hair back to search her scalp. It was spotless, clear.

"I don't understand," she said. "Where's my scar? I remember it, but . . ."

"But it's not there," he said excitedly. "That's not all, of course. I skipped ahead to your most recent memories and found no evidence that you had stopped in a motel and suffered a near-tragic accident because of leaky pipes. In fact, your history ends in a hospital intensive-care unit. And Melissa's history . . ."

"What? What about Melissa?" she asked, her voice cracking.

"Her history ended in the emergency room of the same hospital. You were both in an automobile accident."

She shook her head and stepped back.

"No, this is . . . it can't be true. I don't remember any such accident."

"Because they tailored it out," he said, "and inserted the motel accident memory in its place."

"No," she said, shaking her head. "That's impossible. It makes no sense."

"It's true," he insisted. "My history ends in the intensive care unit at a different hospital. I was the victim of a mugging . . . shot in the stomach. Needless to say, I have no scar there, nor do I have any memory of it," he added.

"So you believe . . ."

Even in the darkness, he could see her face whiten. He felt her hands grow cold and her body shudder. It struck him that they were both standing there feeling like no more than ghouls. He had no easy time putting what they were both now thinking into words, but he had to say it; he had to face up to it.

"Elaine," he said slowly, tightening his hold on her hands, "I think you and Melissa died.

"And I died, too," he said.

MOVING as quietly as two shadows, they climbed the stairs and entered Melissa's room. Elaine put on the Mickey Mouse lamp on her night table. They saw she was fast asleep on her right side, something for which Elaine was grateful, for she could do what she had come to do without waking Melissa. Bob stood right beside her as she leaned over and gently brushed her hair away from Melissa's left ear. Then, slowly, she lifted her daughter's earlobe as tenderly as she could and they both looked closely. Elaine subdued a gasp by shoving her fist into her mouth. Bob helped her to her feet and they quickly retreated, moving again like shadows through the corridor and down the stairs. They left the house and walked back to his car where he embraced her and held her tightly. Safely away from the microphones, she could sob freely.

She pulled herself back and caught her breath.

"We used to kid her about it and say we drew the tiny birthmark with a magic pen to make sure she always washed behind her ears. After a while none of us thought about it; it was in such a discreet place.

"Charles," she said, "what does all this mean? If our memories of our bodies are different from our bodies . . ."

"Then they're not our bodies," he said. "Just as I said— our bodies died, but before they did, they took our minds and with their computer technology stored them on discs for future use. We're the future use," he explained.

"Why?"

"I don't know the why yet, but I imagine these bastards, whoever they are, have been collecting the memory banks of dying people all over the country and placing them in new bodies. That's the essence of their research project and obviously why it's so secretive."

"How can they do this, Charles?"

"I don't know the how yet either. I know that thoughts and therefore memories are the result of what we would call an electrochemical process. In a sense everything we see, hear, do, everything we remember is converted into a form for the brain to store. It's written in a special way. Think of a tape recorder writing sounds and video on tape. It's not unlikely that soon taste, touch, and smell will be transcribed as well. People will not only see and hear a film, but taste what the actors taste, smell what they smell and feel what they feel: a total experience.

"These scientists have gone beyond that, skipped over it because they're on to something greater, more significant: capturing and transplanting memory, but not only doing that, but also tailoring it, changing it to fit some horrible plan. In essence, they're creating people to be the way they want them to be. Can you imagine the power?"

"I'm so scared," Elaine said. "But worse than that," she added, embracing herself, "I suddenly feel so . . . dirty. Don't laugh, but it's as if I'm wearing someone else's underwear."

"I know the feeling. It crossed my mind, too."

"Oh Charles, I . . ."

She stopped and stared at him, her eyes wide as if she were indeed looking at a ghost.

"What is it?" he asked.

"I call you Charles, but you're not Charles; you're someone else, and so am I, and so is Melissa. Who are we?" she asked. The panic and disgust she felt took form in hysteria. *"Who are we?"* she cried.

"Easy, honey."

"I don't know who I am . . . who you are . . . who my own daughter is. Is she really my daughter? Oh God. . . ."

"Easy," he repeated and tried to embrace her, but she pulled away.

"No, I don't want you to touch me," she screamed. He backed off. Something was happening to her, something that might be the result of this flood of truth, this confrontation with reality. For all he knew, some of them were programmed to explode if they were confronted with what and who they really were.

"All right, all right," he said and turned away from her. Give her a chance to calm down, he thought. He leaned against his car and looked up at the night sky. The stars were so clear, so bright. There was the Big Dipper and there was Orion. It occurred to him that much of what people who lived in the same country, grew up about the same period, read the same news and saw the same movies and television knew was common, shared knowledge. Whoever this body was might know the stars, too, might have looked up nights and been dazzled by the constellations.

Elaine's hysteria subsided. She stood there, embracing herself and sobbing.

"What are we going to do?" she whimpered. "What will we do now? Shouldn't we go to the police?"

"No," he said softly.

"Why not?"

"Well, this research unit is the biggest thing going in this tiny village. My guess is they chose this place because of its anonymity, but also because they could manipulate it and its inhabitants safely. In order to do that, they either have to have the cooperation of the police or . . ."

"Or what?"

"Made them over into what they want them to be."

She nodded and wiped her face.

"Before you arrived tonight, Melissa came downstairs because she had had a nightmare about bad men and she said one of them was a policeman."

"Really? What else did she say?"

"She said there were men in white with him and the men in white poked her with a needle."

"Needle? A syringe?"

"Yes."

"I've had a similar sort of nightmare."

"So have I. That's why it frightened me."

"However they got us must relate to that," he said and thought a moment. "If we shared the same memory, there's a chance it happened to all three of us at the same time in the same place," he said excitedly.

"What could that mean?"

"It means we were together."

"But if we were already together, why would they . . ."

"Do this and try to bring us together again?" He thought. "It must be part of their research. They're playing with us, performing some special experiment. Elaine, I remember once I called you Marion."

"Yes."

"And you called me Bob."

She nodded.

"While I was perusing the computer discs, I saw another name that seemed somehow familiar—Boxletter."

She looked up sharply.

"That strikes a note with you, too, doesn't it?"

"Yes."

"There were four Boxletters," he said excitedly. "A male named Bob and a female named Marion. The other female could be . . ."

"Their daughter?"

"Yes."

"And the other one?"

"I don't know. Boxletter, Boxletter, where did I hear that name recently?" He thought a moment and then looked up. "The diner, remember?"

"No."

"When we arrived. The hostess thought we were the Boxletters. I told you that and you said we all have twins."

"Yes."

"We must have come here . . . to this town for some reason and gone to that diner before they did what they did to us. Why did we come?"

Elaine shook her head.

"I'm going back there," he said and started to get into his car.

"Why?"

"I want to corner that hostess and see what she knows about the Boxletters."

Elaine looked back at her house.

"I'm so afraid."

"It's all right for now. They don't know what we know. Go back inside and keep the television on. When you see me drive up, come out again."

"Charles," she said, coming up to him. "Be careful."

"I will."

She watched him drive off and then went back inside. She went into the kitchen to make herself some hot tea and then returned to the living room to do what he said. She tuned into a sitcom and let the canned laughter lull her into a calm. The tea soothed her stomach and settled the butterflies. As she sat there, she fought back thoughts and memories as if she didn't want to be corrupted by her own thoughts, thoughts she now told herself were not really her own.

She couldn't help wondering about people who had transplanted organs, especially transplanted hearts. Did they feel the essence of someone else within them? Or could they eventually forget that the organ came from another living human being? If she had someone else's memories in her, did that mean she had someone else's emotions, soul? Were we only the sum total of our memories, our minds, or was there some other part, some more essential part that gave us our true identity?

All sorts of religious and philosophical questions began to occur and for a while that distracted her. She couldn't help being intrigued by the questions and imagined how these scientists, the monsters they were, were probably driven by many of the same mysteries.

Eventually all this took its toll on her. She fought to keep her eyes open, but the tension, the emotional drain, all of it was overwhelming. Her eyelids grew heavier and heavier. She wanted to doze off, but she suddenly became paranoid about herself. This mind and this body were two separate individuals. Why wouldn't one possibly betray the other? Was her mind trying to subduc her body?

I can't fall asleep, she told herself. I won't. She forced her eyes open and then raised the volume on the television set. Glancing at her watch every five minutes, she anticipated Charles's return. Or should she think of him as Bob? she wondered. For now, it was too confusing. It was best to take it as it came. She hoped and prayed that soon it would all come to an end.

BOB sat in his car in the parking lot watching the hostess through the windows of the diner. He was going to go in to see if she would talk to him, but he saw from the way she was moving about that she was soon leaving. Her shift was apparently near its end. She had her jacket on and was passing some light conversation with one of the waiters. Soon he had to return to his tables and she waved good-bye to the other employees and started out. He watched her enter the parking lot and head for a car toward the rear. He got out quickly and started after her. She turned when she heard his footsteps on the gravel.

The look of fear on her face told him once again that he was someone she didn't like.

"Can I speak to you a moment, miss," he called as she started to speed up. She turned back and looked even more terrified as he broke into a jog to catch up.

"What do you want?" she demanded and stepped to the side. "I can scream and everyone will be out in a moment."

"Oh, no," Bob said, holding up his hand and backing away. "I don't want to hurt you, or even bother you. I just want to ask you a couple of questions. I'll stand right here. Please," he pleaded. His demeanor calmed her.

"What d'ya want?"

"Obviously, you recognize me, remember me, even

though I've only been in the diner a few times, only once when you were working," he said. He smiled, hoping to relax her. She still looked at him askance.

"Not once, twice," she said.

"Twice? I don't recall the second time. Was I alone?"

"What is this?" she demanded and took a few steps away. "What the hell do you want?"

"Please, I'm having a problem with memory and it's very frightening. Won't you help me? I thought I might have been in that diner before when you were there, but I wasn't positive."

"This is stupid," she said, pronouncing it "stupit."

"I know." He smiled. "Imagine how stupid I feel having to ask such a simple thing, but I've got to know."

"You came in both times with your wife and daughter," she said. "Is that it?"

"My wife and daughter?"

"Well, that's who I thought they were. The first time, you made a big stink with the Andersons and the cops had to come."

"The cops?" He stepped toward her.

"Leave me alone," she said and turned toward her car again.

"No, please. All right, all right. I won't come near you. Tell me what happened."

"Jesus," she said, hesitating. "You are crazy."

"I'm not. I was in an accident," he said quickly, "and I lost my memory, but I'm getting it back and I'm trying to learn about the things I did before. That's all," he said, holding his arms out.

She looked at him skeptically.

"Who are the Andersons? What did I do? Look," he said when she still hesitated. "This is really important to me." He reached for his wallet and took out two twenties. "I'll give you this if you'll tell me what happened. And look," he added, stepping to the right so he would be in more light. "We can stand right here where everyone can see us talking, so you won't be in any danger. Okay?"

She considered. Forty dollars. That was a day's wages at Ray's and she could make it in a few minutes.

"Move into the light more," she commanded. He did so and she walked toward him slowly. He handed her the money.

"You really don't remember what happened?" she asked, now that she had the money and felt safe.

"Honest. I really appreciate this," he said.

She looked toward the diner and then at Bob.

"All right," she said. "Here's what happened."

A LITTLE more than twenty minutes later, he pulled up in front of Elaine Stratton's townhouse and waited. It seemed to take her a long time to notice so he was about to get out and tap on her window again. Probably fell asleep waiting, he thought, but just as he opened his car door, she stepped out of her house and hurried down the walk to meet him. She opened the door and got in beside him.

"Well?" she asked. "Did you speak to the hostess?"

"Yes."

"And?"

"We're the Boxletters; we're married. Melissa's our daughter, and I know why we came to Sandburg," he said.

14

NELSON CONGEMI WALKED SLOWLY DOWN TO THE SOUTH END of the fifth floor corridor. It was late; he wanted to go home for the evening, but his sluggish gait was more a result of his being in deep thought than it was his physical fatigue. A meditative posture wasn't an unusual demeanor for him to be in. All his life, or at least all his academic life, he had been accused of being absentminded or "in another world." His ability to lift himself out of his surroundings and enclose himself in a cocoon of his own thoughts was remarkable. Lila Randolph said he appeared absolutely catatonic at times, claiming he reminded her of their subjects in transference.

Almost all of his mental excursions involved his work, scientific problems, theories and applications. Rarely was he distracted by what Lila would disdainfully refer to as "conscience," but lately, that was just what was invading his thinking—these periods of moral regret. He couldn't get away from the growing belief that what had started out as a wonderful and spectacular project had somehow degenerated into something increasingly off course and beyond his control. He felt somewhat like the German rocket scientists who dreamed of going to the moon, only to have their work turned into V-2 missiles, weapons of war and destruction instead.

He stopped at the door to the room in which subjects were kept before and immediately after a transference. He couldn't help thinking that this man, Sam Heller, was an al-

batross, the quintessential rotten apple. Nothing they could
do with him was going to make a difference; it was too late.
He wished Lila would admit to some failures, realize the
reality of their limits and accept them.

He opened the door and stepped in. Heller was strapped
down in the hospital bed as a precaution, and Lila was sitting beside him, reading a report. She didn't look up even
though Congemi knew she realized he had entered. It was
just one of those little things she did to demonstrate her
sense of superiority. Not anything, not anyone, not even he,
was permitted to interrupt her flow of thoughts.

Instead of waiting, he went over to Heller and leaned
over the man to peer into the catatonic's eyes. They were as
glassy as the eyes of death. However, the pupils dilated. All
of the man's vitals were good. The monitor read a decent
pulse and an excellent blood pressure. He was putting out
sufficient urine and his body temperature was normal. Congemi checked the IV and turned as Lila finally looked up.

"Pyle has a program to apply. I think it's worth an attempt and might prove to have interesting results," she said,
holding up the papers.

"What is it?"

"He wants to restore the man's true identity," she said.

"What about the pocket of recent memory we can't re-
move, the glitch?"

"Pyle wants to see if he can shift it so it will seem more
like a nightmare to him than an actual memory. Of course,
we will have to follow up with psychiatric counseling and
convince . . ." She paused to look at the papers. "Convince
Brian that he is remembering a dream and not an actual
event," she said.

"Shift a memory?"

"It's worth a try. This whole view of the brain as being
similar to a computer hard disc with its directories and

files, a separate file for dreams, is very interesting. Pyle surprises me sometimes with his . . . creativity," Lila said. Congemi smirked.

"What do we do afterward should this work? Return him to society?"

"Of course not," she said. "What would be the purpose of that? No. After we have had an opportunity to evaluate the results, we'll render him brain dead and distribute the organs to needy recipients." She smiled. "I would think that would please you, Nelson. After going through all this, we perform a humanitarian action."

"I have always assumed the good of humanity was your purpose for all this as well as it was mine, Lila."

"Oh it is, it is. I'm just a little more circumspect than you are," she said. "Well?"

Congemi looked at the near-corpse.

"When do you want to start?"

"Pyle is working up the computer program now. He needs about a day. Let's say we'll begin the transference tomorrow night at ten."

Nelson Congemi nodded. There really wasn't any point to opposing the plan just because he had a deep distaste for Pyle.

"What will you tell Fryman?" he asked. "You really won't have solved the problem as far as he is concerned."

"We'll distract him."

"Distract him? How?"

"I was thinking in terms of an offering," she replied with that wry smile.

"An offering?"

"Yes. You see, Nelson, I've arrived at a temporary conclusion that will please you, I'm sure. I think you might be right about the effects of conscience. I don't subscribe to the theory that it's in the nature of man to be good or even that it's in the nature of some individuals to have an aversion for evil and violence. Some part of their upbringing, something in their learned experiences has shaped them and we haven't been able to delve deep enough to reach that level. In simple words, we can change memories and conscious thoughts, but we can't redesign their so-called consciences, not yet."

"Precisely," Congemi said, the old excitement returning. This was the Lila Randolph he admired and respected, one who was open-minded enough to consider all possibilities. That Lila Randolph stimulated him and he in turn stimulated her. It was why they worked so well together.

"So," she continued, "what Fryman wants to do is not impossible. What we have got to do, what we should have done, is screen the candidates more closely. Let's try someone who has committed violent acts, someone who already has a predilection toward evil."

Congemi nodded. Lila Randolph was admitting to some limitations. They couldn't simply make people into exactly what they wanted. Working on the human mind wasn't like playing on one of those toy writing pads you scribbled on, lifted the cover and erased, and started again. Some things were beyond their technology.

"Who did you have in mind as an offering for him?" he asked.

"Who better to start with than our own chief of police," she replied, widening her smile.

"Robinson?" Congemi thought about it a moment. "Yes, yes I like that."

"Anyway, first things first," Lila Randolph said, rising. "Review this," she said, handing him Pyle's report, "and let me know if you see any problems before we start on Heller." She gazed at the catatonic man. "Did you notice, Nelson, that from time to time his lips writhe as if he's reliving that one painful memory periodically. Imagine a mind," she said, staring at the man, "that had only one thing to recall and every time it was recalled, it was painful. That would be a whole new sort of torture.

"Why," she said, turning to Congemi, "we could create a punishment to fit the crime."

She smiled and started out. Congemi remained, staring at Heller a moment, and then fled from the room as if what was happening inside the man's head could somehow infect him and cause similar results.

ALTHOUGH they knew every word they uttered was being recorded, Bob and Elaine slept together in her bedroom. Their driving need to be close to each other outweighed their revulsion at being spied upon even during their most personal and private moments. When they spoke to each other, they did so in very low whispers, lips pressed closely to ears. They didn't intend to make love passionately. All they wanted to do was comfort each other and not spend the night alone after the discoveries they had made. But kisses of reassurance became longer and more demanding. Each caress led to another. They became passionate, neither caring that their sounds of love were being recorded. The lovemaking gave them a reassurance they desperately needed and exhausted them so they could finally fall asleep.

Bob woke before daylight, however, and got up to wash and dress. When he slipped out to go down and make them some coffee, Melissa woke and came to the doorway of her bedroom. Dressed in her pajamas, she wiped her eyes and looked up at him tiptoeing down the corridor.

"Hi, honey," he said. Knowing now that she really was his daughter stimulated a rush of affection and he swooped down to lift her into his arms. He kissed her cheeks and brushed back her hair. "You're hardly awake."

"Where's Mommy?"

"Still sleeping, shh," he said. "Want to come down with me and help surprise her? We'll make breakfast." She nodded and then yawned. Bob laughed. "Get your slippers and put on your robe, okay?" He lowered her to the floor and she garnered more energy. He waited for her at the top of the stairway, gazing up cautiously at the sprinkler head in the ceiling of the corridor.

"How come you're here so early?" Melissa asked when she joined him.

"How come? Er . . . I fell asleep here," he said. "You don't mind, do you?"

She shook her head.

"Good." He took her hand and they descended.

Almost twenty minutes later, Bob and Melissa heard Elaine's nearly hysterical cry.

"Melissa! Melissa, where are you?"

"Down here, Mommy," she replied and Elaine came down the stairs quickly. Bob saw from the expression on her face that she had been frightened when she found herself alone and discovered Melissa wasn't in her room. She embraced Melissa protectively, surprising the little girl with her intensity.

"What's going on?" Elaine asked, looking up at Bob, her eyes wide. Bob shifted his gaze to the sprinkler head in the kitchen ceiling as a warning to be discreet. He smiled and kept his tone of voice as calm as he could.

"Nothing much, except Melissa and I wanted to surprise you with breakfast. She made all the toast and I have some omelets ready and some freshly squeezed grapefruit juice."

"Oh," Elaine said, realizing. "Oh, how nice. Thank you."

She put Melissa down and brushed back her hair. "I'll just go back up and wash my face and brush my hair."

"Good," Bob said.

"Good? And what exactly does that mean, Mr. Corbin?"

"Nothing. Only . . . a breakfast as wonderful as this one is going to be deserves a clean face and neat hair."

"Hmm," Elaine said, smirking. "Be right back."

They tried to keep their conversation as mundane as possible. Bob talked about his work at the hospital and Elaine described some of the shopping she was going to do. Melissa needed new shoes. In the afternoon, Elaine was going to stop at the school to speak with the principal about her upcoming teaching assignment.

As soon as they had finished breakfast, Elaine sent Melissa up to her room to start dressing and then she followed Bob out so they would be away from the microphones.

"What are you going to do?" she asked him.

"I'm going back up to the fifth floor and learn what I can about the process to see what we can do about getting ourselves back," he said.

"This conversation . . ." Elaine embraced herself and looked around. "It seems like dialogue from 'The Twilight Zone.' I feel like I'm living a nightmare."

"Both are true. And you will do what we discussed when you get to the school . . . find out who Adam Anderson is so we can . . ."

"It scares me even to think about it," she said quickly.

"I know, but it's something I hope we can eventually do," Bob said and kissed her.

"Be careful."

"You too."

When Bob arrived at the hospital, he found Lady Luck had smiled down upon them. Jeff Livingston had called in sick. His look of pleasure when the hospital secretary told him almost gave him away. He explained it quickly by saying he thought the man was under some strain these days and needed a good rest.

Alone in the office, he began to plan his excursion to the fifth floor. With Livingston out of the picture, it was easy for him to get the access card and go and come as he pleased. He decided the best time to make his reconnaissance would be during the lunch hour. In the meantime, he played around with his computer, searching for pathways to the mainframe and passage into the files stored in research. As he expected, everything required a password and he was denied access. What he didn't know was merely trying to make entry triggered an alarm and launched a trace. His attempt to break in was instantly recorded.

At noon he rose from his desk and went as nonchalantly as he could to the elevators. He carried a small packet of computer printouts as a cover so he could claim he had been sent up to make a delivery. Once again, he waited for an empty elevator and inserted the slot card when one arrived. When the doors opened on the fifth floor, he found the corridor as quiet and as empty as before. This time, he turned left and went down to the corner. He peered around first, saw it was empty, and continued. When he came to a door that read INFORMATION TRANSFERENCE, he stopped. He found the door locked, but he saw a slot above it and tried his elevator slot card. There was a click and the handle turned.

He was immediately greeted by the monotonous hum of a bank of monitors. The information transference room looked like a control room in a television studio. Below the monitors were consoles all lit up. The walls before him were all glass. There was no one seated at the consoles, so he moved quickly to the large windows and peered into a room in which a man was sprawled on a gurney. Over his temples were what looked like large earphones, thick, gray, wide pads, the wires from which ran up into the ceiling. A heart monitor was attached to electrodes on his chest. Although the man's eyes were wide open, he looked mesmerized, his gaze fixed on a large dark spot on the ceiling.

Bob stepped back and studied the monitors. On one of them was the outline of a cerebral cortex. A red tint was spreading out from the center to fill in almost half the cortical outline. As the shading grew larger, a gauge below the monitor ticked off percentiles. Bob watched it a moment and then looked at the man again. They were either taking out his memory or putting a memory in, he thought. So this was where it was done and this was the technology.

The sound of footsteps just outside the door put him in a panic. He saw a door on the left and rushed to it, hoping it was unlocked. It was and he opened it and entered what looked to be a computer hardware storage room. He recognized hard discs, slot boards, chips and the like. He kept the door slightly open and listened as the two technicians, one of whom he remembered to be the man Pyle, spoke.

"As soon as this is done, move him to recovery. I want to set things up for tonight," Pyle said. "We're going to begin at ten."

"Ten!" the other man replied, not disguising his unhappiness.

"Don't worry, Simmons, I don't need you, but I want you here early tomorrow."

"Sure."

"All right. Just run a check on bank two for me. I don't want any problems tonight."

"Gotcha."

"I'll be in my office if you have any problems," Pyle said. "I've got a few things left to do on this program."

Bob saw him leave. The other man went to the consoles

and began checking out bank two. Bob watched him work
for almost twenty minutes. Finally, the technician completed his run-through and looked up at the monitor. He
saw the transference had been completed and went into the
other room. Bob took advantage of the moment to slip out
of the storage room and out of the information transference
room.

Instead of going back to the elevators, however, he went
past them, and quickly entered the library. There was no
one there. He hurriedly found the keys to the cabinets again
and went to the one that contained all the Boxletter files.
After he gathered them up, he locked the cabinet and put
back the keys, but just as he put his hand on the doorknob,
the door was opened and he stood face to face with a security guard whose name tag read ROSS.

"Who the fuck are you?" Ross demanded, his gaze
falling to four files of discs in Bob's arms. He was about
two inches taller than Bob and much broader, with a barrel
chest and hard, chipped-out facial features. A formidable
opponent, Bob thought.

"New man," Bob said quickly.

"What new man? Nobody told me about no new man,
and where's your ID card?" he asked, poking Bob in the
left side of his chest rather firmly.

"Oh, I forgot to pin it on," Bob said, smiling. He went to
the desk to put the files down. Ross followed closely, his
eyes still filled with suspicion. Bob put his hands in his
pockets and pretended to search.

"Shit," he said. "Must have left it in my other jacket.
Here," he said, "let me call Doctor Randolph so she can
verify who I am." Bob reached for the phone on the desk,
but instead of taking the receiver in hand, he grasped the
entire phone and swung around quickly to smash it against
the security guard's head. His action was fast enough and

surprising enough to get past Ross's instinctive arm block, and the phone base cracked him sharply in the temple, sending him sideways. He tripped over his own feet and hit the floor. But he would have fallen anyway. The edge of the phone base had struck him squarely in the center of his temple, easily crashing through with the momentum and force Bob applied.

For a moment Bob stood there, shaking, unable to move himself. Then he put the phone back on the desk and squatted down beside the unconscious security man. He felt for his pulse and was shocked to discover there was none. The man was dead. Bob pulled his hand back as if the body were electrified. His own heart was beating so hard and fast, he thought he might soon collapse beside Ross.

The sound of footsteps outside put him in another panic. He stood up and put his back to the wall, waiting for the door to open again. The footsteps paused and then continued on down the corridor. Bob breathed with relief, but considered the dead security man once more. As soon as this body was discovered, the game was up, he thought. I have to hide it.

He took hold of the dead man's wrists and dragged the body back into the rear of the library. Once there, he searched desperately for a place and found that the cabinets on the far wall were, for the most part, empty. Each was large enough to stuff a man's body into with some effort, even a man as big as Ross.

He started to fold Ross into a fetal position and stopped. The gun, he thought. He would surely need it. He pulled it out of Ross's holster and stuck it in his belt under his jacket. Then he continued to work Ross's body into the cabinet. It was harder than he had first imagined. He had to get the body turned just right in order to get the legs in and close the door. To him it seemed as though he was at it for nearly an hour, even though it was only fifteen minutes. Finally, he was able to close the cabinet door so that it would stay closed.

He went back through the library and checked everything to be sure there was no evidence of any struggle. Confident there was none, he gathered the discs again and slipped out of the library, checking first to be sure all was clear. He hurried to the elevator and pressed the button. Instantly, the doors opened. One had been waiting. Luck was still smiling generously upon him, he thought.

EVEN though Jeff Livingston wasn't there to check on him, Bob remained at his work station until it was time to leave for the day. Every once in a while, he would stop what he was doing and recall the way he had killed the security guard. Whenever he did so, he found himself trembling so fiercely he had to take hold of the desk to stop it. Along with the trembling came that splitting headache that threatened to tear the top off his skull. One time, without even realizing he was doing it, he began pounding the top of his desk. The pain in his hand and wrist brought it to a halt. He considered calling Elaine; he needed to speak to her, but was afraid that her phone was tapped.

Finally, it was time to go and he left the office as inconspicuously as he could, nodding and smiling at other hospital employees. He had all the discs in his briefcase. After he got into his car, he drove away slowly and didn't speed up until he was sufficiently far enough from the hospital. Elaine was outside with Melissa, washing her car, when he drove up.

Perfect, he thought. Everything looks so ordinary; no one would be suspicious. One look at his face, however, told Elaine he had been through a terrible experience.

"Hi," she said. "How did it go?"

He patted the briefcase.

"It's all in here," he said. Her eyes shifted to it.

"It gives me the chills," she said. "It's gruesome, like our actual bodies are somehow in there."

"In a way that's true."

"Did you have any problems?" she asked as he got out.

"Yes. I'll tell you all about it as we go along. We're going to make our move tonight."

"Tonight?"

"They're going to transfer someone at ten. It's an opportunity we can't miss."

He paused and watched Melissa working on the car bumpers with such intensity in her little face.

"How did you make out?" he asked without taking his eyes off his little girl.

"I saw him."

"And?" He turned to her and searched her face, but saw only confusion.

"I don't know. I think I felt something, but then I wondered if I did only because I'm aware that I should. Do you know what I mean?"

"Yes."

"Did you figure a way? I mean . . . how are we going to do it?"

As an answer, he opened his jacket. Her gaze traveled from his face to his waist and she saw the pistol. The shock caused her to bring her small closed fist to her mouth. Wide-eyed, she shook her head.

"It's the only way. It would take too long to explain and they wouldn't believe us anyhow," he said.

"What if we're wrong?" she asked.

"Stay with logic, Elaine. We're not wrong. He's a victim just as much as we are."

She nodded, but that didn't relieve her fear, or stop her heart from pounding.

"Mommy, look!" Melissa called. She turned around. "See how it shines."

"Yes, honey." She wiped a tear from her cheek.

Bob took her hand and squeezed.

"It's all right," he said. "By this time tomorrow, we'll be a family again."

"And what happens to Charles Corbin and Elaine and Melissa Stratton?" she asked.

He thought a moment.

"They died," he finally said. "Let them rest in peace."

15

THEY SAT IN BOB'S CAR FOR A GOOD TEN MINUTES BEFORE they could work themselves up to doing it. Parked in the shadows between the reach of two street lights, they stared with anticipation at the lighted windows of the Andersons' house. Every once in a while, they could see either Mrs. or Mr. Anderson silhouetted in the blinds. Once, they thought they saw Adam Anderson, who they now knew was their Joey.

Melissa sat in the rear with her Mr. Panda. They had prepared her as best they could, telling her they were all going on an adventure and a little boy was going to join them.

"At first the little boy is going to be very frightened," Elaine told her. "But after a while, he won't be."

"Why will he be frightened, Mommy?" Melissa asked.

Elaine looked at Bob.

"Because he doesn't know the secret yet," she said.

"What secret?"

"That he's really your brother," Elaine replied.

Melissa thought for a long moment. Bob and Elaine watched her thinking and waited. Finally, she shrugged.

"I didn't know the secret either," she said, but so nonchalantly they had to laugh.

"That's all right, honey. Now you do. Just be a good girl, listen to what we say, and do exactly what we tell you to do, okay?"

"Uh huh. Can I tell Mr. Panda the secret?" she asked.

"Somehow, I think he knows," Bob said. "But tell him anyway."

Now, a long time from that light moment, Bob and Elaine held hands and watched the Anderson house to be sure the family was alone. Convinced they were, Bob turned to Elaine and nodded.

"It's time," he said.

Elaine felt as if her heart had evaporated and there was just a hollow, empty chamber where it had once been. Oddly, when she moved, her body seemed separate from her thoughts. It had a consciousness, a mind of its own; it was truly a separate individual and every organ, every cell was fully directed on the mission, a mother's mission to get back her child. Her body knew what they were about to do, she thought. It was eager.

Her nervousness was causing her to have these bizarre ideas, she thought. She wanted to stop and tell Charles all this, but his gaze was fixed intently on the house. He, too, looked like a monomaniac, his every move, his every heartbeat directed toward one goal—the rescue of his son.

"You wait right here like we told you, Melissa," Elaine ordered.

They closed their doors softly. As she came around the car to join him, he turned.

"The bag, honey," he said.

"Oh." She had left everything on the front seat. "I'm sorry."

"That's all right. I'm just as nervous about this as you are," he said. She went back and got the large paper bag that contained the rope they were going to use. Bob held her back as an automobile turned out of a driveway down the street. It went in the opposite direction and was gone in moments, returning the residential avenue to its quiet, subdued character.

They crossed the street quickly and walked up to the Andersons' front door. Bob looked at Elaine before he pressed the doorbell.

"We're doing the right thing, the only thing," he emphasized. She nodded and he took the pistol out of his belt and held it down so it would be out of sight for a moment. Then he pressed the doorbell button and they heard the ding-dong. A few moments later, Kurt Anderson opened the door.

"Yes?" he said. Bob didn't wonder why he didn't recognize them. He felt sure the research scientists had done something to erase the memory of the incident in the diner from his, his wife's and Joey's minds.

Bob lifted the revolver into the illumination cast from the fixture above the front door.

"Just do exactly what we tell you to do and no one will get hurt," Bob said firmly.

"What the hell is this?"

"Move back quietly," Bob commanded. "Do it," he snapped.

Anderson considered the gun and the look on Bob's face.

"Jesus Christ," he said, stepping back. "Thieves coming right to the fucking front door."

"Put your hands behind your head and turn around. Quickly," Bob said and pulled the hammer back on the pistol. The click sent an arrow of cold fear through Anderson's heart. He lifted his arms and turned around.

"Kurt?" his wife called from the living room. "Who is it?"

Bob nodded at Elaine. She fumbled through the bag and came up with the thin but strong cord. She began wrapping it around Kurt Anderson's wrists.

"Kurt?"

"Tell her it's all right," Bob ordered. He poked him in the back with the barrel of the revolver. "Tell her."

"It's all right. Just a moment," Kurt Anderson called. Elaine wrapped the tail of cord around Anderson's waist and tied it firmly in the rear, just as Bob had instructed. It had the effect of restricting the movement of his arms.

"Well, who is it, Kurt?" Toby Anderson said, coming out. The sight before her nailed her to the floor. Her scream was quickly aborted when Bob pointed the pistol at her. She could only gasp.

"No one's going to get hurt," he promised, "if you just listen and obey. Do you understand?" She nodded quickly. "All right," Bob said to Kurt Anderson. "Go into the living room. Quickly."

"Bastards," Kurt said, but moved.

"Sit down," Bob ordered. Anderson sat on the sofa and glared hatefully at them. "I'm sorry," Bob said to Toby Anderson, "but we have to tie you up, too."

"Why are you doing this?" she asked. "Are you thieves?"

"No, ma'am. It's too involved to explain right now. Hopefully, you will understand all of it someday."

"I'm sorry," Elaine said and began tying the woman's wrists.

"Just sit next to your husband," Bob said, and with the pistol he pointed to the sofa. "You'd better do their legs," Bob said to Elaine softly. She pulled more cord from the bag and knelt down before them, keeping her gaze fixed on their ankles as she tied the cord.

"What the hell are you two up to?" Anderson asked in a more reasonable tone of voice. Something told him that these two people were not professional house thieves. The woman looked timid, afraid, near tears herself, and the man, although holding the pistol firmly, looked and behaved as though he were in some deep mental anguish, grimacing, his lips writhing.

"We haven't time to explain," Bob said. "I can tell you, promise you that none of you is going to get hurt."

"None . . ." The realization that the pronoun included her son threw Toby Anderson into a panic. "Adam!" she said, turning to Kurt.

Kurt Anderson struggled fiercely against the binding cord. The muscles in his face and neck looked like they would burst through his skin. He howled and kicked his legs out, just missing Elaine. She stumbled back.

"Stop it!" Bob commanded. "STOP IT!" he screamed and stepped forward to place the barrel of the pistol against Toby Anderson's left temple.

"CHARLES!" Elaine cried, surprised and frightened by what he had done herself. Her cry and Bob's action had an immediate result. Anderson froze.

Bob's face was flushed. Anderson's eyes widened in greater fear as Bob's body began to tremble. His gun hand shook, the finger still on the trigger. Bob closed his eyes and sucked in some air.

"Just . . . cooperate," he said. Ordinary speech was suddenly an ordeal. "And no one . . . will get hurt." He opened his eyes and looked at Anderson. The man nodded quickly and Bob's palsy began to subside. "Okay," he said. "Okay." He turned to Elaine. "I'm all right. It's okay."

She nodded and followed him out. It didn't take them long to find Adam's room. The little boy was playing with his Nintendo game, and the noise had covered all the sounds from below. It took him a few moments to realize Bob and Elaine were standing in the doorway looking in at him.

"Who are you?" he asked.

"Friends," Bob said. "You have to come with us, son."

"Come with you?" He stood up. "Where's Mommy?"

"She's downstairs; she knows," Bob said.

"Oh honey, don't be afraid," Elaine said. "No one's going to hurt you."

"I don't want to go with you," the boy said. Bob turned to Elaine. They both knew this was going to be the hardest part.

"Can you do it?" he asked her. She shook her head. "Okay, just wait downstairs," he said, taking the bag out of her hands. "It will be all right."

"Where's my dad?" Adam Anderson demanded.

"Right here, son," Bob said. "Right here," he repeated and moved in.

BOTH Dr. Congemi and Dr. Randolph looked up with expressions of surprise when Pyle simply burst in upon them. His normally parchment-white face was crimson. Apparently, from the way he was breathing, he had run all the way from one end of the fifth floor to the other.

"Pyle, what the hell . . ." Nelson Congemi began.

"There's been an attempted hacking," he said and stopped to catch his breath.

"Hacking?" Lila Randolph moved to the front of Nelson Congemi's desk. "What are you saying, Pyle?"

"I didn't bother to check the readouts on the mainframe until just now. I've been busy with this project," he added as an excuse before he could be accused of negligence.

"So?"

"There were at least a half dozen attempts to break into our files this morning. It couldn't be done of course, but . . ."

"Break into our files?" Congemi leaned forward in his seat. "Who?"

"Well, that's the other part . . . it came from the office in charge of hospital records where we placed Charles Corbin."

"Corbin?" Congemi rose and came around the desk too. "Lila?"

"Are you sure it was Corbin?" she asked.

"I checked. Jeff Livingston was out sick today. Corbin was the only one in the office. The trace goes back to his computer."

"Why would he try to break into our files?" Congemi asked Lila Randolph. She didn't reply. She was thinking and she wouldn't answer until she was ready, but Congemi was too excited, too nervous to wait. He turned to Pyle, who just shrugged.

"I told you that Livingston had sent him up here on a gofer errand, but neither of you seemed very concerned about it," Pyle said.

"Lila?"

"I'm thinking, damn it."

"He couldn't be reverting, could he?" Congemi asked.

"Reverting to what? There's nothing there to revert to, Nelson."

"What about your tapes? Anything you've heard that could explain this?"

Lila sat down and thought for a moment.

"I haven't heard enough to justify a diagnosis, but I have been observing a strong tendency on both their parts to challenge their present identities. Also, this affection they've been demonstrating toward each other seems deep-seated," she added, not without a note of envy. "There haven't been reversions as such, but I have heard some occasional references to their prior identities. Right now, it's confusing, so . . ."

"Why didn't you tell me any of this?" Congemi demanded.

"Because . . . as I just said," Lila snapped, "there's not enough data to form a scientific conclusion. I don't go running amok every time something looks out of sync, Nelson," she said, her implication clear. Congemi blanched. He saw the way Pyle was fascinated by the exchange.

"I'm not running amok, but I don't like this. I don't like it one bit."

"There's something else," Pyle said. From the way he spoke, Congemi got the impression Pyle was enjoying the crisis, enjoying the way it played on both his and Dr. Randolph's nerves.

"Well, what is it?" Lila demanded.

"A security guard, Ross, appears to be missing."

"Missing?" Congemi went back to his chair. "How can he be missing? Either he's here or he isn't."

"Well, that's just it, Doc. He was on duty today, but he never checked out and his car's still in the employee parking lot."

"That's very odd," Congemi muttered.

"Perhaps he neglected to check out and left with a friend," Lila Randolph said. She didn't see the point in wasting time worrying about such a thing. "Is anything missing anywhere?"

"I haven't done a check," Pyle said.

"Why not?" Congemi demanded.

"I just told you, Doc. I've been busy with this new program all day," Pyle whined.

"All right, all right," Lila said. "We're wasting time here. Go through the floor thoroughly and examine everything carefully."

"What about Heller?" Pyle asked. "I can't do both. The man's prepped and we'll be ready on time, but if I got to go through the floor . . ."

"All right," Lila said. "We'll do Heller first and then we'll do the floor."

"Jesus," Pyle said. "We'll be here all night."

"It can't be helped," Lila Randolph said, her eyes cold. Pyle nodded.

"Right, right. Okay, I'm heading for the transference room," he said and left.

"Why would he try to get into our mainframe, Lila?" Congemi asked.

"It could simply be a matter of curiosity, computer games. He was just exploring. Maybe he was bored with his work," she said calmly.

"I don't like this," Congemi muttered. "I don't like it at all. Especially in light of some of your discoveries on the tapes. I'm not panicking, but the whole project's at risk if we miss something here."

Lila Randolph nodded.

"All right, Nelson. Call Robinson," she ordered. "Tell him to pick up Charles Corbin, Elaine Stratton and her daughter and bring them here immediately."

"Right." He went to the phone. He saw she was heading out. "Where are you going?"

"I'll be right back. I want to skim through some of the last few hours or so of the taping to see if there's anything else to concern us," she said. "Maybe I did miss something else," she added.

Congemi was surprised. He had never heard her admit to possibly making a mistake before. Twenty minutes later, she returned. From the expression on her face, he knew they had very serious problems.

"What?" he asked quickly.

"I just spoke with Robinson. None of them are at home, but worse than that . . ."

"What, for God sakes?" Congemi cried when she hesitated. He could see it was something she couldn't understand herself.

"Kurt Anderson called Robinson. He managed to knock a phone off a table and poke the zero to get the operator who connected him with the police."

"Kurt Anderson? Why?"

"He said a man and a woman had just kidnapped his son."

"Christ," Congemi said, sitting back. "How . . ."

"I don't know. Charles Corbin slept with Elaine Stratton last night," she said. "At her house."

"So?" He didn't see why this was suddenly so important. "They've slept with each other before, haven't they?"

"Yes, but he never stayed all night."

"What does that mean? Didn't you hear anything, any clue?"

"I didn't have time to dwell on the tapes, but I didn't pick anything special up in their last conversations. Anyway, I told Robinson to get over here immediately. I don't want to create a major scene. We'll handle this ourselves."

"It's all coming apart," Congemi muttered. "Coming apart."

"Nelson! Get hold of yourself," Lila screamed. He looked up, shocked at her outburst. The phone buzzed before he had a chance to respond. He lifted the receiver.

"Everything's ready. We're beginning in here," Pyle told him.

"Okay." He looked at Lila. "It's Pyle. He's starting on Heller."

"Tell him we'll be right there," Lila said.

"But maybe we should put things on hold until . . ."

"Stop worrying, Nelson. Robinson knows where to find us. We'll learn what's happened and we'll deal with it," she said.

He nodded.

"Let's go," she commanded.

He got up and followed her, but this was one time he didn't have complete faith in their science and technology, despite Lila Randolph's arrogant assurances.

"WHY is he all tied up, Mommy?" Melissa asked when Bob slipped Adam in beside her. Because the little boy's eyes were so filled with terror, Elaine couldn't speak.

"He doesn't understand yet, Melissa," Bob said. "He will soon and everything will be all right. Just talk to him; tell him who you are. Make him feel safe, okay? Show him Mr. Panda, too," he added and closed the door.

He got in behind the wheel and squeezed Elaine's hand.

"You did real good in there, honey. It's going to be all right."

Elaine simply stared at him, amazed herself at what they had just done. Bob started the car and drove off toward the hospital, chanting to himself that it was going to be all right, that they were doing the right things, that somehow they would be able to defeat these powerful and evil people. But it wasn't until they pulled into the parking lot and the hospital loomed above them that he realized just how formidable their task would be. To begin with, how would they get the tied and bound boy into the hospital and up to the fifth floor without drawing attention?

"What do we do now?" Elaine asked when he pulled into a space.

"I don't know." He sat thinking for a moment.

"You don't know? Charles?"

"Just a minute," he snapped. "I'm sorry," he said immediately. "I know you're frightened. I just want to be careful so nothing prevents us from getting things done."

The realization that they didn't have a well-thought-out,

detailed plan put Elaine into a new panic. If they didn't suc-
ceed, they would be arrested as kidnappers and who would
ever believe their story?

"Melissa, honey," Bob said, turning to her. "We have to
borrow your blanket for Adam. Is that okay?"

The frightened child simply nodded and clung to her
panda.

"Thanks, honey." He turned to Elaine. "We're going to
wrap him up and rush into the hospital claiming carbon-
monoxide poisoning. We're to go directly to Doctor Randolph who's waiting. They've used that before in relation
to you and Melissa. Chances are it will work for us."

"What if it doesn't?"

"It will. The main thing is to get to the elevator. I have
the access card, which will get us to the fifth floor. You
take the briefcase," he said and got out quickly. He opened
the back door, took Melissa's blanket and wrapped it
around Adam Anderson. Despite what he knew, he couldn't
think of him as Joey yet, for he was still Charles Corbin
and the boy was still a stranger to Corbin.

"All right, son," he said. "You just be a good boy and
you won't be harmed. You understand?"

The frightened child nodded obediently and permitted
Bob to lift him out of the car.

"Ready?" he asked.

Elaine got out and helped Melissa out. She took her hand
and they hurried behind Bob as he headed for the hospital's
main entrance.

Chief Robinson didn't have his siren going, but he had
his bubble light on when he pulled into the hospital driveway behind them. Elaine caught sight of it first.

"Charles!"

He turned.

"Quickly," he said.

The lobby was relatively empty when Bob burst in carrying Adam. The elderly volunteer manning the receptionist's desk barely had a chance to look up from her magazine.

"Sir?"

"Carbon-monoxide poisoning," he cried. "Doctor Randolph's waiting for us."

The security guard in the lobby was off to the right talking to a nurse's aide. He saw Elaine and Melissa come flying in behind Bob, but he didn't move. He assumed they were all heading for the emergency room and only vaguely wondered why they didn't just use the emergency room entrance.

Bob stopped at the bank of elevators and pushed the up button. A door opened at the far end and he hurried into it. As soon as Elaine joined him, he fished the access card out of his jacket pocket and inserted it. The doors closed just as Chief Robinson came running through the lobby. He stopped at the bank of elevators and pounded the up button. He thought about going to a phone, but decided to get upstairs right behind them instead.

After the elevator doors had closed, Bob lowered Adam to the elevator floor. Then he loosened the cord around his feet so he could walk.

"Just stay calm," Bob cajoled. "Stay calm."

"He was right behind us, Charles," Elaine said.

"I know."

When the elevator opened on the fifth floor, they all stepped out. Bob knew that the second elevator was moments behind them.

"Stand off with the children, Elaine," Bob said. He took his pistol out of his belt and waited outside the second elevator. The doors opened and Robinson stepped out and stopped. Bob had the pistol pointed directly at Robinson's face.

"What the hell do you think you're doing?" Robinson demanded.

"Turn around," Bob said. "Do it."

As soon as Robinson did so, Bob reached out and took his pistol. He handed it to Elaine, then he took Adam's hand.

"All right, walk and walk very slowly," Bob commanded. They all started down the corridor toward the transference room. When they reached the door, Bob inserted the access card and told Robinson to turn the knob slowly. He figured if Robinson had been called, some more security men might be waiting.

But when they all entered, they found only Pyle, Dr. Randolph and Dr. Congemi at the consoles. All three turned in surprise. Chief Robinson was the first to speak.

"He was waiting for me as I stepped out of the elevator," he said.

"Mr. Corbin," Lila Randolph began, "what are you doing? Why did you bring these people here?"

Bob's hand began to shake. He felt a tremor move through his body and travel up his torso like a wave. It was as though he were standing at the epicenter of an earthquake. But he fought for self-control.

"We are the Boxletter family, aren't we?" he demanded.

"Lila," Congemi said, stepping up beside her.

"Shut up," she said.

"Aren't we the Boxletters?" Bob asked. "I want an answer," he insisted and cocked the hammer of the pistol before placing the barrel against the back of Chief Robinson's head.

"Tell him!" Robinson cried. "He's out of control."

"Yes, you are," Congemi said quickly.

"My God," Elaine said, now that the reality was upon her.

"Nelson, you fool," Lila accused. Her eyes were wide with rage and her mouth twisted in disgust.

"It's over, Lila. Can't you see something terrible's gone wrong?"

"Why are you people doing this horrible thing to other people, to us?" Bob demanded, not taking the pistol from the back of Robinson's head.

Congemi sighed.

"Our primary purpose was noble: to get rid of the criminal mind by replacing it."

"Who are all the victims of your noble research?" Bob asked.

"We couldn't experiment with prisoners since incarceration made them highly visible. So we began with what you might call 'invisible people' . . . transients, homeless. People like yourselves were never intended for this. It was all a series of blunders."

"I want you to put us back," Bob said.

Lila Randolph smiled wryly.

"You don't know what you're saying, Mr. Corbin. You're actually asking for your own death and the death of Mrs. Stratton and her daughter and Adam Anderson, as well."

"We know that. They already died; the Boxletters didn't," he said.

"Lila, he's right," Congemi said.

"Shut up. Listen to me, Charles. Your mind's alive. Your memories are alive. That's the *real* person. Boxletter is just . . . just the flesh and bones . . ."

"Oh God," Elaine said, shaking her head. "This is so horrible. You're Frankensteins."

"Hardly," Lila said.

"Exactly," Bob responded. "You weren't content with

just substituting one mind for another; you changed and manipulated thoughts. You think you're gods, don't you?"

Neither scientist responded. Only Pyle seemed to have a reaction and his was one of sick amusement. He pulled his lips back in a grotesque smile. In the silence of the moment, Chief Robinson opted to act.

He spun around, ducking at the same time. Bob's reflexive pull on the trigger sent a bullet crashing into the window behind the monitors and the glass shattered. Robinson tackled him and drove him back against the wall, but Bob held onto his pistol and slapped it against the side of Robinson's head just enough to stun him. He fell back to the floor.

Bob gathered himself and straightened up. He stood over Robinson who rubbed his head and writhed in pain. Then he cocked the hammer of the pistol again and pointed the gun down at him.

"No!" Robinson cried, extending his hand. Bob looked at Congemi and Randolph.

"I'm prepared to shoot each and every one of you," he said. He didn't know from what well he drew his violence and determination, but he was glad it was there and he was sure he could carry out the threat. They saw it in his eyes as well. "I'll kill you just the way I did that security man."

"Ross?" Pyle said. "He killed Ross. Holy shit."

"Mr. Corbin," Congemi said, "you must try to remain calm."

"Put back the Boxletters," Bob said firmly. "The discs are in the briefcase," he added, nodding toward Elaine.

"Mr. Corbin, we were just in the process of a restoration. We've never done it before," Congemi said.

"Then begin with me. Elaine, you'll keep them under the gun. If anything happens to me . . ."

She looked up at the scientists.

"I'll kill them," she said, borrowing from his determination and firmness. She cocked the hammer on her pistol.

Robinson groaned and lay back on the floor.

"All right," Congemi said. "We'll do it."

"Nelson," Lila snapped.

"I said we'll do it," Congemi insisted. "We've got to bring this to an end, Lila. At least for these people," he said.

"I want to retain my memories from the time I woke up in your hospital. I don't want to forget any of this," Bob said. "I know you can do that," he added, looking at Pyle. Pyle shrugged.

"Sure," he said. He seemed totally devoid of loyalty to anyone or anything but the process. It was as if he were an extension of his own machines, but Bob didn't care.

He turned to Elaine.

"You're going to have to be strong, honey. All of us, the children and me, are depending on you. Remember, I love you. It's something that goes deeper than names and memories. Anything that strong has got to prevail. Can you do it?"

She nodded.

"Yes," she said. He kissed her and then looked at the children, who were both frozen with terror. Fortunately, he thought, if this works, they won't remember a moment.

"All right," Bob said. He kicked Robinson in the thigh. "Get up and get into that storage room," he said, pointing to the door. "Now!"

Robinson groaned and struggled to his feet. As he walked toward the storage room door Bob turned to Dr. Randolph.

"I think you should join him, Doctor," he said. "I'd feel better if both of you weren't in here."

"This is ridiculous," Lila Randolph said, not moving. "I happen to be in charge here. I am . . ."

Bob lifted the pistol toward her.

"I doubt that any court of law would prosecute us anyway, but even if I shoot you," Bob said, "it's not Mr. Boxletter, but Mr. Corbin who commits the murder."

She looked at him and realized what he was saying. She flashed a look of reproach at Nelson Congemi and then followed Chief Robinson into the storage room. Bob closed the door behind them.

"All right," he said, turning to Dr. Congemi and Pyle. "Let's begin. And you better pray it all comes out right," he added, taking the briefcase from Elaine and bringing it to Pyle.

16

FIRST THERE WAS NOTHING. JUST THE WHOSH, WHOSH, WHOSH and the sense he was being gently tossed from side to side. He was submerged in some warm world. Suddenly, there was what seemed like an explosion all around him and he felt himself shoved forward. The sound resembled the roar of a great waterfall. Tons and tons of water rushing over and pounding the rocks below, thunderous, the sort of natural cacophony that leaves one standing awestruck and feeling puny in the midst of so powerful an expression of Mother Nature.

Then, there was feeling, the sensation of falling, sliding down an interminable tunnel, twisting and dipping, finding nothing on which to take hold, no way to break the descent. He could actually feel the wash of air flow by; his body folded and unfolded, spun over and over and dropped as if his feet were made of stone.

After that came sight. At first there was only blue-black darkness to accompany the roar and the falling, but soon images began flowing by, pictures liquified, whole faces and places painted on the moving water, distorted yet vivid enough to produce recognizable memories—Marion, the children, his mother and father, houses in which he had lived, villages and towns, cities and airports, a playground on which he played and one to which he had taken Sherri and Joey, a mixing of images, no logic, no chronology, just a random explosion of recollections.

Odors followed, all recognizable, some enjoyable, pleasant, like the aromas of food, the whiff of Marion's perfume, the scent of her hair, even the fresh smell of newly cut grass; some odors unpleasant—the stench of some dead animal, the nauseating smell of burned foods, an overwhelming odor of gasoline, turpentine, nail polish. His stomach churned.

And finally, there was the memory of touch—soft things, lovely things: silks and satins, soft leathers, a snowball in his hands, a marshmallow, Marion's breasts; and then hard things, pointed things, painful things: thorns, needles, a wooden bench, cement, sandpaper, a dentist's drill, scraping his knees.

A burst of light exploded under his eyelids and he thought he heard the sound of an infant's cry, a sound that seemed to emerge from his own mouth. His eyes jerked open and the brightness disappeared to be slowly replaced by a glare of flat white. Gradually, the image focused and he realized he was looking up at a ceiling.

"Charles!" he heard someone call, a woman. She sounded like . . .

"Charles!" Her voice came through a speaker.

"Easy, Mr. Boxletter," Dr. Congemi said. "Don't get up too fast. There's an equilibrium adjustment."

Bob turned and looked at the gray-haired man in the lab coat, and moments later there was a name to go with the face.

"Where's Marion?" he demanded.

"She's watching us," Dr. Congemi said. "As you instructed her to do." He nodded at the windows, one shattered by the gunshot. Bob remembered. It worked. It actually worked!

He moved faster and the room started to spin. Congemi took hold of his arm.

"I'm all right," he said and wiped his face. When he removed his hand, he saw the man on the gurney beside him and recognized him.

"Brian?" He slipped off the gurney. "It's my brother-in-law," he told Congemi.

"I know," Congemi said.

Bob looked up at Marion standing in the window.

"Do my wife next," he commanded. "Then we'll do Brian and the children. Retain the same memories for her, but not the children."

"Mr. Boxletter," Dr. Congemi said. "Are you all right? I mean what do you remember?" he asked. The scientist in him urged him to ask the questions even during this state of affairs.

"I remember who and what you people are," Bob said sternly. He marched out and embraced Marion.

"It's all right," he said, kissing her. "It works. Let them do you now."

He took the pistol from her.

"Go ahead, honey."

"I'm frightened, Charles."

Bob smiled.

"I'm Bob," he said. "Charles is just like . . . like a part in a play I once acted. You'll soon understand. Go on," he coaxed. She looked down at the children. "They'll be all right. Go ahead."

Slowly, she walked through the door and went to the gurney. Congemi gave Pyle the instructions and then he returned to fit Marion with the pads. Congemi nodded to Pyle, who immediately began working the discs. Bob could see that the technician was thoroughly enjoying all this.

"Don't make any mistakes," he warned him. "I want her to be brought up to date, just like me."

"No problem," Pyle said. He started the process and the outline of Marion Boxletter's cerebral cortex appeared on the monitor. The red tint began to expand from the center out. "To tell you the truth," Pyle said with excitement, "I was very interested in seeing if there was anything in your implanted memory, other than what I left at your request, that would remain. We're having a problem with that subject there," he said, nodding toward Brian, "and . . ."

"I'm not interested in your problems. As far as I'm concerned, what you're doing is abhorrent."

"Hey," Pyle said, turning, "if we don't do it, someone else will and they might not be on our side."

"I don't believe you're on our side," Bob responded.

"Suit yourself," Pyle said. Nothing could wipe that smug smile off his face, Bob thought.

Bob drew the children closer to him. They were so frightened by the sights and sounds going on around them, they were almost catatonic.

"It's going to be all right, guys," he said. "You'll see."

Dr. Congemi stepped back into the control room to wait with him and watch the monitors.

"Mr. Boxletter," he said, "you must ˈlieve me when I tell you it was not our intention to use your family as subjects. I never approved of the kidnapping of your son and your brother-in-law. Unfortunately, we are working under the command of a most clandestine section of the CIA and . . ."

"Doctor Randolph ain't gonna like your telling him all that," Pyle said, not taking his eyes off the console.

"It doesn't matter what any of you tell me, what excuses and justifications you come up with," Bob said. "As far as I'm concerned you're all criminals, just a more sophisticated kind of criminal, but nevertheless as evil and as revolting as serial killers or psychotics."

Pyle actually laughed. Then he grew serious and said, "Input beginning."

The telephone rang. Everyone looked at it.

"I'll answer it," Bob said and lifted the receiver. "Yes?"

"Who the fuck is this?" Walter Fryman demanded.

"Who did you wish to speak to?" Bob said calmly.

"Give me Chief Robinson," Fryman snapped.

"I'm afraid he's indisposed at the moment."

"Indisposed? Who the hell is this?"

"My name's Boxletter, Bob Boxletter, but maybe you knew me as Charles Corbin," he added. There was a pause.

"Is Doctor Randolph there?"

"No, I'm afraid she's just as indisposed. But who may I say is calling?" Bob asked.

"This is Walter Fryman. Where's Doctor Congemi?"

"Unable to come to the phone right now," Bob said. "Can I take a message?"

"You son of a bitch," Fryman screamed into the phone and then there was a click. Bob shrugged and hung up the receiver. "A Mister Fryman," he announced.

"Fryman?" Dr. Congemi's face distorted with fear. "Is he coming up here?"

"I couldn't tell you. He seemed somewhat upset."

Pyle laughed again.

"He ain't the only one's gonna be upset," Pyle said.

Bob watched the monitor and saw the percentages climb. When it reached one hundred, the monitor buzzed.

"She's done," Pyle declared. "Medium rare," he added, smiling.

"Get her up and see if she's okay," Bob ordered Congemi and he went to Marion. She stirred and sat up, dazed. Bob went to Pyle's side and studied the console a moment.

"Can you do more than one at once?" Bob asked Pyle.

"Sure. Up to three."

"Do the children and Brian then," he commanded.

"We're having a bit of a problem with Mr. Heller there,"

Pyle said, nodding. "I was already halfway into a restoration using a new approach, when you busted in."

"Just finish restoring him," Bob commanded.

"That's what I was doing, but . . ."

"Then do it."

Pyle shrugged.

"Whatever the man with the gun says," he quipped and flipped the control. Brian's monitor came on again and Bob could see that the cerebral cortex was indeed sixty percent filled, but a tiny spot of red remained.

Meanwhile, Dr. Congemi helped Marion off the gurney and brought her back into the control room. Bob hugged her.

"You all right?"

"Yes," she said although she was still feeling somewhat in a daze. "It's strange, but I remember what they did with us and yet . . ."

"Just as I said, as if you were playing a part in a play," Bob said.

"Mommy," Sherri cried, running to her and embracing her around the leg.

Marion knelt down to lift her and then she saw Joey. Her eyes brightened.

"He looks so frightened, so confused, Bob."

"I know, but we're going to fix him right now."

Suddenly, the storage room door opened and Harry Robinson poked his head out. Bob pointed the revolver at him.

"Stay in there," he ordered and Robinson retreated, closing the door again.

Bob put the second pistol in her hand and cocked the hammer.

"While I'm in the other room with the children, you

point this gun at that door. If that policeman sticks his head out again, shoot. Understand?"

She nodded. She remembered Robinson and she remembered what he and the other men had done to her, Bob and Sherri.

"Keep your eye on this guy, too," he said, nodding at Pyle. "He's not to leave his seat."

"I ain't going anywhere," Pyle said. "This is my place," he added cheerfully.

"Just watch him," Bob said, and started to pry Sherri loose. "Come on, baby. No one's going to hurt you."

"Mommy!" she screamed.

"Sherri, it's all right," she said. "Go with Daddy."

The little girl looked up at her.

"My name's not Sherri, Mommy," she said. "And he's not my daddy."

"Oh, dear God," Marion said, her eyes full of pain.

"She'll be all right in a little while," Bob promised and lifted Sherri into his arms. She screamed.

"It's all right, honey," he said. He looked at Congemi. "Bring the boy," he ordered. Congemi scooped up Joey and carried him into the other room.

"We'll have to strap her in," Congemi said, nodding at Sherri.

"I know," Bob said.

Sherri was screaming so hard and so loud, her voice had reached a pitch nearly beyond human hearing. Her face was beet red. She fought being placed on the gurney, and it broke Bob's heart to force her down and strap her on, but he knew he had to do it.

"Bob!" Marion cried.

"It's all right. She's going to be all right," he insisted and stepped back as soon as both children were set up. He returned to the control room to stand with Marion and put his

arm around her as Pyle began the process. She finally noticed her brother on the other gurney.

"Bob! That is Brian, isn't it?"

"Yes, honey. That's your brother. They made him into
Mr. Heller," he added, glaring angrily at Congemi. "But
we're getting them to make him into Brian again. It will all
be over soon."

"He's right," Pyle told Congemi. "Mr. Heller's nearly
finished." The numbers clicked into the nineties. Congemi
didn't look happy.

"We shouldn't have continued with this restoration," he
said.

"The man insisted," Pyle replied, smiling.

"Mr. Boxletter," Dr. Congemi began, but Bob's attention
was focused on the monitors that told him the children's
implanted identities were well on their way toward re-
moval. "You don't understand all that's occurred here,"
Congemi continued. "Please . . ."

"He's landed," Pyle announced along with the buzzing
of the monitor. Congemi turned to look at Brian's monitor.

"The residue, you haven't removed it," Congemi said.

Pyle shrugged.

"Hey, Doc, I tried. And these aren't exactly the sort of
working conditions I expected," he said. Congemi stepped
up to the doorway and looked in at Brian, who was beginning to stir. They had him strapped down.

"I don't like this," Congemi muttered.

"What is it?" Bob demanded. He saw that the input on
the children was beginning.

Brian's stirring intensified, and when he realized he was
strapped on the gurney he began to struggle vehemently.
He kicked out and swung his body wildly.

"Bob," Marion said. "What's happening to him?"

"He's just afraid. He wants to be freed," Bob said, stepping into the room.

"Mr. Boxletter," Dr. Congemi cried. "Wait . . ."

Bob moved quickly to Brian's side and began unfastening the straps.

"It's all right, buddy. You're going to be all right, too," he said.

Brian stopped struggling a moment and glared up at him. When Bob undid the straps that held his legs fast, however, Brian kicked up, catching Bob in the chest and sending him flying back. Marion screamed and Congemi ran into the room just as Brian twisted himself half off the gurney. His upper body was still fastened down.

With enormous strength, he lifted the entire gurney up with him and got to his feet. The straps snapped like rubber bands and he was free. He lunged forward and seized Dr. Congemi at the shoulders, lifting him off the floor and tossing him easily against the wall, his head smacking hard. The impact rendered him unconscious and he slid to the floor in a seated position.

"*Holy shit!*" Pyle cried. "*Chief,*" he screamed.

Robinson burst out of the storage room with Dr. Randolph behind him. Marion had no chance to shoot, nor did she care to. She was dazed by the action unfolding before her. Bob struggled to his feet and called out.

"Brian, it's us!" he said.

Chief Robinson came into the room and Brian focused on him.

"Restrain him," Dr. Randolph ordered. The chief stepped forward and with his good hand seized Brian's right arm. It looked like he would be able to twist it back and subdue him because Brian seemed confused by his own actions and was unmoving. But suddenly, with a suicidal glint in his eyes, Brian slammed his forehead into Chief Robinson's. The butting drove Robinson's skull into his brain, killing him instantly. The policeman folded at Brian's feet, his face covered with blood.

Now, with a look of more purpose to him, Brian lunged forward and seized Dr. Randolph at the neck. He squeezed so hard so quickly, she couldn't utter a scream. Her face turned crimson as she struggled in vain to pull his hands away.

"Bob, stop him!" Marion cried. Bob grabbed Brian's arm and pulled, but it was unmovable. In fact, he lifted Dr. Randolph off the ground. The redness in her face turned darker and her lips became blue.

"He's killing her, Bob!" Marion cried.

"Jesus," Bob said, "I can't budge him."

Dr. Randolph's eyes went back in her head and, suddenly, her body went limp. Brian tossed her to the side as if she were no more than a rag doll. And then, he spun around to face Bob.

"Brian, it's us. It's Marion and me," Bob said.

The madman's eyes blinked, but he stepped forward. Bob reached for the pistol in his belt, but discovered it had fallen out when Brian had first kicked him away. He saw it on the floor, but it was too far away.

"Marion, you've got to shoot," Bob said. "It's not Brian."

"I can't," she cried. "Oh God." She turned to Pyle, but he was sitting there with his arms folded as if he were watching some television event. "Do something," she cried. "Stop him!" Pyle shook his head.

"I ain't getting involved in this," he said.

Brian lunged forward and wrapped his arms around Bob in a crushing bear hug. Bob struggled, but was unable to budge or break his crazed brother-in-law's grip. Realizing what Brian had done to Chief Robinson, Bob tried to keep his head off to the side.

"Marion!" he cried. *"It's not Brian! You've got to shoot him!"*

Marion stepped into the room until she was only a foot or so away. Tears were streaming down her cheeks. Her chest rose and fell. She closed her eyes and then opened them, raised the pistol, and fired, hitting Brian in the neck. He released Bob instantly and fell back, catching himself on one of the gurneys. Slowly, he sank to the floor. Bob rushed to him and he looked up, his eyes blinking.

"Bob?" he said. He tried to form another word, but his lips stopped and his head fell to the side. Bob got up slowly and went to Marion, who was sobbing hysterically. He embraced her and led her back to the control room, just as the children's monitors buzzed.

"They're all done," Pyle said, shaking his head. "Wow!"

Marion and Bob went to fetch the children. While they were doing so, Nelson Congemi regained consciousness and began to struggle to his feet. Pyle finally left his ringside seat and came in to help him.

Dr. Congemi gazed around at the carnage.

"You missed it all, Doc," Pyle said. "Better than the Friday night fights."

"My God," Congemi said, looking down at the twisted body of his associate.

Bob knelt to pick up the pistol on the floor and then stopped before them, his dazed son in his arms.

"Was your experiment, your project, worth all this?" he asked.

"No," Congemi said, shaking his head.

"I want you to show me exactly how this is done," Bob said.

"Are you kidding?" Pyle said.

"You know I'm familiar enough with computers. I just want to know how to do the process."

"No problem," Pyle said. "I got it down to one, two, three, especially for someone with your background. But why do you want to know?" Pyle asked. "You want to go into business for yourself now?"

"No. I want you out of business," he replied.

EPILOGUE

"JUST PULL UP TO THE FRONT AND LEAVE THE CAR," WALTER Fryman snapped when Bruno turned into the hospital driveway. Almost before Bruno had brought the vehicle to a stop, Fryman jumped out. He didn't even bother to close the car door. Bruno had to run to keep up with his boss. Travel delays—mechanical problems with his personal helicopter, a mix-up with vehicles—had made it impossible for him to get to Sandburg as quickly as he had wished. Chomping at the bit, the veins in his temples looking as though they would explode, he charged through the hospital lobby and punched the elevator call button. The instant the doors opened he was in, Bruno beside him. Fryman plunged his hand into his jacket pocket to produce the access card. The doors closed slowly, far too slowly for him, and then they were finally on their way to the fifth floor.

"I'll have their asses," he muttered. "I'm sick of their screw-ups. I don't care how brilliant they're supposed to be; they're nothin' but fuck-ups to me," he said.

Bruno nodded. He had seen his boss enraged before, but never to the point where he looked out of control. Usually, Fryman had that cool manner about him. He could kill a man and maintain an indifference that made the act look no more significant than brushing some lint off his shoulder.

The doors opened and Fryman shot out, not looking anywhere but in the direction he was heading. He was as fixed on his target as would be an infuriated bull. The only thing

259

that made him hesitate was the sight of the door of the transference room open.

"What the fuck's going on here?" he muttered and entered slowly.

"The window," Bruno said. Fryman saw the shattered glass, the door of the storage room open and the door to the operations room open. Someone had also smashed the consoles.

"What the hell . . ."

They heard someone whistling a monotonous tune, and they both walked cautiously to the door of the operations room. The carnage still lay before them: Dr. Randolph's twisted dead body sprawled on the floor, Brian on his back, his head turned so that the bullet wound in his neck was visible, and Chief Robinson, his glassy eyes peering through the ribbons of dried blood drawn over his forehead and down his face.

"Holy shit," Bruno said.

To their right, Pyle, dressed in a custodian's coveralls, glided a push broom over the tile and whistled.

"Pyle," Fryman shouted. Pyle continued to push the broom and whistle. *"Pyle!"*

Pyle paused and turned their way. He shook his head.

"What the hell went on here?" Fryman demanded, approaching. "Who did this?"

"Work, work, work—that's all people do, make work, work, work," he said and turned back to his sweeping. Fryman reached out and seized the broom handle.

"What the hell are you talking about, Pyle? Who did this? What happened?"

Pyle stared at him, his eyes blinking rapidly.

"What the fuck's wrong with him, Mr. Fryman?"

"Who the hell knows? Pyle," he said, "what the fuck are you doing?"

"My name's Marty," he said, smiling, and grew very serious again. "Work, work, work." He turned and began pushing the broom.

"Where the hell's Congemi?" Fryman said. He looked at Bruno. "Let's find him and quick."

Bruno nodded and they started out. They marched down the corridor toward Congemi's office, but not halfway there they paused when Fryman noticed a man standing in the open doorway of the library. He had his back smack against the jamb.

"Who's that?" Fryman said.

Bruno looked and took out his pistol.

"I'm not sure, Mr. Fryman."

The man was in the shadows and had his face turned so that it was masked.

"Hey, you!" Fryman called.

Slowly, the man emerged and they saw it was Dr. Congemi.

"Jesus," Fryman said. "The stupid bastard."

Bruno shook his head and put his pistol back into its holster. Then the two of them walked toward Congemi. About ten yards from him, Fryman noticed the pistol in Congemi's hand.

"What the fuck you doin' with a gun? What went on here?" Fryman demanded.

Congemi took a step toward them.

"I've been waiting for you," he said. "Waiting for you to come out."

"Come out? Come out of where?"

Congemi smiled, but there was something so odd about his smile that it drove a chill up the normally hard Walter Fryman.

"Nelson, what's going on?" he asked.

"Nelson?" Congemi laughed and raised his pistol to

point it directly at Walter Fryman. "My name is Ed Walters," he said. "The real Walter Fryman would have known that."

"Huh?" Fryman said. He didn't have a chance to say anything else. The report of the pistol in Congemi's hand thundered down the corridor and the impact of the .38 drove Fryman back against Bruno. Fryman's forehead exploded with blood. Bruno held him for a moment and then released him so he could get his own pistol out. He had plenty of time, for Congemi didn't turn the gun on him, or even look at him. It was as if he didn't see him. Bruno emptied his revolver quickly, riddling Congemi's body with bullets, spinning him around and driving him back. He fell face forward on the floor of the corridor.

Meanwhile, about twenty miles along the highway leading away from Sandburg, Bob Boxletter made a turn that would take him to the New York Thruway. He was driving a late-model, light blue Mercedes sedan.

"Where did we get this car, Dad?" Joey asked. He was sitting between his father and his mother, and Sherri was on her mother's lap.

"Oh, I borrowed it from a friend," Bob said, smiling at Marion.

"Why are we all sitting in the front? It's crowded," Joey complained.

"I just wanted us to be close together for a while," Marion explained. "After we pull into the rest stop for snacks and bathroom, you and Sherri can sit in the back."

"Won't your friend care that we're taking his car so far?" Joey asked.

"No, I don't think he's going to mind." He smiled at Marion again. "I don't think he's going to mind at all. He knows we'll take good care of it."

"Won't he need it?"

"Nope. Where he is, he doesn't need a car."

"Where is he?"

"He's . . . er . . . resting comfortably in a computer," Bob said.

"In a computer? How can he be in a computer, Dad?"

Bob glanced at Marion, who was obviously waiting for his response.

"Well, son, it's a long story, a helluva long story."

"Don't say bad words, Daddy," Sherri chastised.

"Oh, right. Sorry, Sherri. It just slipped out. Almost as if . . . someone else said it," he added.

Marion's eyes widened.

Bob smiled and reached over the back of the seat to squeeze her shoulder gently.

And then they drove on to complete their journey home.